COMMISSIONAIRE DU GUI'S LAST CASE

The Missing Celebrity Chefs

A host of celebrity chefs have disappeared without a trace leaving the Metropolitan Police baffled and the British public outraged so forcing a mistrusted political establishment to react.

On the brink of retirement, Commissionaire Du Gui, the debonair master crime solver of the macabre, gets a call to go to London to act as an informal advisor on the case. Can the freethinking Commissionaire, without treading on the toes of Scotland Yard, save the day?

The last case in the distinguished career of Commissionaire Du Gui is a humdinger with help coming from an unusual source.

First published in Great Britain in 2017

Copyright @ David Dow Millar 2017

First Published 2017 by The Misty Tree

The moral right of the author has been asserted

All rights reserved.

Any errors of commission or omission remain my own

ISBN 978-0-9929340-8-8

EBook ISBN 978-0-9929340-9-5

DISCLAIMER

All characters and places mentioned anywhere in this novel are fictitious and any inference to real people, dead or alive, is coincidental. Any familiarity is simply because most people's lives and events are similar, and the interpretation is only different.

CHAPTERS

BOILING OVER

"In the cold darkness, sensing a rare hint of nourishment, they lie delirious for something delicious to eat."

*****

The normal ripples of discontent swelled by fury washed above the flood defence barriers of officialdom. Happiness levels had fallen and dissatisfaction in the powers that be engulfed the British Isles. After weeks of political inaction and public emotions stirred by an impatient traditional media releasing spoiler stories to counter the 'process was being made' reports from the police and Home Secretary, frustration at the failure to quickly expose the culprits responsible for the mysterious disappearance of the celebrity chefs was reaching dangerous proportions. A situation so serious a gracious Arab potentate had discretely offered to leaseback UK made riot control equipment to quell the anger that was spilling on the streets.

Protesters from the world of celebrity further stirred undulating anxiety into a full-blown tsunami by marching down Whitehall, shown live on the TV networks, to demand better protection for this key stratum of society, which provided the nation with important placebos to ease life's pains. A stellar cast of 'A' list theatrical and movie stars jostled for the best positions at the front. Top professionals in their field not known to give up an assignment by insisting that it was time for someone else to have a chance. They were followed by fading stars, resting actors down to the 'Z' list hand cream and voice over actors, who put their own slant on peaceful protest by wearing gloves and staying silent. Hairdressers and makeup artists to the stars initially refused the right to join the ranks, quickly got a place near the rear after threatening strike action.

Rejected reality stars organised their own march and deliberately coincided it on the same day as the televised event, as well as ending it with a rally at Trafalgar Square, the final destination of the main event. Battalions of YouTube broadcasters and wannabes swelled the numbers in this counter-demonstration. The most publicised *refusniks* to this alternative show of displeasure were Mum's Ne*t* out of disdain for many of the other accepted participants.

On the day, the reality stars stole the limelight off the celebrities by having bare breasted glamour queens at the head of their procession, their modesty covered by a banner announcing their support of the chefs' families. This visual treat created the desired excitement and frenzy among photographers.

In a doomed attempt to stop the paparazzi from given their full attention to this screen-stealing spectacle, Sarah Peccadillo, an impeccable actor in work and away from it who had made a name as a disrobing screen heroine, volunteered to strip topless, not an appealing sight as her best days were long gone, but thankfully cries of oh no quickly deterred the woman. Instead the organisers of the official march retaliated by pushing strutting catwalk queens to the fore. This move caused a pile-up of photographers riding outback on motorcycles when some of the aforementioned vehicles attempted to return to the official march by doing one hundred and eighty-degree turns. Above this undignified melee of motorcycles, a near miss between BBC and SKY helicopters occurred when both camera crews demanded their pilot to hover in the same space.

Elsewhere, footballers and pop stars showed their solidarity by driving a convoy of chauffeur driven stretch white limousines around the Mall. A reporter who had later dared to insinuate that these cars with one-way visibility windows only contained a hired driver felt public wrath when his house was petrol bombed. It did not help the affronted stars' defence to have the limousines festooned with asinine sponsorship advertisements, mainly own brand perfumes and casual wear.

At its peak, some quarters claimed that two hundred and fifty thousand celebrities amassed in Trafalgar Square and the surrounding walkways. Again, the reality stars one-upped their rivals with impromptu food stalls set up around Nelson's

Column, manned by naked chefs, a headlining steal considering the reason for the protest. Millions of viewers instantly switched to live coverage on Channel 4, knowing this network aligned itself on the side of controversy and had no qualms in showing naked flesh before the watershed hour.

Completely ignored, up against a wall and away from the main action, the actors' guild of maniac depressives gathered, decked out in cassocks to denote their internal struggles. They just wanted to be left alone and got their wish. Naturally, this did not please everyone. The cycle from extrovert to introvert was not like menstrual synchrony. Some declared depressives would now have gladly worn bright colours and told any interested reporter about a life long struggle to overcome anxiety, stress and depression, probably brought on by sex abuse when young; all the while emphasising that it was not their fault when they were rude or downright odious, it was a chemical imbalance in their brains aggravated by suppressed feelings. They were misunderstood troubled individuals besieged by a death wish and human vulnerabilities manifesting as a masochistic tendency to relish suffering. Any acquaintance lulled to sympathise with their plight, neuroses and persecution mania when not in the limelight would eventually be driven mad.

As artistic temperament flared, the inevitable confrontation between discontented factions within the supporters of the different rallies occurred with little the keepers of the peace could do to intervene. The catalyst was generally agreed to be the taking

of unauthorised photographs and live streaming
on the multitude of YouTube and dot net channels
broadcasted by reality stars. Others said it was the
running out of goody bags for celebs entering the
square too late. The commotion started around a
fountain. There was nothing much to start with just
some pushing and shoving to outright fighting
when rougher elements joined in. Soon becoming a
right sorry lament of lost dignity from these role
models.

When petite Elspeth Barbel was on the receiving
end of smacks in the face from the swinging breasts
of a glamour queen, the renowned impartial
Metropolitan Police had to take sides, primarily as
this scene was broadcasting live with the frantic
sobs of an aggrieved commentator echoing off the
walls of every living room in the land.

"In the name of God, someone has to help our
beloved dame."

A three hundred strong rapid response force made
up of heavy horse and bulletproof-shielded body
armoured constables charged into the crowd to save
the world of entertainment's first lady. Alas, the
bold efforts to re-address the balance failed, this
was no Thermopylae. The battered and bruised
thespians fled the field, leaving the law enforcers
with nothing to defend. Later, conspiracy theorists
had a field day when it later emerged that no
arrests had been made. The most common believed
machination was that adult entertainment
participants in the rally threatened to release
names of prominent constabulary officers if any
charges came to court. Officially, broken bones and
the nation's favourites being ducked in fountains

were blamed on a yobbish element carousing with the reality stars. In the weeks to come the inevitable barrage of defamation and counter writs arrived, boosting the profile of many involved.

In response to these demonstrations, the great British public spontaneously took to the streets. In the subsequent news coverage, the Muslims were criticised for not showing support for the families of the chefs, while the fact that the Chinese community remained completely indifferent went unstated.

While these shenanigans were happening, in a nice Oslo suburb, Commissionaire Du Gui sat in a comfortable chair having a commiserating chat with the widow of a murder victim. His face was one of industry rather than that of sheer genius with a smile without any hint of superiority, only kindness. They were passing the time of day like old friends yet three weeks before they had never met. It was the reported death of her husband that had caught his attention out of that day's stories from the assortment of European newspapers deposited on his desk. Noted as worth pursuing, the roaming investigator booked a flight, diverted his phone to voicemail, leaving a recorded message stating his unavailability for a few days and left the office unmanned. In his view, the only person that would really miss him would be an elderly neighbour whose dog he routinely took on a long walk. In return, she would do a bit of dusting for him, pick up his mail off the floor and put it on a sideboard.

The unspoken truth was the Commissionaire

looked forward to getting away from the banality of office life. Not surprising when taken into account that this old-fashioned investigator still firmly held the quaint idea that law enforcers should go out on the streets to prevent crimes. In his books, villains rarely volunteered to walk into a police station to confess to planning a crime and doing physical harm, while the practice of paying and protecting informants well placed within criminal networks was unethical to him. Furthermore, despite many efforts to take an interest in the latest policing methods, he stubbornly held to his own.

His interest in the goings-on in Norway's capital arose when it seemed peculiar that a man of that age would apparently do away with himself by trekking up to the 1952 Winter Olympic ski jump, climb over a two-metre-high safety barrier and slide down, head first, onto the solid cement basin of what remained of the landing area. This act contradicted a lifestyle expressed by the widow in the newspaper reports as peaceful and that her husband only left the house to go to work or to play chess. On the day of the alleged suicide, as by habit, she spent that afternoon preparing *fiskesuppe*. The thought of a chess enthusiast doing something interesting, even in death, did not comply with the sleuth's experiences, nor did the idea of a sudden despondency overcoming this man due to finding out that his partner for many years had been cuckolding him seemed very likely: a woman that spent the afternoons preparing evening meals from scratch was not one that was having an affair. Indubitably, these were feelings and not facts, but feelings based on solving the causes of unusual deaths over the last thirty years.

This incident was due to mistaken identity. The deceased man was a facilities manager based in the commercial sector of Oslo in charge of a team of hard working gophers who ensured everything from the correct working temperature to toilet paper was in place. By pure chance, this man had a doppelganger that worked a few doors away in the headquarters of a petroleum company. His double was chief accountant in the procurement department and was lining his own pockets by accepting costly contracts from a construction company owned by a prominent well-regarded leading businessman in Norwegian society who coveted political power.

In the cutthroat world of business, a billionaire was just that, a man rich and powerful enough to demand the best deals and to have bevies of paid heisters in the accountancy and tax industry to scurry about to stop his money being wasted by governments on things like national defence and welfare. None were angels, otherwise they would not be in the position they were in. In spite of this, in the world of mass media, there were favourably portrayed tycoons deemed to be on the side of progress not a megalomaniac wanting to either control or exploit everything. All this ignored the harsh fact that double-dealing and backstabbing took place daily in boardrooms and over business lunches with the booty buried deep in spreadsheets.

Although morally questionable transactions were inconsequential to this businessman, publicised knowledge of it could affect his embryonic political ambitions. Thus, it was the fear of these dodgy dealings hitting the fan and destroying future political ambitions that led to the issuing of an underworld contract to erase links to the doppelganger. The supposedly crack gang of hit men manhandled the wrong man into the back of a car and drove up to the tree-covered hills overlooking the capital city. Their aim was straightforward: first torture the victim to find out if any discriminating information existed anywhere before silencing him for good. With the intervention of Du Gui, things did not go to plan. Everything was now in the hands of the legal system, destined to take at least ten years to complete as defence lawyers argued the legitimacy of every accusation raised. It did not help the state prosecution that the intended victim had subsequently vanished.

Asking open questions and giving the correct expected respect was Du Gui's prime *modus operandi*. His strengths were a deep knowledge of human behaviour and compassion from which people that met him believed he cared, sympathised with what they said or done. This made them talk freely. With his reputation preceding him, culprits sometimes declared their guilt once they knew his interest in their felony. Not directly linked to the judicial system helped him as well. This was beneficial in circumstances where it was not clear-cut between right and wrong allowing those involved to disclose information without perjuring themselves. When it turned out to be an innocent forced by cruel circumstances into his or her actions, the milk of human kindness prevailed and he would quietly drop his interest when a compassionate juridical verdict looked unlikely. Why condemn someone to hardship when he or she had already suffered. When comforting a survivor or a nearest relation to the victim, the detective

never dwelled on any vulgar or forensic aspect,
but focused on his felt heart joy on helping a victim
and revealing a felon's true motives.

The inwardly quiet and peaceful widow, young
compared to the deceased husband and to Du Gui,
remised about the last few weeks and her marriage,
describing a life together that had been good, a
rewarding relationship rather than adventurous.

"You are my knight errant. Thank God for people
like you. How could I be expected to cope by myself.
Without your intuition, I would have been lost.

The saddest thing of all is my husband's voice has
faded from my thoughts and dreams."

Like love grief was not the same for everyone, it
affected people in different ways. The end of life
experience was not pretty for anyone, cosmetically
less hallowing for families of the rich but with a
similar outcome. These personal sorrows placed
everything else into proper perspective.

She continued:

"The ground is full of dead ordinary men whose
intelligent voices were never heard or heeded."

Du Gui listened as he sat with a cup of coffee
grasped in his left hand and a thick slice of sour
cream cake in the other. Opposite him the
mourning woman whose hair was just starting to
turn grey was preparing herself for a possible
future of being aware of the least sound that echoed
through the rooms of her house. There was no

television in the room for company which implied that the couple had not ran out of nice words to say to each other or needed a distraction to avoid touching upon forbidden topics. However, it was inevitable that marriage led to the loss of many things, including friends and the need to go out to socialise.

With rekindled sparkle in her eyes, she articulated her thoughts.

"The money now coming should secure me. No need to rent out rooms with plenty to allow me to get out and about. There is enough to visit my daughter in Cork, posted there by her employers Norwegian Air International."

He returned a smile, convinced she was grieving without guilt of past things said or done. She was going to make a go of it, thus stopping her becoming old too quickly and withering away. No sitting alone and looking at obituaries and ticking off recognised names. Aware of the emotional state of female survivors, he made sure his natural empathy did not lead to the transference of possible heightened emotions to feelings of affection for him. Even taken it for granted that when a loved one died you died a little yourself, he expected going forward she would be ok. The first significant test faced will be to go out into the world alone for the first time in many years. Yes, she was going to be fine, recover and not succumb to retreating into the shadows of mental illness or loneliness. Meeting new people would ameliorate her spirits.

Looking at his watch, he stood up, went over, gave her a kind hug and courteously told her that a plane back to Brussels awaited him. His final remarks were:

"It has been a pleasure to clear up this mystery."

The insurance company that had to pay up after the recorded death changed from suicide to murder would not miss him.

*****

Although a spruce dresser, the effort to maintain a high standard was getting harder at each passing day. The older Du Gui could hide if desired the muskier smell about him, but the overuse of deodorants and male perfumes was not the path for him. Like anyone else he was a man of his time, shaped by what was going on around him in his youth. That time was the 1970s when his musical and dress sense came from epic American crime movies and exciting designs coming out of England and Italy; a time when jazz sound tracks became the dialogue of magnificently tight-lipped and sardonic overcoat wearing detectives tracking down villains. Disinterest in the flower power scene with the pretentious happenings did not stop him enjoying the arrival of mass-produced youth garments with vivid designs shouting out eagerly perceived non-conformity. Gone were the days of hardwearing dirt hiding dark clothes, essential apparel in industrial dust ridden streets.

In later life, achieved success came with rewards and the pleasure of having a personal dresser, the only person who knew his waistline, how to make clothes hang well on his compact muscular frame and who remembered his client's partiality for a good British pullover. The only remit was the well-cut street clothes should be inconspicuous to allow him to go about unobserved and shoes that were good for walking.

Walking always won hands down in his view. Running was alien and in his line of work, it would advertise his presence or indicate an unanticipated denouement. For the public, a uniformed officer on the beat reassured them. For him, it helped to focus his thoughts as legs muscles stimulated the heart to pump blood up to his brain. Anyway, he was never built to be a sprinter or an agile martial arts expert. Therefore, in his early days, his brain was nurtured and with a physiognomy that gave no hint of his true mental faculty, lulled opponents into a false sense of security, giving him an edge as his sharp, incise thinking belied his years.

What you never had you never missed so a slowing down of pace that came with age did not worry him but the other symptoms linked to getting old and along with a stiff hip joint from falling on it after slipping on an icy pavement did annoy him. Recent annual private health consultations made him fully aware what happened to the body after sixty years on Earth. Tests showed signs of an overactive thyroid, tinnitus, and inflammation due to a hyperactive immune system. As well as inheriting a broad nose and a strong jaw, there were congenital disorders from a legacy of coming from human stock that once came out of an overcrowded slum. A boy can escape deprivation but the effect of it stayed with him with the dead passing on their fatalities. The worse scenario for him was to wake up blind and deaf but the doctors told him not to worry and that these emerging medical complaints were natural indicators telling him to slow down and enjoy his remaining years in more leisurely pursuits.

The last consultation resulted in a permanent prescription of statins and a mild sedative when headaches flared up. He did believe the tales that the statins accelerated the ageing process but was not brave enough to stop using them to find out. Doctors and health experts harping on about obesity, hypertension, heart disease, cancer, diabetes and dementia put the fear of god into his age group, with many believing all were utilised to get them to act their age and do as they were told. In his case, at least, the well-paid consultant treated him as an adult and did not lecture him on his lifestyle and merely pointed out the consequences of it. This was appreciated by a man that believed a little bit of weight never hurt anyone, it gave you reserves. However, the advice received did periodically change his ways: a strict diet for five days of the week, multiple vitamin and omega-3 supplements, and worse still giving up smoking and reducing the intake of caffeine and wine. That said, in the tempest of an investigation, all these impositions went out the window.

Cause célèbres, as a rule, did not attract his eye when browsing the newspapers but the missing chefs was an exception, in a nutshell, the motive for it seemed beyond any rational explanation or attributable to a base instinct. It gave him food for thought. On one hand, besides legions of well-wishers, the celebrity had to contend with ill-wishers some of whom could be deranged.

Consequently, Du Gui followed reports with interest and was perplexedly amazed that a country with a CCTV camera for every subject could lose so many celebrities in one night. It was always important for this investigator to keep an open mind but the elimination of unknown natural causes or coincidences looked straightforward. For the disappearances to be attributed to a series of unfortunate coincidences was virtually nigh impossible. If it were an organised crime operation, then quietly paid for information would bring dividends and unravel the mystery, and besides, many top ranking criminals and their spouses were food connoisseurs and acquirers of fine things, so increasing the possibility of an underworld crime lord stepping in to help. For future reference and habit, some salient points of this conundrum were noted down.

> *Audacious abductions on a night*
> *when all were in London*
> *Lack of crime scenes*
> *All a matter of speculation*
> *No who, why, how or where*

In a world where publicity was everything, the English language media sources at every opportunity obliged by blazing the faces of the chefs. Social media was jammed with hundreds of alleged sightings of them. Look-a-likes earned a fortune parading around shopping centres and turning up at stag nights. The release of alleged sex tapes blamed on impersonators and inventive video editing.

Everyone has a worth allocated to them, the effort assigned by the authorities reflected this value to society. Most of this score comes from job role and reputation. The considerable effort and money spent on the discovery of the whereabouts of the chefs amply illustrated their value. Furthermore, the huge resources spent was an attempt to mollify the hysteria that had consumed the British Isles. This despite, as many experts in the field privately acknowledged was a waste as they were probably already dead; this likelihood increased further by the amount of publicity generated which would panic any abductor to extreme measures. Although it was a forlorn hope to expect to see them alive, nevertheless, the mass media demanded on behave of the nation for a crumb of hope.

Du Gui added another comment in his notes:

> *If it were mass murder, why would it*
> *be of interest to anyone to choose chefs*
> *as the victims?*

Without facts and the news industry awash with spurious information, it was hard for the Commissionaire to pit his wits. With so little factual information available to him and many imponderables, it was far too easy to create false premises, unfounded assumptions that led him astray. Thankfully, it did not concern him and anyway the best criminal brains in England would be on top of it.

*****

Conscientious officers in the CID, Special Branch and Special Operations beavered away day and night to get the breakthrough. Even anti-terrorist organisations and GCHQ helped. Competition was fierce as there were instant promotions for those that solved the case but without specific leads to follow they were in a pickle, beginning to become skittish. Only queer nefarious activities of certain leading figures came to light when CCTV footage throughout the city was analysed. In the meantime, the news and publishing industry showed a complete lack of decorum by deliberately stirring up the emotions by making mountains out of mole holes with manufactured kiss and tell stories about the missing chefs, alleged incompetence in the investigations to date and rushing to cash in by re-issuing old cooking DVDs and rehashing biographies. On the main, the manufactured 1D shrouded descriptions of the missing chefs were just kind eulogies. Well-paid publicists had done their job to promote and protect them by keeping a rigid control of their projected profile and preventing indiscretions reaching the public eye.

Spewed out verbose nuisance knocked real news off the headlines. Debating the unknown made better copy and gave more potent headlines than undisputable facts. This preoccupation allowed the government and City of London the freedom to dump detrimental facts and figures that otherwise would not have passed the attention of journalists worth their salt.

Five chefs were missing, three males and two females. The men ran restaurant franchises while the women specialised in the home cookery market. One of the men was a stereotypical hard drinking wife beating loud mouth macho for late night TV viewing when male drunks came back from the pub. Another was a gentle northerner, child of a village vicar for Sunday morning viewers. The remaining male purportedly came from Scottish inherited wealth stock and entertained midweek viewers with weird and wonderful impractical ways of cooking food.

In his notebook, for something to record, Du Gui had written:

> *Male chefs having affairs with*
> *protégées?*

Of the females, you had a flirting former model and a homely West Country lass, one teased and other melted the heart; and both had a wild upbringing and a sugar daddy in the wings. For these females, he wrote:

> *Hated each other?*

All the chefs naturally had their own brand of culinary products and links to a major supermarket chain. The fact that the personas of the chefs were drastically different to capture a specific audience made the idea that a crazed fan had incarcerated them all seemed incredibly fantastical. The only thing that they had in common was a love of recipes using lots of butter, cream, sugar and red meat. The main benefiter in the culinary world of this riddle was another chef nicknamed the Preacher, who brattled on about good eating habits and the benefits of a Mediterranean diet.

In the bizarre times of today, it was not beyond the realms of possibility that a new health lobby extremist group had decided it was time for drastic action to stop the rise in obesity; maybe even, epigenetic preventive health warriors out to protect yet unborn innocents from the habits of unthinking future parents.

Was it really an act of subversion against the idols of the day?

More important matters such as ennui with work occupied Du Gui at this time. Policing was veering off in a direction that had little attraction for him and with many years of service under his belt, he could easily walk away from it. Because he did not want to overstay his welcome this idea was never far from his mind. Best to go soon and let the new generation of sleuths take the reins. Mind you, there was not much evidence to suggest that there were many waiting in the wings to take his place. Crime solving had a new paradigm and wearing down shoe leather no longer held much friction.

He had turned down offers of becoming a security consultant for the rich and powerful. Enough funds rested in his bank account not to have to waste spending his remaining years repeating obvious advice on how multi-national executives and rich quick sport and media personalities should protect themselves. Along with an excellent civil servant pension a comfortable life was there for the taking.

There was also a multimillion-euro contract on the table for his memoirs. The premonition that humanity would see out only a few more decades was additional motivation to see his memoirs published and read before it was too late. In saying that, the idea of sitting down and typing his life story was unenticing. Being able to write up case histories did not mean that he had the ability to convey events in a manner that expressed his true opinions and feelings. Facts and storytelling were two different things and if not done well too much emphasis on one would deprecate the effectiveness of the other. On a higher plane, he wondered if memoirs could tell the whole story or even an abridged version of it; did the written word not corrupt the reality; was the inexpressible not unexplainable and were all biographers really just butchers of the truth. Actually, his main worry was the incapability of expressing what he meant. The publisher offered assurances that this was not an uncommon apprehension. They could find an acceptable ghost writer to draft the book from interviews that their legal team and he would later vet.

A particular remark clinched the decision to not deprive the public of his case histories:

"It was a well-trodden path with only a few memoirs ever written by the subject. Many hands will contribute to the finished article as it is passed through editors, copywriters and proof readers."

With the book money, many a dream could be realised. Through work life had taken him where he had to go, now he could go where he wanted. There was nothing to keep him in Brussels and the list of active friends in his address book was these days dwindling fast. The idea of owning a vineyard was quickly dismissed as too cliché. Nevertheless, ensconcing himself in the countryside away from the humbug of the city was a tempting thought.

The smell of the earth replacing the underlying stench of a petroleum driven city. Peace and quiet that comes from being surrounded by stillness. If humanity made less noise the world would be a better place. Thus, why not escape from human folly and return to the familial roots in what was Nord–Pas-de-Calais. Buy land with apple trees and do his bit to help the bees by preserving their habitat. Continue a tradition initiated by the Romans when they brought the seeds with them. The cider would not go amiss either. Glorious isolation with the hullabaloo that accompanies everything from reported news to movies.

"Hops for beer and honey for cider, why not. An untroubled life then with good luck a good death. Did the great emperor Constantine not give up his deity and urbane life to retire into the countryside to grow cabbages? Besides, it would be great to be able to see sunsets over a sea horizon. If being a hermit is too much, maybe find an understanding childless widow to share it, be trusted to look after me and give me the burial wanted, but would it be an untroubled life? Life was never that rosy. I have always been a metropolitan animal and acclimatising to a rustic life will bring its own set of problems. With no financial need to sell the flat why not have the best of both worlds. Knickknacks gathered over time had to be kept somewhere, they created a visual eulogy with the flat being the mausoleum."

The centuries of spilt blood in Flanders made the men guarded, and then again, maybe this was just a load of twaddle as his ancestors mainly worked at the coalface, lived hard lives in deprived overcrowd conditions and could bellyache like any other

Frenchman. It was thanks to his father that he avoided the mines, a man who pulled himself up by his own bootstraps by studying hard during his meagre leisure time to eventually get a clerical job and in later life circulate in a higher social sphere, allowing him to meet and marry an attractive school matron who came up from the Midi-Pyrenees to teach children in a region devastated by the war. Apart from meeting his future wife, carving out a better existence did not bring happiness: he never settled in it, never at ease. This new world to him was inhabited with a petty bourgeois that by upbringing knew the ropes and were complacent to the radical changes occurring around them, dismissing them as unwanted with the non sequitur that life would return to normal once society came to its senses with their rigid conventions followed again. A class that had an ordered set out approach to everything, even bereavement, as if all human interactions were a business transaction, a straightforward transfer of funds.

He was based in the headquarters of the European Directorate of Judicial Affairs, within the department of serious crime. His office walled with heavy file cabinets with paperwork organised in his own unique filing system with overflowing manila files containing newspaper clippings, hand written notes and coronary reports. Everywhere high stacks of old notebooks visible on his desk, on top of the cabinets and along the window shelf.

The days of running off on the hunch of a miscarriage of justice or the macabre were ending. Due to recently enforced budget controls, his spending was being scrutinised by officious superiors, people with a limited emotional and empathetic range who only wanted solvable crimes investigated. He would no longer have unfettered freedom to roam and hated the idea. The tedium and rigmarole of briefing pencil pushing managers and attending staff meetings went against his methodology of crime solving. He was a man of instinct and human insight engaging directly with the world and other beings. From this perspective, it was amazing how some people thrived on paperwork. In his early days, before they gained power, there was an appreciation of their efforts to record criminal proceedings, now they had become a pain in the backside. Cost efficiency and the belief in the infallibility of scientific evidence ruled the roost. Modern techniques, excellent for trapping persistent known criminals were not so effective for obscure one-off acts with no obvious criminal intent.

He was actually past the usual retirement age for investigators and hints to do so by his superiors came in the form of assembling a team of information technologists brought in to digitise past cases onto databases with the aim of removing any dependence on his knowledge, making it easier to replace him. The age of high-speed cyber networks and open international travel necessitated the forming of specialist teams compartmentalised to look into the parts rather the whole nature of a crime, channelling effort down specific paths. A crime had to fit a category to allow it to be logged on a database and accessed by searching a designated key word. Modern criminology only demanded a DNA sample and access to a reliable database of suspects. It had occurred to him that maybe his perceived usefulness was just a protective illusion to justify picking up a wage. Could he, like so many in his age group, merely be habitually going through the motions. Another self-esteeming ploy could be that he was the exemption to the rule that elderly workers just passed their time at work or if in management used the gift of the gab or blatant ruthlessness to hide ineffectiveness. His approachability and plain speaking ruled out the latter but delusional opinions about his worth could not be ruled out. At least work was not a form of umbilical that maintained his manly status in the family household so preventing him becoming uxorious.

No matter where he looked, the future for lone wolves was bleak with stimulating work usurped by good salaries for those content to do administrative chores and where love for committee work was essential. Equanimity when dealing with mountains of paperwork was the be it all. Becoming prosperous by regurgitating tautologies and showing willingness to pass down directives. Vocation could never be the reason for desiring such employment. In effect, the creation of a broad strata of bureaucrats. Working under bean counters was another ominous sign. Finance teams busied themselves by collating cost plans that presumed an expected clear line of investigation without any deviations. The inevitable refusal to accept that a plan was not a road map but a demonstration of prudence before entering the unknown domain of uncertainty and blind alleys. When delays happened, more time was spent on discussing additional costs than dealing with the unexpected. A circular progress thus ensued as most staff maintained a silence, reluctant to argue viable causes for over spends, predicated by top down pressure and fear of losing a future promotion. Even the ergonomic reasoning for open-plan environments to create solidarity within a team felt impermanent to him; a setting ever ready for dismantlement.

Hard work was still required but that translated into hours of studying computer-generated data. Technology preferred to dexterity, the death knell of traditional nose down detection. Computer algorithms even predicted where certain crimes occurred and the profile of the offender. Detection and arrest decided by the highest calculated prediction probability, but useless in providing explanation for the inexplicable. Mind, did the apparent success of these algorithms demonstrate the lack of lateral or original thinking within the criminal fraternity and within humanity in general.

In lighter moments, he was philosophical about having the rug pulled under his feet. In every field of human endeavour, the twenty-first century was about collective effort. In some way this fact about postmodern life helped to explain the cult of the celebrity that gave the illusion that individuals still mattered. Naturally, the corporate world exploited this desire by promoting the idea that everyone was special when selling its products.

*****

Public outcry continued. From tenements to country houses there was disdain at the Prime Minister's bread and circuses utterances in having confidence in the police's handling of the mystery, that the country had the best forces in the world and that everything possible was being done. Even the monarch raised concerns about the inadequate response from her government.

Politicians hated being forced to take an interest in public concerns, preferring to abstractly wield power without worrying about the consequences of their actions on individual cases. As with every type of public umbrage, a reaction soon followed as anarchists and other complainers took to the streets. Violence erupted; distort subjects fought with extremists angry that third world disasters, famines and fuel poverty deaths were being ignored. Freedom of speech and the right to demonstrate hailed when demanded by the underfoot populace in evil states was a bitch when directed against the government at home.

Of course, the Prime Minister had to try to quell and pacify public anger by agreeing that these were harrowing times as well as pleading for patience. Off the record, he was extremely annoyed with the celebrities for stirring the masses to insurrection instead of doing their day job as the nation's trend setters; the sooner all the classes were back in their proper place the better. He even admonished *Equity* and threatened their members with exclusion from the honours list.

Continued establishment reassurances did not help to calm the nerves and mainly fell on stony ground as social media rumours and other allegations unrelentingly flamed unrest spreading throughout a disaffected population still reeling from backtracking on stronger immigration control after the EU referendum victors promised it. The rumours believed depended on held prejudices. Hence, many supposed the authorities had not been telling the whole truth. Some believed the involvement of Islamic terrorist cells and even fantasised vegan extremists to be behind this latest outrage against the peace loving Britons. Some assumed it was a hoax carried out by cunning TV executives about to announce a new up and coming show for celebrity chefs based on a tropical island, a walkabout in the Australian outback or in a gorgeous countryside mansion. In defence, when interviewed firm denials of a stunt were given but many executives regretted never coming up with these ideas themselves. There was a desperate need to refresh the cookery variety show as the ratings of terrestrial channels had been suffering since an internet competitor started broadcasting *Drone Wars*. A show attracting millions of regular viewers hooked on aerial combat between pellet firing drones flying at 1000 metres over the most beautiful cities and landscapes. A glorious idea based on the glamour bestowed on First World War dogfights, made all the more spectacular by adding a superfluous fuel tank to the drones' fuselage that exploded on a direct hit or when it nosedived out of control.

Beneath the reassurances, the prognosis based on the little information available for general consumption seemed glaringly pessimistic and the best chance for a satisfactory outcome was that important details had been kept back.

Meanwhile, as night follows day, there was the inevitable rush by publishers to print biographies before the public's ardour diminished. Quality did not matter. The only remit was to produce over two hundred pages of non-libel chitchat interspersed with agency library photos. Publishers with copyright on old biographies had a march on rivals, re-issuing them with a new cover and an amended last chapter while competitors had to resort to hashing together complete books from freely available reports, quotes from unsubstantiated media gossip and relying on the imagination of the author. This unexpected rich lode saved many a job by allowing some publishers to avoid administration for another year.

Behind the scenes, the government threatened to dismiss the Met Police commissioner if nothing substantial surfaced soon, and MI5 were ordered to investigate the personal lives of the chefs to see if some sort of perverse activity had taken place: a drug induced incident or some group sexual activity that got out of hand. Maybe, after a weekend party at a chef's country retreat, they ended up dead and floating in an indoor heated pool. MI6 used their contacts in the Middle East to see if an objectionable despot had richly rewarded them for cooking for him and they were now hiding in shame. To cover their backs, police investigations into some of the outlandish claims on social media were carried out to ascertain whether any truths were associated with them. This only exacerbated morale as well as wasting precious time. Needless to say, the Prime Minister continued to ask the public to show patience, as this was a difficult worldwide operation. The chefs had country estates, properties and yachts spread over the world and had the use of private aircraft to leave the country undetected. Therefore, conducting thorough searches and evidence gathering was a painfully slow process. The honourable gentleman additionally went out of his way to squash mischievous rumours that they had defected to Russia, saying that security sources here and in America had confirmed that the chefs had no links with this evil state and if they ever surfaced in that country it would be under duress and tantamount to an act of aggression against the free world.

In such a defensive state with damage limitation in mind, the Prime Minister forced the euro-sceptic mandarins at the Home Office to swallow their pride and the invite went out to ask for the services of the famous European special advisor of strange criminal investigations to have a go at unravelling the mystery. He had assisted the Met before but only behind the scenes with his name never mentioned when the offenders appeared in court. Now the government insisted on a visible profile, they required a game changer, an impact player that would satisfy the public, quell unrest and get them off the hook. The irony in asking the EU for help did not go amiss in Brussels.

Rumoured to have had lost the chance of high office in his own country because of his unlovable eyebrows, the European Director of Serious Criminal activities, *Geschäftsführer* Brüning, an overweight man with black hair parted on the left, thick bushy eyebrows and hound dog cheeks pulled Du Gui into his office to inform him of the invite but really to censure past nonchalance to his authority.

"You see Du Gui, this is the way it should be done. Our department has been formally asked to let you assist in England. None of this running off to help a presumed victim based on a newspaper clipping. What's more, you always conveniently forget that your jurisdiction is limited to members of the union and its trading partners. You have even ran off to Canada in pursuit of a felon."

"The man on the run was an Italian senator."

"We have international agreements on criminal extraditions for that sort of thing!"

On his way out, just as his hand touched the gold plated door handle, the director said his final piece.

"Listen well, be on your best form and try not to antagonise them. You know how sensitive they are towards us."

It was water off the back for Du Gui who knew that Brüning's two-year tenure in this office was ending soon, as the EU bureaucratic merry-go-round would replace him with another key member's choice. A two-year tenure was ample time to enhance the pension pot and reduce without the need of surgery the politician's bags under the eyes. According to Du Gui's recollection, it should be the turn of the Spanish to reward their man. He would miss this current director for his idiosyncrasy of not being able to find a shirt with a collar that comfortably fitted him. When meeting him, he wondered how the man's collar shirt button held under the enormous pressure of a bulging neck trying to burst out. One day, the top button would jet forward taking the eye out of some unfortunate.

The news of the invite through the grapevine had already reached Du Gui's ears and he was back in his element. He had not been to London for over a decade not since the mass rollout of surveillance on its population and where policing was now a matter of rolling back recorded footage to identify criminality. Its police force, although loathed to admit it, were no longer proactive crime fighters.

His memoirs publisher was ecstatic to hear about this consultancy assignment with the Met: money could not buy such worldwide publicity and it would give a good ending to a distinguished career. Their endorsement summed up with a cheery parting comment.

"Enjoy yourself. You revel in a good crime!"

A sigh of relief spread across the UK with the news the man dubbed by the tabloid press as l'*infatigable* was on his way. Their sensationalism in the gory aspects of some of his most unusual cases had boosted his reputation. In the City of London, the Stock Market rallied recovering several billions in earlier losses. As was the nature of sudden fame, prior to the invite, only keen followers in the chronicles of crime could identify him. The day after the announcement of him coming to help, every man, woman and child across the land could now put his name to a face.

The news of this appointment was not universally welcomed. No organisation liked outsiders forced upon them and like other infallible institutions, the famed Metropolitan Police had its reputation to protect.

To reinforce the point that Du Gui worked for an accountable EU organisation, an assistant, Estela Vermeulen, a person deemed to have a good positive mental attitude was assigned to help him and ensure reporting procedures were followed. The director said he had chosen a level-headed woman with a bright future ahead of her, an asset to the department. In a world once the preserve of tough men, opportunities were there for all sexualities. On meeting, Du Gui saw a svelte female with a southern European face that made men aware of their hormones. Beauty if accompanied with charm was power indeed. Smiling and offering her hand, it looked as if she belonged to a gym. The firm handshake confirmed this observation. About one hundred and sixty centimetres in height, tanned, probably just back from holiday, and looked late twenties. Attractive that is in the modern sense with a thin framed muscle toned body and a lean face that had high cheek bones, a small slightly pointed nose and feathery eye lashes protecting maroon coloured eyes; a head held high by a graceful neck; and a posterior that would not look big in everything. On the downside, the musk of the physically fit lingered longer than the fragrance of her scented shampoo and body deodorant. There was something unromantic about an overly fit woman in the eyes of men of Du Gui's generation. Maybe the smell reminded them of East European shot putters.

Vermeulen gave the impression she did not want a man so that she could improve him, anyone chosen would have to keep up or be left behind. Considered serious minded, hardworking, amiable and helpful to superiors, she was ambitious to get on, which implied being naturally manipulative or learning to be if she wanted to succeed, and be prepared to flatter the boss or even to sleep with him or her if the rewards were sufficiently high. This last bit of dedication was an extreme act and being just an apple in eye of an influential manager normally sufficed. Obviously possessing an activated psychopathic gene would be of great use to her.

On a personal note, Du Gui mulled over the proposition of would she consider him a person who could advance her career or dismiss him as a yesterday man. Her looks shouted out middle-aged man's *little girl'* but though seemingly forever trapped in this ever expanding age group, he excluded himself as too old to be worth the expenditure of her charms, old because his body felt old.

Nodding sagely at his assigned colleague, he was mindful not to see her as an unwanted burden and looked for the positives. Better to have a cultivated young female colleague than a testosterone driven male thug dressed in a suit. This hormone was blamed for many health problems and Man's lack of empathy as it impaired relationship-building behaviours like easy-going eye contact and the ability to understand someone else's motivations. If testosterone was a handicap, then it was a problem that affected all keep fit fanatics regardless of gender. For the ambition driven female in this group, it was a matter of swings and roundabouts, with the increased threat of an earlier death being one of the downsides.

*****

After all the paperwork was signed off, the pair arranged to travel to London on the Eurostar. Du Gui decided to reside in the large French quarter that had sprung up in the last decades, shunning the opportunity to stay at a top class establishment in Piccadilly, lodgings Miss Vermeulen would not give up for all the coffee in Java. The chance to receive deferential treatment by immaculately attired room servants in an establishment famed for its rococo furnishings, spas and comfort was too good to miss for this young woman, a residence where everything a princess would require was a phone call away. For him, a single room with en-suite bathroom was sufficient. The only prerequisites were that the walls had adequate soundproofing and the plumbing was in good order. This would allow him to have a peaceful night to reflect on his day and unwind with a good book and a glass of cognac.

When he did not sleep well, his work suffered.

Du Gui was first to arrive at Brussels Midi railway station. At a news kiosk, he bought an English broadsheet and a book, a tale about a narcissistic crime writer's dinner party for loyal fans. The cover of a new *James Bond* story had initially caught his eye but a dynamic secret agent, who was older than him, jumping from rooftop to rooftop and rolling his car to avoid exploding grenades and guided missiles fired from shoulder held launchers did not appeal to him, *quelle connerie.*

Next, he headed to the Eurostar platform with the intention of meeting Estela on the train. There the known face of an incorrigible rogue with a wonderfully resourceful mind was spotted. When travelling between destinations, the man dressed well.

Genuine rough sleepers cannot conform to the norms of society, possess poor interpersonal skills, spend time just aimlessly wandering, always confronted by the law, become petty criminals and due to bad experiences are mistrustful of others. Their lives spent revolving round soup kitchens, squats and prison with drugs as constant companions. Comradeship existed in their world, someone to share a fag and relate their problems but encounters with fellow rough sleepers could quickly turn nasty with unreported violent outbursts occurring as good folk slept peacefully in their beds. These were the true down and outs. Hunger reduced them to a diseased inflected docile spineless painful condition.

This image contrasted with beggars seen on many a street, although visibly dishevelled, signs of not existing in a desolate state were detectable. It could be the good condition of a fashionable pair of boots, the use of a high-end mobile phone or a recognised face who had bagged a good spot with friends regularly stopping to see how business was faring.

Not being an expert or motivated to do the research, he often wondered if there were more beggars today than in the Middle Ages. He did know that there were different types of beggars and that one in five of them were genuinely dissolute, the others obtained state benefits of some kind, and among a few percentages a good income was derived from sitting out on pavements. The self-assured man seen boarding the train was one of the latter.

Du Gui went over to this prince of beggars and
interrupted his perusing of a visitors' guide to
London. Undoubtedly reviewing the best latest
haunts to ply his trade. A jolly scallywag called
Radu, a Romanian with an impish grin, reddish
brown hair, dark almost black eyes and a light
ivory brown skin. A medium build man with a
straight back when not begging and noticeably
arched when working; one smart cookie who slept
with an eye open.

"Where is your accordion, your old swindler?"

"What! Oh, it is you, *mon ami*. I only carry the
concertina when travelling. You are also on
business?"

The unabashed fraudster claimed benefits in
London, Brussels and Paris for a wife and six
children back in Romania. To keep social services
and fraud investigators off his back, his paperwork
affirmed him as a paid part-time kitchen helper
requiring support with his rent as well as child
benefit. The world of business supplemented by
social benefits, principally in the restaurant and
food industries, used to hide this deception. A
seasoned con man extraordinaire, a swindler who
knew his target audience. In London, he had
lodgings in a Lebanese's boarding house near Earl's
Court. When begging, his clothing reflected the look
of an indigenous down and out to differentiate him
from the foreign beggar. As a rule, he stayed clear
of his own community, not due to any grudge but
because in his profession the threat from

compatriot gangsters and subjugation to their will was an ever present one. Escape was impossible once under their dominance with passport and earnings confiscated.

"*Mon ami*, corruption is the great enabler in human society, it oils the wheels. Only a fool has scruples. Honesty is rarely rewarded. May as well be crooked," philosophised the prince.

"I should get you arrested."

"Stop threatening me, *mon ami*, I have residency rights, save from prosecution or deportation. I am a free man. A self-employed entrepreneur with a keen eye for ways to get money. It is hard labour to beg, freezing to death while trying to get blood out of stones with insults and harassments routinely endured."

"Yes, it is hard work being a citizen of the world."

Both laughed and before leaving the Romanian in peace his contact details were taken. Undercover help from his son was no longer guaranteed as he had his own family to look after, so unorthodox inconspicuous assistance from another source could come in handy.

At his window seat, Estela was spotted coming along the platform with a porter and baggage following on behind. Her gait had not yet mastered the power walk that came from authority and still betrayed hints of a skip, hopefully due to feeling excited about the assignment.

The train departed on time. Estela sat opposite

him, made a morning greeting in a neutral voice then proceeded to open her laptop, Du Gui read the newspaper.

As far as the case was concerned, the paper proved to be an absolute disappointment. A two-page spread opening with a leading question with the same question repeated in the final sentence. In between thousands of words that did not illuminate anything of interest or reveal any insight on the investigation, just page fillers from a longwinded feature writer who loved nothing better than to postulate and expostulate his stance. After that annoying read, a ten-minute search through the rest of the paper resulted in two articles receiving his full attention: a restaurant review and a story about a discovered plague pit in East London. The pit near Liverpool Street railway station believed to be the final resting place of at least 100 victims of the Great Plague of 1665. Archaeologists made the gruesome find during excavations of the site exposed by heavy digging equipment for preparation to laying the foundations of a new office complex, a tower that would become the latest tallest structure in the City of London. Initial examination suggested the mass burial occurred in a hurry and could shed light on the catastrophic epidemic, which wiped out a fifth of London's population.

The restaurant review helped to decide where to eat while in London. The food critic discussed current food fads and gave his opinion on an evening spent at a top Knightsbridge hotel where the mezzanine grill room had been taken over since January by a chef currently lauded in France for his fusion of French and Tahitian cuisines; a chef leading a revival in Gallic gastronomy by the name of Jordan Lemanu, who appropriately enough was of mixed breed. The critic seemed to have something against diners who enjoyed nothing more than to go out for a good meal and return home to fall asleep on the couch or bed after filling their mouths with everything put in front to them. The least scathing comment was the food was no better than surf and turf drowned in rich sauces. Another commented observation was the night out was a chaotic collision of primitivism with *fin du siècle* opulence. The article created the impression that the intended readership must spend most of their time in the gym or bopping about town after *un epas léger*. The smugly written article epitomised that weird haute cuisine fallacy that less was more. It inferred to Du Gui that this critic believed that intellectually there was nothing in favour of comfort dining. Whereas, in his homeland, great chefs came from a peasant ancestry, believed in generous portions and happily spread the joy of having a full stomach.

When the train powered through the tunnel, the change in mood that comes from being aware of entering an unnatural environment, prompted him to discard the paper and browse the novel. A fiction about a novelist giving a reception to winners of a short story competition. He wanted to give something back to the readers of his detective series so why not have a soiree to celebrate the end of the series. Reward the readers rather than go to a backslapping event organised by the publishers and other trade bodies. The winners had to write a three-thousand-word plot outline depicting the exploits of the detective. To make the event even more interesting the winners had to dress as a character from the series and received a pre-release copy of the final instalment to discuss over the dining table. The evening broadcasted over the internet to gain maximum publicity for the shortly to be released book. The blurb on the back cover suggested that not all was as benignant as it seemed.

*****

At St Pancras railway station, they were guided straight through customs by a Met officer. For Du Gui, not seeing the Channel or having to wait at border control took the magic out of traversing countries. The waiting car pulled out into the busy London streets and immediately grinded to a halt. The Met officer was in his early thirties, fair headed and physically strong, wore a well-tailored black suit and had a wedding ring on his finger. He introduced himself as DC Williams, Welsh heritage, played rugby and would be their liaison officer to help them settle in and obtain all that they required. A fine example of a leaner, fitter and stronger law enforcer than previous generations, but unfamiliar with chasing down and tackling crooks. Du Gui's first impression of this man was that of a muscle bound sickeningly polite jockstrap, but this type of impression always entered his head when encountering a confident young buck.

The first day at Scotland Yard was spent on formalities. They were shown to their desks in the inquiry coordinating centre; everything smelt new: an open-plan area accommodating all the various teams that contributed to the daily briefings. There

was a quick welcome from the chief investigator
and a command for Du Gui to see the Met chief in
the early afternoon, then they were brisk off to
obligatory lectures on health and safety, data
protection, the dos and don'ts in behaviour and a
reminder of the dress standards expected from all
officers, uniformed and non-uniformed. Afterwards,
Du Gui and Vermeulen received their identification
and fob access badges and taken around the
building by the office monitor to be shown the
muster point in case of fire, the canteen, toilets and,
importantly, the smokers' corner.

At the appointed time, he entered the offices of the
high command and made his presence known to a
secretary who pointed him in the direction of the
PA. Not everyone was equal in this person's world,
she knew whom to show respect, and whom to treat
abruptly, but everything always said with
emotionless perfect diction.

The moment he walked on the thick and silent
carpet of the commissioner's office behind the stiff
well-educated, barely polite PA, his outspread
palms closed. The drinks cabinet with high-end gin
and scotch and sparkling crystal glasses ready for a
VIP was not going to be opened for him. The large
space that met his eyes with appropriately sized
furnishings with everything in its place was not a
scene that imbued approachability or the
impression of hard work. Quite the opposite, it was
the well-practiced ploy of humbling the visitor in
the presence of a powerful man not open to
persuasive argument by creating an imposing
space. The dour-faced close-chopped grey haired Sir
Anthony Middleton Edwards and a high-ranking
toady stood waiting for him. The room was stifled

with rewards and framed pictures of previous commissioners and an out-sized writing desk with papers neatly stacked waiting to be signed. The room gleamed from that just polished look; nothing showed signs of patina.

In complete contrast to his proposed offer of introduction, it was a cold reception for the invited advisor. This was to be a private conversation with nobody recording minutes, just a stern word about the ground rules from a man unused to being contradicted and not able to vent his bile on the Home Secretary for imposing a foreigner onto his team. With an assertive CEO voice used to being obeyed in and out of uniform by underlings that never looked him in the eyes, the stipulations for allowing this intruder freedom to roam within the investigation were about to be spelt out from lips that slanted to the upper right.

"On my part, the pleasure in meeting you is muted. This is a serious business. Your appointment is only a sleight-of-hand decision and a waste of money by a feckless jittering political establishment desperate to restore public favour. Our records indicate that your commission is honorary, that you have a track record of being a lone wolf and hostile to superiors. The last thing I need is a smart-ass with the ability to pull the wool over the eyes of the Home Office into believing his usefulness."

Du Gui patiently stood still, noting that his thick collar length hair swept back to curl naturally at the back of the neck and tinted brown glasses must be sending out the wrong message, and not that of a man with many years of crime solving under his belt.

"Make no mistake and get his clear in your head that you will have no direct involvement. We require you to confine your activities to providing support and confirming to the press that everything that can be done is being done.

Everything by the book and no sharp practices. This is a tight ship. You have no jurisdiction to make an arrest or enter premises without supervision and a court issued warrant. With this in mind, the officer at your disposal will act as your guide and keep you honest."

Du Gui dreaded to think what his socialist father would have made of this man. A man brought up to give commands abetted along the way by cronyism and the old school boy network. The teleological dream for society shattered on the concrete floor of realism with the divide between the masses and the elites onwards widening.

The Met commissioner continued:

"I wish to make it clear from the start that I do not welcome the interference of a professional nosey parker like you.

You are only an observer to provide insights. Remember, media pressure brought you here, not a request from within my organisation. This is a team effort whilst you have never lead men or been responsible for their welfare. I am charged with maintaining discipline in an organisation that employs over forty thousand officers, many routinely armed. The last thing we need is an amateur meddling in this business and most likely breaking rules and established procedures making a conviction impossible. I will not allow pain-stalking work destroyed.

Access to any suspect will be restricted to thirty minutes a day and that after my teams have completed their interrogations. Your name will be added to the list to receive transcripts of interrogations.

Divulging the nature of our investigations or offering opinions without passing it through our Press Office first is strictly forbidden. One last thing, never attempt to hold press interviews in front of the revolving sign of the headquarters. Enter and leave the premises by the side entrance to avoid any photographers."

After the unwanted guest left the office, the nodding toy dog ventured to offer support to his superior.

"At least his words will be more credible than the dreaded vote of confidence coming from the Prime Minister's Press Office."

"Really. No good will come from this. The last thing we need is a venerated Belgian to tell us what to do!"

"He is not Belgian, sir, French."

"My God that makes it worse, what will the old Etonians say in the Civil Service club. Not worth thinking about. Dreadfully rum lot those

Frenchmen."

Back at his desk, Du Gui shrugged off the
disparaging remarks, knew enmity towards Europe
still festered in high places and to put things into
perspective he recalled how much warmer was the
earlier meeting with the chief investigator in
charge of the day-to-day running of the case. He
had been smart enough to know to speak in
monosyllables to the blunt autocrat, repeating 'I
appreciate your frankness' three or four times. The
secret when in the presence of those that deemed
themselves important was to say nothing
controversial. The best way to prevent
disagreement was to automatically agree as if the
matter was clear and not worth bringing up in the
first place. This policy had its risks as acting as a
piece of furniture could one day find you the deputy
head of the organisation.

He had expected nothing more and as a rule never
concerned himself with the fate of the high-
powered. Yet, there was some sympathy for this
irritated and put upon prickly pear, who put the
nail on the head by guessing his allergy to
authority and bureaucracy. The Met commissioner
was the biggest fish in the UK police force but all
the same a civil servant accountable to elected
politicians, compelled to spend his time firefighting
and being the butt of any ambitious Home
Secretary or Mayor of London. For a man that
expected deference, this would more often than not
be a demeaning experience and not good for his
health. The poor bugger's bright red face screamed
high blood pressure. Elected politicians were past
masters of transferring accountability and the
Ministry of Propaganda known as the Prime

Minister's Press Office was quick to point the finger at its appointed scapegoat when mismanagement saw the light of day. All they needed was the instigation of the first rule of leadership which was make sure any shit did not stick on them. Mind, the stab in the back for him will be a handsome golden goodbye to buy his silence.

What was incontrovertible was his presence rankled the Met and they did not want his type of practical help. Although forewarned was forearmed, the unambiguous statement of his duties would, as a matter of course, be ignored. He was obstinate by nature and not anyone's puppet so would go where his nose led him. The diktats would only be followed within the confines of Scotland Yard while his lunchtimes belonged to him.

He observed a hive of activity at their desks as Estela gladly accepted the assistance of the liaison officer to set up their laptops and request access to the networks and databases, odd considering that her EU personnel file indicated attendance at all the IT courses going and the security clearance given to them granted access to everything. At least the computer technician sent to help could sit back and enjoy his coffee.

"Anything you want to know I can find out for you," said the helpful Williams.

Du Gui wanted to ask how anyone could think while sitting in front of flickering screens, better to stare at the blank wall behind their desks.

Close by some of the watching female officers gave the distinct impression of not appreciating Estela's presence. In their eyes, the female had it all and got the attention sought after: strikingly black hair unprofessionally fell on a bare neck, five centimetre heels, clothing a bit too tight under which a bra just covered her nipples; terrible attire for chasing down criminals, outrageous work clothes.

Noticing Du Gui's pondering face when he had returned from upstairs, the liaison officer commiserated with him.

"It is a pity that your meeting with the top brass did not occur in the late afternoon after his nibs' nosh at his club."

"*Ca m'est égal.* Pardon, it makes no difference to what we have to do."

Du Gui made a mental note not say anything of importance in front of this man as it would go straight back to his superior. Someone with his alacrity to please was too good to be true.

GALLIC RESURGENCE

London had the sixth largest French population of any city. Four hundred thousand souls had jumped across the Channel, many to find work but a significant number to live in Kensington to avoid taxes. Along with Russian bankers who stole clients' assets in the motherland and financiers fleeing Iceland after the banking crash to avoid imprisonment, London attracted the cash rich financiers voluntarily making themselves exiles by buying immunity from extradition.

Despite his face being all over the national media, Du Gui believed residing in this quarter allowed him to hunker down anonymously permitting him to come and go without drawing attention. This belief stemmed from the natural disregard of his compatriots for the affairs of others, and this included celebrities. With this in mind, the chosen residence was the Excelsior, a fine five-storey solidly build dark brick facade hotel, probably early sixties, with a pretentious mock Georgian ornate entrance intimating promised comfort. The quiet location off a main thoroughfare was another reason for choosing it. When he arrived, a different room was requested, one away from the front.

The room now given was on the third floor and had a placid décor that pleased him. Its blandness did not offend the eyes and would not distract the mind. Moreover, it was pleasing to him to find that the window opened, allowing the temperature to be manually regulated as it was currently too high for his liking.

Alone for the first time that day, he unknotted his tie, unbuttoned the collar of his shirt and released a sigh when an unflattering face came back at him from the full-length mirror fixed into a closet door. Although never seduced by narcissistic gazing at his own image there were some days when seeing it made him feel young but delusion was impossible when suddenly confronted with his true physical form. A shagging face looked back at him, which deflated him and forced another involuntary outtake of breath, a reactive gesture that happened a lot recently. He had to admit that his debonair days were fast coming to an end, well past the age to be the love interest in a romance movie.

To avoid the mirror, he stepped sideways and continued disrobing prior to showering that day's effort away. Physically, he was getting more like his father: burlier, wearier with an expanding stomach. The major difference was that a cushier life slowed down the ageing process. His face was softer and hair had its colour, a mousey brown, not bad for a man who was older than his father ever was. There were downsides to a lifetime of enjoying rich food and wine increased the likelihood of suffering from the modern afflictions of obesity, diabetes and other linked illnesses. Once under the hot gushing water, he realised that he had forgotten to bring shampoo.

Again, for a moment, the familial face manifested in front of him, this time from the bathroom mirror, the face seen when his father and he had sat down together and enjoyed a very expensive bottle of cognac. It was the day before his father went to hospital, to never return. It occurred to him that in his final days he would not probably enjoy a fine drink with someone who knew him inside out. Yes, there was his own child but he had grown into a man without him knowing of his existence, only to meet later in life by chance on an outing in the suburbs of Paris to apprehend a blackmailer of a junior minister at the Élysée Palace, so in many ways the son was a stranger to him. Even the time spent with the mother was brief, entering his life when an injection of the *joie de vivre* was needed, leaving a sweet lingering taste on the tongue. Like everyone, he was sometimes upbeat, rolling along, and other times down and going through the motions. Marie LeMoël had cleared the decks and gave him a new lease of vigour.

After drying himself and putting on a pair of slacks, polo shirt and jumper, he opened his suitcase and brought out the gizmo for detecting electronic bugs. He did not know how it actually worked but it gave confidence when it did not buzz. Advances in bugging technology may have already outdated this trusted device but the ritual of checking was now firmly set into his routine. It did not take long to scan the simple laid out room. The bed, chest of drawers, closet, striped venetian blinds and the television bolted to the wall, as expected, returned no signature. The exercise would be done again tomorrow in case any interested party found out the new room number. The ritual of checking for bugs relaxed him rather than gave him much concern. A more important task was the purchase of two second-hand refurbished pay-as-you-go mobile phones to use as confidential communication with Estela.

Next, a bottle was unconsciously taken out of the opened suitcase and a large measure of cognac poured into the provided toothbrush tumbler. He then proceeded to reflect on his meeting with the Metropolitan Police commissioner. The fit of pique was expected. His arrival was a slap in the face from those on high. Anyway, as it turned out, he was happy to keep his distance from the official investigation. Let the Met follow tedious leads, tick all the boxes without any real enthusiasm of making a decisive breakthrough but ensuring that they had protected themselves against an unforgiving news media pointing the finger of incompetence at them so not allowing headline grabbing politicians to make a name for themselves.

This evening, Du Gui would have something good to chew on. What was more this will be the only occasion Miss Vermeulen would venture out with him: their tastes were to prove not alike. They arranged to meet in the restaurant mentioned in the earlier read broadsheet review section, his choice.

*****

A crouching photographer clad in leather and swamped with hanging lenses called his name and snapped him with a flash on the way up marble steps. From that angle, the partially shown name of the renowned hotel where the restaurant was located would clearly show up. The snapper knew his stuff.

The restaurant refurbished for the new season was not anything like a gaudy kitsch slice and dice sushi bar as asserted in the uninformative broadsheet. This hotel would never allow itself or its guests to be associated with anything so tacky. In addition, French culture had influenced the South Seas for many centuries so this Garden of Eden using Gallic know-how could only produce titillating food. Perhaps, the esteem food critic was friends with rival restaurateurs and knowing what side his bread was buttered ran a spoiler on their behalf. Attracting the in-crowd was a cutthroat business. Whatever the reason for the poor review, it did not matter to Du Gui, as tonight's meal was eagerly anticipated.

A great deal of effort had gone into the design and layout to produce a modern take on an often-portrayed primitive and in the past barbaric land to bring the true Polynesian experience to the European diner. For that reason, although not all tastes can ever be satisfied, the work done could have at least been accorded some credit. The foyer had an original Tahitian welcome canoe as its centrepiece. The lounge was walled with 3D black and white transparencies of Gauguin primitive paintings showing idyllic scenes of bare breasted young native women surrounded by lush greenery with partially hidden staring wild beasts. Dotted around the seating area white waist-high pedestals displayed encaged in glass cabinets fine examples of South Seas indigenous art. The waitresses in native costume greeted guests with smiles and grace. The décor was devised to be a mood modifier as the diner moved to the lounge into a world of calm created by an atmospheric interplay of colour, space and light. The use of parallel and horizontal lines on the walls in muted colours of the South Sea Islands signified the islands raised above the Pacific Ocean and breaking waves rolling onto the beaches. Du Gui accrued this information from the description that came with the drinks menu. Piet Mondrian would have appreciated the backhand compliment. What Gauguin would have thought was a different matter. The standing of this painter contested in modern times as recent revelations accused him of being a wife beater who despised being poor after turning his back on a lucrative stockbroker's life. This had added credence to the growing argument that this man had cut Van Gogh's ear. Even so, the detective had his reservations. The psychological state and life story of the Dutch painter made him more likely to do a rash self-inflicting act when pushed by a bully. To boot, there was the question of practicality. A left-handed person like Van Gogh would naturally cut the left side ear by pulling it down taut with the weaker right hand to execute a cut with a blade held in the stronger hand. The right-handed Gauguin would find it awkward to cut it no matter how he approached it.

The restaurant was more or less full with French diners and some other adventurous souls. The English instantly recognisable by their haughty bad

French when ordering, no nasal vowels for them. The place was patronised by financiers, drug barons and, of course, criminal investigators.

While Du Gui was looking forward to the meal, Estela seemed distracted but not by the presence of sartorial splendour. The ostentatious panoply of the latest fashionable evening dresses and the show of jewel encrusted *Rolexes* and gold bracelets as diners supped their aperitifs drew no interest. She even did not blink an eye when their drinks arrived in a *coco de mer* carved tray. When it occurred to Estela that Du Gui was observing her with a detective's curiosity, she composed herself by sipping her drink and by keeping a well-practiced expression of enjoyment on her face when queried for her opinion.

When seated, diners could look into the kitchen through a soundproof viewing window. The clean-shaven, small and stocky head chef wore the tallest toque, a little Napoleon of gastronomy dictating instructions with an economy of movement and seemingly few words as the sous chefs in white and kitchen helpers in blue dashed about. These missionaries of roasting large joints of meat like African Christians had come to Europe to re-acquaint the natives with what they had lost.

The whole scene was a feast for the eyes as the alchemy of slow roasted sizzling seared dishes created an olfactory charm. To Du Gui's delight, not many saucepans simmered on the stoves. Being of northern extraction, he did not like the flavour of food concealed by rich sauces; such dishes were a perfect metaphor for the deception and sophism spun to hide simple truths that would otherwise be difficult for the public to digest. Not being a great follower of the aesthetic arts either, he was nothing like the stereotypical image of a sophisticated foreign detective.

The menu offered many delights: wahu; poke; whole grilled beef ribs with a truffle jus; smoked pork; marinated jumbo shrimp, clams, crab legs, mussels, oysters and scallops; and fish in coconut.

Du Gui asked Estela about her family.

"Belgian father and German mother. There is also Spanish blood on my father's side. The family background is of civil servants and functionaries. Since its conception we have been professionally involved with the European Union."

"So the bloodline has its veins dug deep into the apparatus of the EU allowing offspring to enjoy the benefits of access to excellent free education and employment opportunities, thus explaining her speedy progress through the ranks. Her self-assurance coming from always getting what was wanted."

He found the getting-to-know-you exchanges a bit of a challenge as Estela with her inherited stuck-up cheekbones was reluctant to engage in a flowing conversation. His joke about her being the second sister meant she was the perfect child as her parents learnt from their mistakes with the older daughter just raised a quick sharp smile. As the protracted silences lengthened, he began to find himself looking at her penetratingly, trying to read her true thoughts.

Confronted with an insurmountable barrier, he gave up and decided to disregard her good looks, stop making small chat, preferring to dwell on the food being prepared behind the viewing window. With roasting of the whole animal becoming a lost art, the scene was evocative of a medieval cookhouse. The gastronomic juices stirred in his stomach as meats slowing rotated on spits over wood chip fires with juices braised over them and igniting in the flames below. Succulent wild boar, mutton, goat and beef, the animals recognisable, delicately absorbing the warmth and smoke of the fire. The menu listed grain fed Boer goat, Gloucester Old Spot pig and slow-growing Belted Galloway cattle meats, crustaceans flew down from Scotland and vegetables and fish picked up in the morning from New Convent Garden and Billingsgate. It was a pity that the days of eight to ten courses at one sitting were long gone. The health lobby would go bombastic if a culinary entrepreneur attempted to re-introduce this type of fare back to the masses.

For his starter, there was bisque surrounded by crispy battered shrimp and langoustine, crab and crayfish miniature breaded cakes. The main was pure carnivore: mixed roasted meats served with young root vegetables pan cooked in an herb butter sauce and a drop of broth. The natural flavours enriched by herbs and spices, not oppressed by them.

The wine, red naturally, was from the Loire valley.

Du Gui positively purred.

On a smoke break, he went out and sneaked down the back of the hotel to avoid being seen at its prestigious front. In the gloom of a dark alley, he observed blue-cladded kitchen helpers huddled near bins and this fellow smoker joined them to get gossip. With backs against a wall drawing on cigarettes, keeping the smoke in their mouths as long as possible before expelling it, they seemed reluctant at first to chat in his presence, suspicion flashed in their eyes. They lowered their guard when it dawned on them that the stranger was French.

"*Salut,*" reverberated from their lips.

When asked how they found London, the consensus was it was too busy for their liking and they looked forward to returning to French Polynesia. They did not venture far from their place of work, only the head chef was adventurous. He selected the suppliers himself after spending days travelling around to ensure the best possible quality was purchased from the many purveyors of fine rare breeds of organic meat that had popped up in England. Du Gui learnt that for the last couple of weeks the head chef had confined himself to the premises after initially being keen to spread the word of his cuisine.

As what happened when smokers gathered together, a silence descended as they stared at the smoke rising from cigarettes held between their fingers. The sight of blue *Elastoplasts* drew Du Gui eyes to the small cuts and grazes on the hands of the skivvies and the tattoos that ran up their arms. Taking a last drag, the butts were flicked away. With addiction satisfied, without any apparent signal, the kitchen helpers parted, re-entering a rear door and from his close position he saw a pair of bouncers marshal them back in.

He returned to the table to enjoy a dessert and coffee. On seeing Estela fixated on her smartphone, feelings of pity aroused within him for a generation compelled to believe life existed in a mobile application, always searching for news that his generation happily accepted took days or even weeks to reach them. Like behaviour behind the wheel, its use beamed out a strong signal of a person's true temperament. Here, the device was put away. Closer to home it was another manifested sign that he was not scintillating company.

Slices of mangos, papaya, pineapple, orange, and grapefruit served on a crepe and topped with cream and slivers of crystallised ginger was the only course that united Estela with him. Her starter and main courses lighter choices than his: marinated shrimp with asparagus and roasted rolled pork with a blue cheese and olive stuffing.

The evening ended briskly as his younger colleague was eager to depart. It was noted that she went away from the direction that would take her to a taxi rank and a tube station for Piccadilly.

"Must have friends nearby, which was not surprising given her background."

In the event that the UK press turned against him, it was decided best not to be seen dining again in an expensive restaurant; why give them an easy target, as media adoration was a fickle business.

*****

With the evening ending sooner than expected, Du Gui, after showering, picked up the bought novel, laid in bed and commenced to read the opening chapter, voiced by the host of the reception.

Once established as a crime writer of note, readers expect that your novels meet the same levels of consistency and familiarity as previously acquired. Fans organise themselves and debate about the most trivial of facts about their idols and love to point out any discrepancy found or in the reported life of the novelist. The coming of cyberspace has only intensified reader participation with the inevitable heated discussions that can turn the smallest of fault into the Grand Canyon. Therefore, there can be no let-up of standards and you must indulge the wants of your fans. Loved characters cannot be unwarrantedly dropped or allowed to veer off to conduct out of character acts. Your fiction has to follow the crime solving modus operandi that brought you a large audience in the first place and after twists and turns to spice up the story, the finale must have the accustomed one with any failure to do so to the readers' satisfaction not tolerated without an excusable ploy. Like any product, the readers' loyalty cannot be tested too often. There are others waiting in the wings to entice them away. The choice available is many from cosy reads, hardboiled crime stories to psychological terrors. The long, the tall and the short of it is the writer becomes shackled and subordinate to his protagonist, a prisoner of his own making forced to provide fodder to feed his hungry audience. The bonus side to this submission to the will of the reader is the free publicity generated by forums and websites dedicated to your good name, a marketing dream of self-perpetual publicity from treasured admirers. Followers of my adventures inundate newspapers' book clubs and reviews, on some occasions, their comments so touching that signed photographs of me have been sent by my publicist to these adoring devotees. Through my hero, they love me and bestow many confidence-building riches in a world designed to knock the unwary down. Every time an honorary doctorate in literature is bestowed on me, my gratitude to my fans excels further.

Apart from the commercial rewards and the public adoration, there is an addictive element to committing oneself to writing a series of novels. Your protagonist becomes an alter ego and the settings familiar and reassuring. It is like going home and putting on that pair of old slippers that should have been thrown out months before. Comfort and ease are so hard to give up. It also keeps you sane when writing to order has turned a loved vocation into a job with a signed contract requiring a set number of books to be available for trade book fares at prime buying times.

With all this in mind, I thought I would have a bit of fun by offering readers the chance to entertain me with their own literary compositions, hence the invite to enter a story competition. The winners must clearly believe my books are their friends and, in addition, their entries must convey a raw spirit and a plainness denying the possibility of membership to a writing society or being literary snobs.

In return, the winners are invited to a soiree, not a

maudlin occasion but a convivial evening to celebrate the literary life of a wonderful fictional detective. This coming of together will be a bit of spice to liven up the plain fare conferred upon them by life's injustices. The main proviso is only adventurous hearty eaters who enjoy a good red wine and are willing to debate anything should apply, definitely not an evening for vegetarians or alcohol abstainers...

"A novelist celebrating being made rich by gathering his most devout fans to shower paeans of adoration on him. Suppose making tales rather than living life is one way of creating your own reality. What's more, who has the copyright on the submitted short stories? Smells like a ploy to gather new plot material for another series of books," the heavy-eyed Du Gui mused.

*****

The next morning, the bedside phone rang at the requested hour. His breakfast consisted of an omelette served with English muffins on the side, helped down with piping hot coffee and *le Monde* placed in front of him. An article with picture about a high profile defender of moral values found dead by a patrol car in a red light district with his trousers down caught his attention.

Leaving the hotel, the liaison officer stood waiting for him by an unmarked car, the displayed permit allowing it to be parked anywhere, a sure sign that it either was a diplomatic service vehicle or it belonged to the force.

When he entered the open-plan floor, it immediately struck him that last night's long effort to make a breakthrough had once again ended in failure. The place had a depressive reek of stale sweat with takeaway cartons overfilling the waste paper baskets. The cleaners, if allowed in, were going to have a busy morning.

The ingratiating Williams headed off to sign out documents for them. Because workstation security cabinet space was scarce, each day he would have to sign out and return everything they required.

Putting on his reading glasses and turning on the desk lamp, a necessity that started in his late forties and the first noticeable sign of his physical decline, Du Gui perused the provided case notes before studying them in detail. The act of putting on his glasses aided his thought processes as it triggered the mind and body to expect increased brain activity and reduced sensual stimulus.

First impressions were not encouraging, nothing to raise the spirits, small potatoes only. The rigid reporting format dictated the pace and scope of the investigation. Each day, the blue book, the internal name for the case overview document, was updated. Each investigation department had its own section to maintain with subsections for every investigation within that department. The chief investigator along with a Met deputy commissioner, the Crime Prosecution Service and a Press Office representative then approved what information to release to the press. In terms of manpower, the Chancellor of the Exchequer agreed to release funds to permit two hundred officers and thousands of support staff to bill their time at a daily cost of a million pounds sterling. Each line of inquiry was commanded by a chief inspector with five detective constables assigned to him and 24/7 access to the uniform branch and technical resources. To date, only tenuous leads from unreliable sources had been uncovered, nothing found to take to the CPS. All other ongoing criminal investigation operations, including *Yew Tree*, reported no prior interest in the missing chefs. None of them admitted to seeing this coming. It went without saying that all underworld stool pigeons were lent on and that none squawked anything useful.

There was a set course of action laid out for the different departments. After sounding sessions to get consensus and weed out obvious wrong tacks, each department put forward their best conjectures to the chief investigator. After prioritisation of the most feasible theories, a team went out to find corroborating evidence to build a case. Energy sapping work when there were no encouraging leads to raise confidence but the alternative was to admit defeat and that was unthinkable so they had to try to remain optimistic and continue to work for the best. Within the force, the investigation was codenamed *Operation Floyd,* after the TV chef that the chief watched in his student days.

With no crime scenes, there was an absence of lab and forensic reports. This helped to explain the glum looks on most of the faces of the officers around him, his fellow investigators were lost without them. With no fault attributable to them, from the early stages of the investigation, police efforts had been fruitless. The Yard had reacted as soon as concerns reached them, immediately searching everywhere conceivable, except evidently where the chefs actually where; not knowing the precise last movements hindered efforts. The partners of the male chefs were not expecting them and the partners of the female cooks had stone wall business alibis in New York and Rome. When working up town the chefs stayed in nearby flats. It was suspected, some of the sous-chef protégées or friends did not want to admit that they were expecting their company or had been in their company. No one volunteered to be the last person to see a chef out of fear of becoming the prime suspect. The upshot was no one knew the destinations of the chefs with timelines ending with the last sightings on CCTV footage at their regular haunts. Another surprise was the GPS trails from their smartphones ended early that evening with nothing detected since then. Narcotics detected some traces of drug use at their residences but nothing above the expected for people living their type of existences.

On the ill-fated night, a firework gala on the Thames to celebrate the berthing of a flotilla of luxury pleasure cruisers along the Embankment with blasts and flashes of colour exploding in the night sky for hours and an international football match with jostling fans were major distractions for the public and police resources. A particular concern being permission for a Russian tycoon to moor his state of the art vessel close to Westminster, a couple of hundred metres away from UK Intelligence Headquarters, Scotland Yard and Whitehall.

Mobile communication activity around the last observed sightings was just the usual mundane noise with recordings being a mix of pay-as-you-go and annual contract. Nothing clandestine. The pay-as-you-go callers mainly conversed in ethnic languages about low-key matters implying ownership by cleaners, waiters and lowly restaurant staff.

Du Gui wrote down his initial suppositions on the possible motivations behind the curious occurrences.

Act of revenge
Grudge
An insightful act of terrorism
Just a series of unfortunate accidents
A suicide pact
Media stunt gone wrong
Kidnap attempt gone wrong
Professional rivalry

The background descriptions of the professional lives of the missing revealed the mechanics behind the world of celebrity cook shows. State supported TV tended to favour regional chefs and the national independents opted for London based ones. Every major region had a representative except the Welsh. From show recordings, guest chefs tended to come from within a limited circle of close associates and fellow TV hosts who returned the favour, blatant cronyism creating a cartel. Although he did enjoy how English sponge puddings were prepared, the popularity of these shows did not seem to make any of them more interesting; pleasing to the eye, they emitted a stale predictable repetitiveness where costs, availability of fresh ingredients and tidying up did not matter.

With home bases as far afield as Scotland, Cornwell, Yorkshire, Ireland and London, the investigation had a lot of ground to cover. Reconnoitring these heartlands to unearth useful information about the chefs appealed to him. There were large remote hunting estates in the far north, owned by tycoons and offshore registered companies. The chefs could have ended up as the sport for crazed survivalists, and it would be up to him to stomp through heather covered hills to rescue what was left of them. Adorning Highland dress to emulate the fictional character that in his youth got him interested in investigative work. In the south west, their bodies could have been thrown down a steep shaft of a disused tin mine, too deep and unsafe to attempt to scale down. In the land of the white rose, miles upon miles of underground caverns existed beneath the green rolling hills, where a collapsed spur would conceal bodies forever. The capital, sitting on top of many forgotten rivers feeding into the Thames, massive sewer systems, and communication conduits where a body dumped in a manhole could remain undetected for months until a fault forced a service provider into action. If buried in a cellar, then they may never be detected unless by chance.

Out of curiosity, Du Gui checked the lunar cycle and confirmed there was no full moon that night. Old wives' tales did have an element of truth, as the insane and perverse liked to add drama to their activities. As if to confirm there were crazies out there, sacksful of mail from every sad nutter in this great nation offering advice to him care of Scotland Yard landed on his desk. It could have been worse: body parts had been known to be sent to the police.

With the ground rules for his role firmly stated, he wrote down his proposed daily itinerary; an ordered life was a good life. It read:

8.00 a.m.	Breakfast
10.00 a.m.	Carry Out Duties
1.00 p.m.	Walk and Reflect
2.30 p.m.	Lunch
4.00 p.m.	Own investigations
7.00 p.m.	Hotel & dinner
11.00 p.m.	Bed with a good book

A mental note was taken to restrict himself to two glasses of wine at lunchtime, otherwise it would be difficult to keep a clear head when the vapours reached his brain. In addition, keeping punctually to a planned schedule was not only a sign of respect to others but to him as well. Today, after lunch, he would continue with his reading and instruct the mailroom to redirect any correspondence from the public to the paper-recycling bin; he could do without this encumbrance.

At one p.m., Du Gui vacated the building. Fully engrossed in her laptop, Estela would not miss his absence.

Incognito undertakings may have been compromised by the publicity of his arrival but he dismissed fears of it stopping him getting about on his own by rationalising public behaviour, in particular, that seen in capital cities. On the tube, passengers ignored others around them and on the street people had their own appointments to meet. Anyway, as a people watcher, it was important to be out on the streets and see the sights. He admired Hawksmoor's baroque stamp on this city's architecture and hoped to set aside an evening to go on a conducted night tour of this man's churches and facades fronting some of the famous sites, including St Paul's.

London was an emancipated city that did not normally notice if anyone was missing or died, where ethnic migrants and the liberal minded fought for breathing space, with each community keeping to themselves and sheltering their own kind from the outside world, including from law enforcers. It was a magnet for eccentrics and the single minded to make a mark. Like *Quality Street* chocolates there was a variety for every gender. For those who could afford it, style was everything. Shock provoking eclectic attire to attract attention. On reflection, in his younger years, it mattered to him as he too had taken pride in his dress, now compared with metro man a conservative label applied to his clothing. In saying that, nowadays, dressing for some had a stronger statement behind it. It did not indicate an age group but a mental state, whether that was a religious one, a state of spirit or a show of wealth. Old men dressed as hipsters wearing knee length shorts, designer tee shirts and extra wide American basketball snickers on their sockless feet. Young men grew Edwardian style manicured beards and were into every conceivable revival in music, clothes and hairstyles as a reaction against industries that flooded the planet with manufactured orthodox music and images of boy and girl bands. For sure, good fashion sense was in the eye of the beholder and what goes round comes around. Revamped headgear once instantly identifiable trademarks of shunned physical-comedy icons the likes of Benny Hill and

Norman Wisdom had become must have fashion
items. Oversized headphones associated with nerdy
losers proudly seen as the best audio for the digital
age.

*****

The next morning arriving at his desk, he could not
help noticing a change in Estela. Her dark pupils
enlarged, eyes sparkled and flashed towards
Williams, who displayed a wry smirk in her
direction.

"The liaison officer is living up to his name," as his
face registered a fleeting surprise.

Sex made the world go round and so long as it was
two consenting adults consuming each other, it was
none of his business.

He resumed his review of the backgrounds of the
chefs. They had their own peculiar social habits
from which any resulting notoriety enhanced their
popularity, the usual stuff: sex addiction, social
drugs, speeding cars etc. Financial affairs had
raised questions especially for those paid by the
public through the BBC and revealed something
they all had in common. While wills, where they
existed, contained nothing unexpected and declared
bank accounts showed no unusual sudden
withdrawals of large amounts or regular payments
to persons' unknown, the amounts found in these
accounts along with taxes paid seemed low
considering how successful they had been. It did not
take long to discover that the same accountancy
firm managed their affairs. This on its own was not
unusual as word of mouth led people to the best

specialist help. However, when asked to explain the unexpected discrepancies in the declared finances, the firm declined and pleaded client confidentiality. Because an accountant was the modern day equivalent of the old butler who knew the family's dark secrets and could use this knowledge for extortion, and what was more, other clients with this firm included exiled foreign nationals and known criminals, the chief accountant, the founder and major shareholder, was subsequently called in for questioning. His persistence in being uncooperative made him disliked and resulted in surveillance on his company's activities. The fact was he received the highest score for criminal involvement from the official list of drawn up suspects with a likelihood percentage of 43%. Unfortunately, the score was not high enough to justify an arrest warrant. The discovery of a smoking gun was required to get bang to rights. The use of enhanced interrogation techniques on the only viable suspect to date was reluctantly dismissed. The last thing the police needed was anti-establishment lawyers to make hay at the expense of the public purse. Instead, to put him under pressure, a follow up interview under caution resulted but the accountant in the presence of a top solicitor maintained his nerve, and walked away unperturbed. This despite effort to intimidate him by arranging to have two of the biggest detectives available to arrive at his office to bring him in to assist with their enquiries and after that a long wait in a cell as they delayed the interview as long as possible. This proved a fruitless ploy. Years of stone walling tax collectors had given this man a thick skin. The solicitor rubbed salt into wounded pride by threatening a lawsuit against the Met for preconceived notions about the honesty of the honourable profession of his client, reminding them to only ask relevant questions and not try to lead him to say what they wanted to hear, that he was fully aware of the law and the redress for false arrest, and that this whole exercise smacked of a fishing expedition, a desperate one at that.

Peeved and in an attempt to recoup some costs for the taxpayer, a notice of probable tax avoidance was sent out by the investigating team to the Serious Fraud Office. The possibility of financial irregularities, led to another line of inquiry opening up when a report in *Reuters* drew considerable interest. It stated that a hired jet with an undisclosed passenger list had gone missing after shortly taking off from the Cayman Islands.

Reports from officers assigned to give support to the chefs' partners indicated that they were bearing up fine. Hardy any grief was displayed by the sugar dads but they rarely did as they could have their cake and eat it; passion for pleasure was what kept them young, and at their time of life they had to move swiftly on to find replacements before the arteries hardened. While, after the initial shock and weakened by the lost, most of the wives had picked themselves up and got on with the business of running a home for the children. Uncontrollable sorrow replaced by stoical necessity. They found housework was less of a chore, no skivvying in the kitchen to scrub away splattered fat from overheated frying pans or have to put utensils back in their proper place.

On his walk, he reflected on what was happening in

the office. Respecting his assistant's privacy did not stop him making a judgment that she was not a serious contender as a confidante: her loyalty was compromised, compelled by the fact his gut feelings had straightaway warned him not to trust Williams and having an affair with him showed poor judgment on her part.

"Did a rose always have to have a thorn?"

In truth, as it takes two to tango, maybe, they suited each other or she had had a lobotomy, either way, she was now distracted.

"Did the blindfolded cupid choose a gold or lead arrow for this pair?"

He knew that this initial opinion might be wrong and obtained using contrived values, and she may, in fact, be a beacon of postmodern womanhood, a tough cookie, completely self-confident and devoid of any neurosis brought on by absorbing culturally learnt feelings of guilt and shame.

To get any useful work out of her it was best policy to keep his own counsel as well as not waste his time on an intrigue between a married man and a colleague. Staff being inured to sexual affairs playing out in the workplace was the norm with infidelity common and monogamy rare. It all boiled down to how much oxytocin a creature possessed. Regardless of biological reasons, Du Gui could not help thinking the woman was selling herself short. They probably were not the only ones mixing business with pleasure in the department, as the long hours, heavy drinking and time away from home probably challenged many a relationship, testing it to the limits. At the end of the day, drinking alcohol and copulating for pleasure was all that distinguished humans from other animals.

"These chefs had a lot to answer for."

A big bonus for personal relationships that survived was the monetary rewards; maybe afford that dream extension to the house, a luxury car or go on a long indulgent exotic holiday.

Although the state of lust or as *Rabelais* put it libidinousness made Miss Vermeulen useless to him as a detective because, in his view, her cognition prowess would take a back seat until the addiction for sex diminished. At least, she might allow him to evade the unwanted attentions of his minder, and as self-harm rarely occurred while in lust, duty of due care to her in the workplace should be fine. On a positive note, team spirit was guaranteed to be good.

These last premises turned out true, Williams would keep close to his assistant. The affair with an attractive alluring woman enhanced his standing at the rugby club, giving his mates a bit of fun listening to his amorous tales. Trysts enhanced by the plush setting of a hotel suite given to his assistant courtesy of the taxpayer. She astride him on an armless Queen Anne chair or frolicking in a spa bath.

Du Gui's doubts about his assistant did not mean she would not find herself in a good position within some department in her next assignment. All that was required was to land administrative roles that matched her skills and have an immediate boss susceptible to her charms. Life never changes, the well-liked can cruise through causing as much damage as they liked without the finger of rebuke pointed at them, defence for their behaviour always forth coming. Of course, if unlucky, she may get a future manager not warmed by diminishing physical charms, thus hitting a glass ceiling.

*****

Returning to his desk, he asked his assistant to bring up information about the working lives of the chefs with emphasis given to the use of bodyguards. He wanted to know if the same personnel were assigned to them and if they were on duty the night of the disappearances as well as had large amounts of money deposited into their bank accounts. It had occurred to him while having lunch at a café by the Serpentine in Hyde Park, that a minder knew who was doing what to whom. Lunch itself was satisfactory but slightly spoiled by the hurly-burly of joggers, cyclists and other exercisers passing in front of the waters; seeing people of advanced years refusing to accept a graceful decline was particularly disheartening. It was a pity the siesta never caught on here, as it would have made the English character more relaxed. The best part of that day's stroll was the sight of the hawthorns in full bloom.

He did not like giving orders or pulling rank to confine the efforts of others so was relieved when the assistant seemed contented to use her expertise. Happy to remain in the office, she was to attend the regular morning briefings, monitor

Interpol alerts, follow official announcements on the screens dotted round the office, collate process reports and comment on the efficiency of the various investigating teams. When he was away from the office, she was to alert him by text of any breakthroughs. This freed time to conduct his investigations away from a liaison officer distracted by his assistant's charms.

His itinerary was updated by inserting a comment to switch on the mobile phone at five p.m. to check for updates. He had never learnt to like speaking over a phone, especially a mobile one. When forced to speak on them the terse use of a few direct words made him come across abrasive and eager to end the call.

In the car back to their hotels, stopping first in South Kensington, Du Gui mused about the anatomy of love and the trouble it caused.

"Strange that the word love was not part of the nomenclature of psychiatry and cognitive behaviour where experts in these fields classified relationships in terms of emotional blackmail and dependency."

When dropped off, he told Williams not to bother picking him in future and that he did not need a chaperone to get about, as the tube will be handy enough for him and probably quicker. His guardian remonstrated about this decision but Du Gui remained adamant, insisting:

"I need exercise to get the brain juices flowing."

The liaison officer decided on a tactical withdrawal and to report this outcome to his superiors. The car shot out into traffic and immediately came to a standstill. The advice about being at the mercy of the media circus if he travelled alone by public transport ignored.

In the hotel, he approached the reception desk and asked about tube travel and where were the nearest stations from the hotel and Scotland Yard. They pointed out that it was only a couple of stops down the line to Westminster. In total a trip of around thirty minutes to get to the Yard. Next, he went to the tube station to buy an oyster card to allow him to get to his destinations swiftly without leaving a detectable trail. The initial thought was to get a moped but the consequence of a tabloid getting a picture of him on route and unkindly linking him to *inspector Clouseau* or the raunchy activities of a French President in the Champs-Élysées put him off. It was not a good idea to give too easy a reason for pillorying him after being built up as a hero.

*****

Back in the hotel bedroom, that day's reading of available documentation was mulled over. No hint of suppressed evidence had been detected. There was just a complete lack of it, nothing to categorise and build a case. This immediately ruled out a logical approach to understanding the mystery. A psychological approach seemed a pointless waste of time as well as it was unheard of for a serial perpetrator to act out multiple wrongdoings in one night. Obviously, this assumed that they did all disappear for the same reason.

To relax his mind, he picked up the novel he had placed on the bedside table.

Situated back from the narrow street on the edge of a Hertfordshire village, the large house with a nice-looking surrounding garden was an old rectory once owned by a famous nineteenth century playwright. It was built when the garden provided all that the kitchen required and life revolved round the village calendar. A time when nothing of the slaughtered beast was wasted. Larders and medicine chests packed with products from cultivated beds and from within the locale. Root vegetables, pickles, dried herbs to add to meats and soups, berries turned into jam and border flowers cut to adorn indoors, the scents of some used to keep pests and bad odours at bay. Meats cured, flour milled and beer brewed in the village...

The five winners, already adorned in costume, arrived independently at the house. All ready to ask questions about how the novelist organised his working day, why his detective never held onto love interests from the previous novels, never had a great passion in his life and did the detective's personality reflect any of his own. The writer of 'the parrot that bit the hand of the vicar' was the first at the door and came as the mild mannered female reporter that helped solve the mystery of the missing pages in the diary of a famous ex-military general. Next, came 'the murder of the man that held the world's debt' and he opted to be the villain of the piece in a blackmail tale centred around the world of high finance. 'The fifteen skulls', dressed as the femme fatale in the spicy tale about art gallery theft, made her appearance as the prior guests and the well-tanned novelist, made up as the Chinese criminal kingpin from the tale that took

his hero to Macau, were sipping pink champagne.
'The shenanigans at the court of the Duchy of
Alsace' and 'the non-existence of the Italian tax
collector' arrived together after bumping into each
other at the closest railway station and agreeing to
share a taxi to the given address. Both easily
recognised each other's character from their
costumes when departing from the uptown train.
'Shenanigans' came as a murderous tail coat
wearing neo-Nazi aristocratic sympathiser and 'the
non-existent tax collector' as the khaki wearing
archaeologist who discovered a two-thousand-year
old testament of an until then unknown disciple.
The former's bearing and high forehead perfectly
suited the guise while the latter being Jewish was
hoping that the other was just playacting.

Not only were the guests instructed to not reveal
the plot of the final book but also not to mention
attending the soiree as the recorded event was to be
released prior to the book launch.

*****

Getting up the next morning before the break of
dawn, he went off to do a round of breakfast radio
and TV interviews then later in the morning
serious news interviews. The staff and technology
at each broadcaster were indistinguishable, only
the interpretations of the presenter to his answers
and choice of newspapers in the green room were
different.

At each venue, a scrambling crowd of reporters,
inanely screamed questions at him as
photographers pushed and shoved to get the image

that would show the most desirable expression on his face wanted by the newspapers. Everywhere he went the same gaggle waited for him. At first, the thought entered his head that someone must have leaked his schedule to the paparazzi but it was soon realised that they were following a long established circuit.

Doing the rounds in front of the camera did have a curious effect on his mannerisms. A sickly sweet self-importance overcame him most noticeable when confronted with eager to listen to every word said presenters. Before all else, he was determined as quickly as possible to nip this unpleasant discovery about himself in the bud.

When confronted with the press there was no standing room left in the hall and questions rained on him. He did have trepidations about the prospect of addressing the gathered media circus. The task required him to provide steadfast support by offering optimistic opinions and remembering never to apportion blame for perceived lack of progress when facing their music. With a strong desire to avoid being caught in the headlights of press anger, these objectives were firmly set in his mind. However, it did puzzle him that for a nation known for its hard mindedness, he had to refrain from hinting that the missing chefs were already dead. Regardless of this, his given role was to relieve public anxiety; an important role in a world reported by instant and often hysterical coverage. Unfortunately, having to meet so many strangers and to remember instantly their first names and what organisation they represented was a daunting prospect for a man suspicious of anyone asserting to be a friend after a quick introduction. To be fair

to the Met, they briefed him well beforehand on
questions to avoid as the sting lay in the follow up
question and who would come to the rescue if it got
hostile: Joe from the *Daily Truth* would stick his
hand up if the going got tough. Most importantly of
all was to remember the pecking order with TV
first, broadsheets then tabloids and if time allowed
the freelancers and assembled foreign press.

*****

His port of call in the afternoon was a visit to the
discovered plague pit to see the progress made by
the archaeologists. This took him along Brick Lane,
through tightly cluttered passageways with fast
food vendors packed together, a bazaar of
competing noises and smells of Asia Minor and the
Indian continent with unshaven surly patrons
aggressively selling identical meat offerings of
unknown provenance by yelling and manhandling
anyone into their premises bold enough to walk
down the lane. To survive the onslaught, Du Gui
quelled his natural curiosity and avoided eye
contact by staring straight ahead.

His journey was halted by the sudden seething
movement of believers leaving afternoon prayers to
recommence their secular duties. Powerless against
the force of the exodus, he pinned himself against a
wall to prevent being propelled by the unstoppable
tide of human flesh as wave after wave excitedly
flowed past him. This temporary confinement
permitted him to scan the state of disrepair of the
upper levels of the buildings. It was hard to believe
that this was highly valued real estate within the
City of London, a poverty trap in the richest city in

the world.

Back on the lane, a struggle took place. A flailing
unkempt blood-shot eyed youth, who looked as if
the last few days were spent on an alcohol-fuelled
pleasure bender, had turned into the lane to find
himself face to face with the full force of believers
and immediately dragged backwards. A visible
discomfort overcame this youth surrounded by
what he did not understand and the startled
realisation that his intended destination lay beyond
his reach. His garbled cries faded like his struggle
to push himself to the safety of a doorway. With all
hope gone, the youth accepted his fate and vanished
from sight, seemingly trampled by the vigour of
insurmountable energy.

At the plague site, mechanical diggers and pile
drivers stood idly by while health and safety
inspectors made sure that anyone entering the site
had the proper attire. From an open-to-the-public
advantage point high above the vast hole that
seemed to go thirty odd metres into the earth, Du
Gui observed ubiquitous orange cladded figures,
young students of different nationalities, on their
hands and knees in carefully laid out grids of two
square metres scraping away thin layers of soil.
Similarly dressed but in bright yellow supervisors
rushed around when a volunteer raised a hand. The
precision of the undertaking was impressive and
contrasted hugely with the earlier work done by
men using heavy-duty machinery. The slow pace of
the archaeologists belied the few weeks given to
conduct the dig before building work recommenced
with the site flooded with concrete. Once laid, the
foundations would stay in place for at least fifty
years.

His attention switched to a bullying common gull
swooping down and scattering some black heads
into the air, the cries of the disturbed birds reached
him a moment later. An inquisitive scraper with
trowel in hand wandered over to the commotion to
see what caused the fighting. Pulling out a pair of
binoculars brought for the occasion, he perceived
what seemed to be dirt-smeared remnants of
discarded meat delicately prodded by a nonplus
white looking girl, probably a vegetarian not keen
on the smell of rotting raw meat. Curiosity satisfied
she made her way back to the main activity of the
dig. Adjusting the focus of his binoculars, the
unearthed remains of distinct parts of overlapping
discoloured skeletons poking out of the soil came
into view. The great financial centre was literally
built on the corpses of the broken.

A small crowd of spectators circled round him when
finally recognised, some craning their necks to get a
better glimpse of the famous Frenchman. A
freelance photographer took a snap of him, which
made it into most of the tabloid papers the next
day. After signing some autographs and posing for
pictures, Du Gui decided to make his way back
towards Liverpool Street station with the intention
of visiting *Dirty Dicks*, a famous public house curio;
its walls and ceiling copiously festooned with
stuffed mouldy cats. Behind him, the dispersing
crowd of admirers gossiped about how small this
celebrity was in real life and how soft and hydrated
his skin was.

Along the streets leading to the railway station and
links to tube stations businessmen and women
hurried for late afternoon meetings or to get home

before rush hour. Immersed in capital stupefied many of them by dominating conscious thinking with spreadsheet data and client instructions. Others depending on the state of their private lives agitated or pleased with themselves. The endeavours and bustle of these pedestrians along with the hawking of tousled young vendors trying to give away free newspapers, the roar of noise from traffic and shouting into mobile phones all spoilt the intended amble to what was going to bring back reminiscences. Construction work was also everywhere. Dust blocked the pores, choked the nose and clotted taste bud receptors on the tongue.

The energetic, healthy and confident stubbed faces of the building site workers, covered head to toe in dust, stood out from the clean cut and smartly coiffed office worker and the hungry looking vendors of newspapers. Even glancing up to admire the design and décor of the City brought no pleasure. The impression created by heavy rumbling machinery was of sunlight retreating in fast time as new buildings rose up and redundant ones came down. Block by block, perfectly sound structures replaced by taller ones with faster lifts, larger open-plan space to enhance networking and allow greater monitoring of subordinates. It was not only an example of Big Brother watching you but everyone having the right to hold judgment over a colleague's behaviour.

One day, some great architect would see a dream realised with a dome put over the City to encase it, protecting it from the elements, a world of dark shadows, the blotting out of the sky, a place without children or wildlife; one-upmanship on the financial centres in New York and Shanghai. Du

Gui pondered how many of the air conditioned office dwellers when looking out of the closed windows dreamt of the possibility of the hairy strong armed labourers levelling the City of London so freeing them from long commutes, or did they sit in their artificial environments feeling smug watching hard labour performed in harsh conditions.

Unfortunately, for Du Gui, a former popular historic landmark that had dubious associations with ladies of the night was completely obliterated. In its place was a comfortable drinking hole for well-paid office workers. It was over twenty years ago since he was last there, working on a case involving a crepuscular *Jack the Ripper* copycat. Given the circumstances, the pub then was empty as one brave streetwalker stood in the adjacent dim narrow lane, a passageway cleaned up to become a thoroughfare for the business community converging on Broadgate. The caught mass murder turned out to be a lesbian social worker, which helped to explain how the killer continued to get close to her victims without arousing fear.

Facing the public house brought back memories.

"To this day, criminal psychiatrists and cold case teams question the sectioned prisoner to find out her motivations and actual number of kills. For every incarcerated psychopath, a host of specialists made a good living from analysing the causes of the crimes. But who cures a psychiatrist of mental delusions and breakdown of social inhibitions. My exposé of Dr Arnaud as the serial murderer with a taste for relieving troubled patients of their woes

causing the gutters of Poitiers' steep narrow medieval streets to run red with blood not only destroyed the misbelief that such killers were only found in Anglo-Saxon countries but still baffles the profession to this day."

Instead of sitting in the revamped bar and partaking in a consoling libation, he walked up Bishopsgate to Leadenhall Market. There to have lunch at a bistro recommended in his tourist guide, a refined venue in a sheltered setting. The decision to do so did not disappoint as a half bottle of exquisite *Domaine de la Romanée-Conti* was consumed with an excellent lunch consisting of a starter of crispy whitebait followed by sea bass with capers and samphire *en papillate* as the main and a lemon tart to accompany his coffee.

Along the road to this venue, champagne cocktail bars buzzed. The clientele, mostly traders in their late twenties, retold their boastful tales over the same drinks every weekday. When a colleague not able to cut the ice anymore was dismissed they smirked and when someone left for a better opportunity a silent moping united the drinkers.

*****

Heading back to the Met it was impossible not to notice his face splashed across all the newspapers on the newsstands around the tube station. On the train, he picked up a free paper, ignored his face, and glanced at the lonely-hearts column then read his stars during the commute. It was foreseen that his immediate future would not be easy and to expect a bumpy ride.

While he was observing the archaeological dig, a
man voluntarily entered the Yard to come clean
about witnessing the last sighting of the chefs
leaving Portsmouth. A tough as old boots, small
wiry man of indeterminate age due to the
possession of a bald head and a timeless face, and
depending on the angle his pronounced nose and
slightly weak chin could make him look attractive
or bizarrely grotesque. The man claimed to be
British and initial enquiries based on fingerprints
reported no criminal record. The interrogation log
on him stated his pockets contained some coins and
notes, wore discount store clothing and had badly
looked after teeth. The good news, if this was an
authentic sighting, the police, the social services
and the judiciary could not be accused of negligence
by allowing a persistent criminal, a bailed felon or
an early released prisoner to re-offend.

People walking off the streets to confess were
common occurrences in high profile cases. A
publicity-seeking fabulist of the macabre would
happily be prepared to spend several months in
confinement for the privilege of being able to sate
his appetite for attention. This latest arrival was
given some credence. Apart from not being one of
the usual lot, his stated days and the rough times of
the chefs' abductions were close to the last known,
not only that, the times stated were just after the
last confirmed reliable sightings. However, this
person like all the others was not detained as this
information could have been ascertained from press
reports.

Du Gui first caught sight of this man when going
for a coffee break, walking past him in a corridor

sitting patiently on a bench outside an interview room. It was a small thing that drew his attention, the scratching of the back of a thick rugged callused right hand. Engaging with a uniformed officer on guard duty, he asked who this person was.

"A singing canary, sir."

"What?"

"A nut claiming to know what has happened to the chefs."

"Know anything about him?"

"Not really. Best to ask someone on the investigating team. I am only on guard duty. But I did overhear that he was a sailor. Expect him to be sent on his bike with a flea in the ear."

The best place for bonding and gossip was at the coffee machine. Office friendships formed more by close proximity than personal leanings. A setting where an intelligent manager neither dwells nor dissuades socialising. It was there that Du Gui inadvertently learnt something; the gossip was about his pair.

"Wait till she has a bun in the oven that arse won't be so pretty then," a woman officer sneered.

People had a warped sense of humour and needling was inevitable in gatherings of more than one. Apparently, the liaison officer's wife had only just given birth a few weeks earlier. Who knows, maybe, by providing bedroom gymnastics, his assistant was going a good thing for William's relationship with his wife and new born. Easing the wife's pressure when hormones demanded she spent her attention on the baby. That said a surge of testosterone in this man's body made him more likely to be abusive.

The much talked about pair remained impervious to these rumblings; both had a job to do and they decided that they might as well enjoy it.

Anyway, it was not his problem. He shrugged his shoulders and walked out of the building, deciding that it was best to go to the nearby *Starbucks* to avoid overhearing anything, tolerate a South American bean blend, which was better than instant but still not as good as a French roast made with West African beans. For security reasons, the police force banned officers and staff to use this coffee house, but Du Gui decided he was exempt from this prohibition, as the Met commissioner had said he was an amateur.

After ordering a tall filtered coffee and a slice of pumpkin pie, he found himself a table, sat down and waited for his order to be called. The waiting was utilised by recalling the spotted expenses of his assistant. Items related to late night dining made him wonder if the liaison officer claimed overtime for their nights of passion. The amount did not bother him, a mere trifle, as there would be a flood of wildly abused expense claims and *ad hoc* spending on infrastructure. The extended working hours meant many officers returned home in taxis or stayed overnight in inner London hotels.

He enjoyed the pie. The eccentric use of vegetables

as a sweetener in desserts worked as far as he was concerned.

On his way back, the confessor still sitting on the same bench stood up to engage in dialogue with him.

Later, he asked his assistant if she could access the records from all the investigating teams. She replied in the affirmative that this should now be the case. The absence of facts meant no likelihood of building a solid case against anyone, so he may as well go by intuition and see if anything of relevance could be flushed out by sticking his nose where it was not wanted. It was not necessary a gamble, more like a calculated risk. The hand dealt was sparse but the shape of it and reading what his partner and the opposition possessed had made him a good bridge player capable of bagging six spades with a poor hand. In addition, it was best not to dwell on an unsuccessful outcome by remembering that even the unlucky get lucky sometimes.

"Can you bring up records on unsolicited reports?"

Standing behind her back as she typed database queries, he observed the speed of thought and ease in which she found the correct query to bring back the desired result. A list of names with a brief description flooded the screen. The one he was looking for was there.

"Gabriel Smith. Claims to come from Southsea and had been on a vessel that sank with the chefs on board," declared his assistant.

"Southseas?"

"Yes, Southsea, Portsmouth. You will have to bear in mind that his testimonial cannot be collaborated and his identity has not been verified."

"These fantasists rarely give their true identity. They think they can come in, say their baloney then disappear. It never occurs to them that their stories are checked and time wasters prosecuted," volunteered the liaison officer.

"Sometimes they reveal something without meaning to when they embellish their story with some truth," aired Du Gui.

"You have found something?" She twigged.

"Not really. A know-it-all will assert to know the truth and a rationalist insists to be able to ascertain it, I on the other hand query everything."

She just nodded in return without saying anything further and printed off preliminary interview transcripts and psychological impressions of the confessor Gabriel. These stated that he showed the capacity in holding a logical conversation and appeared not being used to police interviewing procedures. The closing remarks classified him as a new face, harmless and with a bit of encouragement would not waste any more of their time in the future.

Before leaving Brussels, the European Director for serious criminal activities in a separate meeting told Estela about Du Gui's ways. Her role in this assignment was also stipulated and it demanded her to embed herself within Scotland Yard to learn all she could about their internal procedures and systems. The performance of cutting edge signal analysis tools used in real time visual and sound surveillance monitoring of the public to allow faster reaction times to criminal and terrorist threats were of special interest as the EU was in the progress of adopting a similar authoritarian mantra to protect democracy at the expense of individual freedom and the right to privacy. Along with charging top dollar for the services of their personnel, the directorate was determined to gain as much insight as possible into UK civil control arrangements.

Du Gui then asked his assistant to request CCTV footage of this suspect of interest going back a few hours prior to entering the Yard to volunteer information and to review existing witness statements to see if any of the paparazzi had been interviewed. The chefs, chiefly the glamorous ones, must have been on the radar of some of them. It was more than likely that an image of one of them on that night existed in a memory card somewhere. If there was a paucity of statements, then she was to recommend to Williams that this omission be flagged and that all the newspapers and magazine editors be contacted to determine if they had been offered last seem prints. Any interviews should be under caution, as these people were notorious for withholding information.

FISH AND CHIPS

After a detour, Du Gui made his way to Charing Cross Station. Ignoring as much as possible the relevance of its name, the destination was Trafalgar Square to feed the birds with some rolls taken from the hotel breakfast tray and to meet Radu to cajole him to provide assistance.

The hustle and bustle of tourists navigating through the tight walkways in the tube station did not bode well as far as obtaining a brisk walk was concerned. At street level, the road traffic added to the discomfort and dissuaded him to forego exercise before his luncheon date. On the off chance that a recital was in progress the decision was made to struggle over to *St Martin-in-the-Fields.* Loosening the muscles would have to wait until the evening and until then obtaining a good dose of vitamin D would have to suffice. After being hooted at twice and shouted at once, he managed to get across to the front entrance of the church to be rewarded with Handel's rapt oratorio *Solomon.* Standing close to the doors, the liturgical sounds immediately transported him to his youth and the imposing surroundings of mass. When the beep from his watch told him it was time for his rendezvous, the traffic and streams of tourists were once again crossed.

He seated himself on a bench in the sun, toyed with the bread rolls in his hands, a signal that the pigeons and a brave solitary sparrow could not ignore. Their diligence in gobbling up the crumbs only interrupted when an unhurried Radu arrived, lit a cigarette, crushed the empty packet and tossed it on the ground with a typical smoker's indifference before sitting down. This caused the feeding pigeons to flutter in the air, regroup a few metres away then scamper back to the crumbs. The sparrow had just carried on feeding regardless.

After some perfunctory salutations, Du Gui unwrap deli bought sandwiches to share with his guest. There was a choice of oak smoked Scottish salmon with cream cheese and American pastrami spread with mustard and topped with thinly sliced gherkin. Both sandwiches made from seeded bread had a few leaves of watercress in them for decoration purposes. From his inside jacket pocket two miniature bottles of Chilean Chardonnay wine were produced and opened.

Radu listened and nodded as Du Gui outlined what was required of him, which was to visit the last whereabouts around the times of the disappearances and report back his findings.

"Illegals and criminals nervous of the law were more willing to talk to a low life like them," intimated Du Gui.

Not much of a compliment but once Radu knew that his finances would not suffer, he took it all in his stride to do his best whatever that would be. Anyway, his own commerce could continue at the same time. As an incentive, Du Gui handed over an oyster card and a few hundred pounds with the promise of more the next time they met.

"Ok, I will start tonight."

"Good, I appreciate it."

On parting, Radu remembered a vital request to make.

"Do you have any cigarettes?"

Du Gui handed him one and lit it for him.

Leaving the square, the detective noticed a small band of in-between work actors manning a candle vigil for the chefs.

Squeezed into the airless tube train and having to tolerate the stench of body odour and bad breath, the judder and unexplained sudden halt in the tunnel, forced him like everyone else who was standing to cling to the handrail and bump into the nearest neighbours. All of them packed in like boiled in the can sardines or more appropriately herrings fermenting in a barrel.

"Did the underground operator not know that they had a celebrity on board entitled to a first class service?"

In an attempt to take his mind off the elbow that rammed into the back of his neck, he pondered about what lay hidden in this underworld. Beneath or parallel to the tube lines would be forgotten closed off lines and secret paths accessible to allow those with an authorised need to travel quickly without any observation between government and security service buildings. Maybe a phantom made this world his home or subterraneans chased from the world above lived on fricassee rat and caught river fish poached in the abundant trickling down gutter water.

Not much work was done when he eventually got back to his desk. The information requested would not be available for a few days. His time was mostly spent finalising travel arrangements for the next day.

*****

An early night meant a glass of cognac and the recommencement of the novel to clear his mind.

A mixture of awe and apprehension when meeting their idol was soon surpassed by happy radiating faces. The novelist was everything the authorised biography said he was, down to earth and gregarious. He did look rounder in the flesh but that could be attributed to the costume and applied makeup and even possibly the prosthetics around the eyes to give him the appearance of a lavish living ruthless Chinaman with thick waxy black hair seen on many for their aging leaders. The large dining room with wall-mounted cameras was splendidly laid out in the style of a grand Edwardian household, right down to an oval silver centrepiece containing freshly picked blood-red wall garden flowers cradled in wild arum leaves; not just lush and sweet smelling but handy for camouflaging microphones. The room itself displayed original fittings and art nouveau decorations. A preparatory dry run shortly before the fixed unmanned cameras went live was done to allow the guests to loosen up, get comfortable in the surroundings, be at ease and relaxed when eating and drinking. Polite nonsense spoke to check the sound quality and make sure the lighting did not turn anyone into a grotesque. Being watched and judged was not everyone's cup of tea so the guests unaccustomed to being in front of the camera welcomed this consideration. When the lights dimmed and a red spotlight above their heads went on, it meant audio was off, the intention being to run commentary or adverts at set intervals and to allow smooth serving of the courses. Intimacy was maintained by the presence of a sole inconspicuous manservant to provide for them.

The menu was a meat eaters delight:

Menu
Brown Windsor Soup
Scallops and Black Pudding
Steak Tartare
Braised meat served with selection of root vegetables
Wild Fruit Suet Pudding
Coffee, cheese and biscuits
{Red wine served with every dish}

Guests could skip a course but they were encouraged to try everything…

The opening preamble to set the scene and tone continued. While welcoming drinks were served, each guest had a short separate on camera interview to express tributes.

*****

Paddington station, the gateway to the southwest, with a modern concourse bolted onto Brunel's high wrought iron glazed roof facetted with massive timepieces.

When Du Gui arrived, the activities of the bomb squad practicing the detection of explosives with sniffer dogs confronted him. As passengers waited at platform gates with silenced TV screens above their heads repeating news the channel chose to emphasise, including the obligatory images of the chefs, the four legged scent detectors and their handlers worked the concourse to track down the phoney bomber. Armed body armoured officers with guns pointed down strolled around to give added reassurance or unease depending on your state of mind. Translators were also on hand to explain that this was a practice drill for those that did not understand the meaning of the displayed signs placed around the station entrances.

Some of the public, although completely innocent in their activities found it difficult to look so or to maintain a casual stance. More so when a dog took an interest in what they were munching or had in their bag for the train journey. Others rightly worried when approached by an animal able to discern illegal substances.

To avoid being accused of stereotyping, the bomber turned out to be white and some of the handlers were from the ethnic communities.

Du Gui felt some sympathy for bemused travellers who had missed the public information notices about the security exercise, as the entrances and passageway were awash with posters of all kinds. Many defaced, some with Arabic writing that for all he knew could contain the vilest obscenities. Graffiti on a missing poster for the chefs had some artistic merit. The five faces transformed into penises and breasts of all shapes and sizes. Satire, the last weapon of the suppressed was alive and well.

The long Riviera train to Plymouth promised a picturesque introduction to delights found away from London. A five-hour journey in first class with a window seat, fresh coffee, sandwiches and newspapers. For lunch, there would be pork with a honey sauce, early Jersey potatoes and baton carrots. The chief investigator after consulting with a deputy commissioner was happy to give Du Gui the go ahead to visit the home bases of the chefs. His peregrinations outside the capital would show the regions that the investigation was not London-centric, give the local chief constable some needed publicity, keep the press interested in the Frenchman and get him out of their hair for a few days.

The daily report from Williams, although always identical to the previous one due to a lack of creative thinking showed nothing to worry them. Du Gui was keeping his nose out of it while Vermeulen aided the investigation by making herself a good conduit for assessing reported sightings in Europe. As they presumed, Du Gui's reputation exceeded his fading abilities and the assignment was being treated as a jolly. Spent most of his nights in his room with a radio and a novel

titled *'Dinner with Deserving Fans'* for company.
Behaving like a low paid travelling salesman living
out of a suitcase and shunning the opportunity to
take advantage of the many available special
personal services. The report on Williams asserted
he was getting too close to Vermeulen. This was
dismissed without a second thought as a buddy-
buddy role was the remit given to him when called
up as a late replacement for the more prepared
officer from the Special Operations Unit. The
original plan was to assign a young female officer to
directly keep tabs on Du Gui but news of him
coming with an assistant got them to change tact
and deploy Williams to work on Estela as a way of
indirectly monitoring him.

Du Gui browsed a tourist guide and reviewed the
trespassing laws to find out where and where not
roaming was permitted. Coastal trials, historic
public pathways and bridleways seemed the safest
bets. Minor country roads were to be avoided
mainly as the revival in cycling and the
affordability of 4x4s made them dangerous for
hikers. The guide had colourful images of happy
tourists under blue skies enjoying the many
available activities on offer: coves jammed full with
yachts, cliff walkers, some with dogs, admiring the
view with busy channel traffic in the distance, and
surfers riding the waves. For the traditionalists
there were folk hornpipe music and dancing, later
adopted by the Royal Navy supposedly to keep the
jolly jacks fit on long voyages to the new worlds but
probably it also provided entertainment for the
ship's captain as well.

At Plymouth, a car picked him up and drove to the
headquarters of the Devon and Cornwall

Constabulary to receive a review of work already done and to be given guidance on what and not to say to the gathered press. Afterwards, he headed west in an unmarked car taken from the police carpool.

The Tamar, once an impregnable barrier to stop the spread of Anglo-Saxon migration, was quickly crossed. Centuries before, crossing the waters represented a change, something different, for many something for the better, a safe haven from pagan migrants from northern Europe. It was the remnants of the Celtic world in England later subjugated by class division and racial purity based on pseudo-scientific proofs of superiority and a nineteenth century State wishing to push non-conformity to the fringes of its domain. Now breached by bridges hordes of tourists descended into the western tip of England while many incomers bought property, one of them was a missing chef.

Along this route, the highway suffered from a lack of overtaking lanes with traffic control relying heavily on cameras.

Even in the face of an influx of affluent southerners to both regions, rivalries between Cornwall and Devon continued to this day with traditions on how to eat the humble scone tea delineating the two tribes. The Cornish preferred the jam on the bottom to stop the cream melting on a warm scone and the Devonians insisted that the jam be on top to allow the eyes to savour the delight to come. Relations further soured by Devonian claims that they invented the pasty first.

His first stop was to see the rural retreat of the chef and take a sally round the area. Although, nothing was found in previous searches, he wanted to make his presence known and to get a feel of the lay of the land.

Back at Scotland Yard, he had reviewed visual and infrared footage from cameras mounted on drones. The footage showed a renovated extended stone farmhouse. A glass sheltered topped balustrade balcony supported by hardwood pillars ran the whole length of the upper floor and looked down on a heated swimming pool on one side and a full size tennis court on the other side. A high spiked brick wall surrounded the perimeter and along with the driveway closed off by metal gates, everything looked new. A report on the examination of military satellite photographs by specialists in soil disturbance taken before and after the disappearances eliminated recent activity that would point to human burials.

Parking the car, he replaced his town shoes for an old pair of scuffed brogues, comfortable footwear, once his favourites, twice thrown in the bin and recently resoled with thick rubber treads.

At the closed gates, above his head, a CCTV camera peered down at him. A voice from a speaker asked what was wanted.

"I am from the police investigation team."

"I know who you are. Your face is on the news. This is private property and unless you have a warrant you cannot come in."

"Are the family at home?"

"No."

Du Gui left it at that and decided to skirt at a leisurely walking pace around the area. He already knew that the family had moved out for an extended holiday in the Seychelles.

The path taken, littered with cigarette ends and dog pooh, went up a gentle slope. Going by the amount of litter, the press pact must have laid seize for days. Unlike the open fields seen from the train coming down, the fields here were small quadrilateral enclosures dictated by the contour of the land, every shape except squares and rectangles. The fields were cultivated with orchards, flowers and root crops, interspersed with isolated coppices.

Following a sharp turn in the path, a growling beast confronted him, its eyes on fire, savage jaws wide open presenting huge teeth. A confident animal gained from its enormous size.

A shout from an unconcerned handler, a tall man around fifty years old, dressed in wellington boots, moleskin trousers, *Balfour* jacket and a deerstalker hat, coming up behind, halted it.

"That is a big dog?"

The uppish handler spoke through rather than at him.

"Yeah, it is a Dane, a Doberdane."

"What lies ahead?"

"This path takes you to the kennels which are private property."

Reaching the kennels, a large sign stated that this was a private licensed breeding establishment. Private was printed in red and underlined. Straight ahead, the commencement of loud howls articulated the detection of his presence. He turned right to continue the wide berth around the walled house. The turning took him through paths and lanes, occasioning him to bump into fellow walkers and sporadic road traffic. Single-track tarmac was quickly crossed to pick up the path again. Through the trees, all the properties seen were in an excellent state of repair and large enough for several families to share. The ground beneath him revealed a history of a thousand footprints while to his right hand side beyond the undergrowth a field with straight parallel rows of young vegetables showed signs of a good return at harvest time.

He stopped and passed the time of day with a man walking his ferret on a lead, a sociable character belying his gloomy looking down turned cheeks and lips.

"No pet. It is a working animal."

The man wore a baseball cap, jeans and polo neck top, all with washed out colours. A large canvas bag hung over his left shoulder. Offering Du Gui a cigarette, an explanation of the lineage of the animal and hunting habits were freely given.

"This one is the grandson of the first ferret I ever

had. That was a good one. I know these paths well, been hunting hereabouts since a lad. Early mornings are best and back at dusk if nothing caught earlier."

"Rabbit is good eating," said the Frenchman.

"Agree. Don't understand why it is only used in pet food. Squirrel makes good eating as well."

"Do you come from here?"

"Not now. I drive across from Falmouth. When I was a youngster this area had new age communes living off the land. Replaced by new incomers keeping themselves private."

"Anything unusual happen recently?"

"Quiet. It is why people move in. Locals been pushed out by the prices. Walkers in the know tend to head along beside the kennels to get to the coastal path."

A blast from a shotgun interrupted them. Both men looked across a field to see where the sound was coming from.

"Someone looking for a wood pigeon for his dinner," conjectured Du Gui.

"Doubt it. More likely a clay pigeon shoot. The moment anyone with money moves to the countryside they buy a gun. Plenty of guns around these parts."

They stood listening for a moment then in opposite directions parted with the report of guns fading in the distance.

His improvised winding route eventually took him downhill. It was a route unlikely to be undertaken in the dark of the night, especially without local knowledge. With time to reflect, Du Gui again reluctantly accepted that this latest assignment was in some way an escape from an office in Brussels that no longer had any attraction for him and which allowed him to keep his mind busy so delaying a decision about his future; a luxury many others did not have.

Walking along the right of way the joy of birdsong and a pleasing breeze reverberated in his ears. Around him wild primroses and periwinkles added colour to the green hues of the ferns and vines. A pair of luminous orange eyes a few feet away in the shade of some thicket grabbed his attention, mesmerising him until it was identified as belonging to a common blackbird with satiny feathers. Its vivacity broadcasted an unmissable statement that the male and female of the species could not ignore. As the thicket became denser external sounds and sights became less of a distraction and for the first time that day inside an acoustic shadow, he felt alone cut off from any road or building. The sun descended from the clear blue sky behind a canopy of branches and green leaves, deepening the shadows that dissected the path. The stillness around him heralded the approach of dusk. In front of him, a narrow gap in the thicket running perpendicular to his walking direction informed him that this was the only direction open to him.

Quoi! The whole world seemed to turn into a blur right in front of him at the same time as an invisible wave of pushed air struck him. He teetered just missing the full concentrated force as a powerful horse and rider at full gallop passed him on a bridleway barely two-metre-wide trellised by thicket, oblivious to his presence rode on, leaving a fleeting glance of a raised rump, soles and heels pinching the flanks of the horse. The sound of hooves barely heard on a rucked soft ground kept damp by perpetual shade and probably by sweat running off regularly exercised horses. So close was the encounter the exhaled breath of the horse stroked his cheeks. If it had hit him, he would not have felt a thing. Alive and physically unhurt but giddy, he rubbed the back of his neck, it felt damp. He tried to bring his mind back to the present day as it raced through his past life then like a transfixed frightened rabbit with a pulsating chest he hesitated to cross the path before making the leap of faith to the other side.

Traversing those few metres shattered him. A stiff drink to settle him would have been nice but he had to continue and hold on until back in civilisation.

At the parked car, a cigarette was lit and a final look at the closed gates brought a smile to his face.

"Even that massive hound could not jump those defences.

Perhaps the walls separated family life from the outside world and the chef's other activities."

*****

He had already decided to spend the night in Falmouth and the next morning drive to the small harbour town made popular by the chef.

The scale of the historic naval port nestled within Carrick Roads surprised him, all the larger by the paucity of ocean going ships in its long docks. Now the Roads and rivers that fed it were havens for pleasure boats with the presence of the Royal Navy reduced to a minesweeper on exercise and a radar installation. In the streets, early summer tourists and locals steadily went about their business. Above the shoreline, an evening breeze fluttered the flags on the ramparts of the fortress dominating the promontory.

He parked the car in a space reserved for guests of the small hotel and on entering found it to be silent with the only movement coming from the swinging pendulum of a wall-mounted clock.

"Alright, my handsum. Sorry for keeping you waiting."

The friendly welcome of the returning receptionist who seemed to materialise in front of him immediately relaxed Du Gui. Picking up his key, he politely asked a trivial question.

"Are you busy?"

"Ere, not really. Emmet season starts proper next month then the place will be overwhelmed with squalling kids. Have you been out and about?"

"Yes, I passed time walking round the countryside for some peace and quiet. Emmet, what is that?"

"Oh, a southerner, from the Home Counties. Walking eh. That was a fair old slank for a man of your age."

Catching the drift of her conversation, he rebuked the girl by informing her of his decision to eat out after an evening saunter up to the fortress. The lasting fond memory of the hotel would be the effect of decades of direct sunlight hitting its charming warped windowpanes and not the cheeky young receptionist or the creaking bed.

Next day before the road headed downwards to the small harbour, the car was parked. The place was already teeming with vehicles competing for parking space. At breakfast, checking his guide, it alerted him to the lack of amenities: no car park, family friendly beach or green space, the harbour front being its main outdoor attraction with streets that became narrower the closer to it. Going any further in the car chanced the risk of getting stuck in a traffic jam or crushing an unfortunate pedestrian.

Walking down, modern detached bed and breakfast houses soon gave way to continuous rows of slate stone terraces, then came the village shop and pub and further down there was a DIY and fish tackle shop before the renowned open all day chip shop appeared on his right. Across the road also owned by the chef was a restaurant offering more upmarket fare. A table had to be booked well in advance to eat inside both premises.

He queued for an hour to buy fish and chips. Not the healthiest of foods, but who wanted to eat

healthy on holiday. Time spent in the company of
bored kids and listening to their parents repeat
drooling comments about how nice the fish looked
when served customers left the chip shop with their
purchases. A rival chip shop just around the corner
had a fight on its hands to attract passing trade. Its
well-placed advertising sign informing the visitor
that their fish was fresh today ignored; like
teenagers queuing all day to see their favourite pop
act, tourists wanted a frustratingly long wait.
When served *comme McDonalds*, Du Gui followed
tradition by going down to the waterfront to eat his
takeaway while standing against the sea wall,
where disused water troughs home for flowering
annuals and civic floral planters added colour but
constricted free movement.

The blue sky, the shining sun and the rhythmic
sound of waves lapping on the other side of the wall
helped to de-stress the mind and body. In the
Channel, sensed not seen were unyielding lanes of
container ships. Closer, a sailing yacht in full sail
glided past using a backing wind to bank. He eyed
it and thought that with Falmouth down the way
and Portsmouth up the other end, naval
intelligence would surely have anything that
entered these waters tracked.

The seaside evoked different feelings for land
lovers, testified by a nearby child voicing his
opinion.

"I like sand and real chips, the ones that come with
a toy."

His father swiftly passed the blame.

"I like women in bikinis and soggy chips but today is your mother's choice. Moan to her when she finally comes back from looking for a toilet."

A pleasure beach would have been nice, a safe place to get sea air and view deep waters, under which danger lurked, a domain that Man had never mastered and where existed creatures fearless of him.

Nearer to home an act of thief was about to be conducted in broad daylight. The distraction of sea traffic allowed a herring gull the opportunity to dive down from a roof gutter to snatch a portion of fried fish from an infant. The startled child proceeded to gaze at her feet waiting for attention before commencing to wail. Meanwhile the victorious gull became the subject of a mugging from its compatriots as an alert hawker waved a helium balloon in the distressed child's face to pressurise the parents to buy it. An identity parade of usual suspects for this theft would be interesting.

The half-eaten snack was disposed of discreetly to avoid condemnation and even cries of sacrilege from fellow consumers. Next Du Gui went off to collect gossip from the rival chip shop.

The owners of this quieter chip shop served a more restricted traditional menu during shorter opening times. Apart from that, everything seemed to look similar to that of the celebrity chef: a clean colourful frontage and interior, and a warm buttery smell emanating from it.

The genial smiles on the faces behind the counter

beamed out good service.

"It's a lovely day," proposed a white coated woman.

A conversation informed him that the servers were the proprietors who lived above the shop. They fried *Maris Piper* chips from the same potato deliverer as their busier rival. They did not come originally from Cornwell. In fact, they came from Kentish Town and moved the family home a decade before. The husband did the frying and the wife the serving. Their voices and mannerism easily betrayed their origins and both agreed the locals had accepted their presence. As the wife went out back for paper trays and forks, the fryer told him that the missing chef was a notorious lecher and young women on the make flocked to him for work.

"Was his face a regular feature in town?"

"Not really but I would instinctively know when he was about. Know your enemy that sort of thing. He is treated like the lord of the manor. His presence still felt by the missing posters tacked on front windows and white ribbons of support pinned on blouses and jackets."

The subject matter immediately changed when his wife re-entered.

"It does not matter what time of year it is, there always traffic around, but the place comes to a standstill in high summer," said the husband.

Thanking them, he returned to the waterfront to make judgment on this takeaway. Like the previous takeaway, the quality was good. The British knew their potatoes and how to fry them. The chips were again crispy and explained by the fryer due to not rushing the process and using separate oil. The fish dipped in a beer batter tasted excellent as well. This family run business was more generous with their chips, which was put down to him being recognised.

He remained for a while beside the sea walls to let the rays of the sun warm his face. In the last few days, human activity was observed everywhere he went from ramblers, people walking dogs, people on horseback, on bikes, in cars and on boats. The general opinion gathered from the locals was that trade was brisker than normal and the mystery of the chefs had nicely filled the gap between Easter and summer. That aside, the sun and fish and chips kept the tourists happy. His presence gave added pleasure to autograph hunters.

Staring seawards, it occurred to him that France was beyond the horizon. Apart from the use of hedging and not stone to separate enclosures and the absence of galette stalls, Cornwall was like a split at the hip conjoined twin of Brittany.

On the way back up to the car park he dropped off at the pub. The landlord informed him that his picture was in the front page of the local rag and it said a specific line of inquiry was being followed. He in return jested the hope that his presence would not put the regulars off their drink. The spin on the visit had been swallowed by a newspaper. Looking round, the dark wood mantelpiece above the open fireplace was found to be impressive. Sipping the cider recommended by the landlord, it occurred to

him that the only thing missing to make the day
out perfect for culinary pilgrims was a statue of the
missing chef. After all, Plymouth had *Drake,* a man
only credited with defeating the Spanish Armada.

*****

Nothing happened while he was away.

There were good days, bad days and uneventful
dull days, and his return would be the latter. The
latest progress reports stated the closure of dead
end investigations and a refocusing of effort on the
core motive for kidnapping, ransom. All criminal
gangs having the capability and audacity to conduct
such high profile abductions now had a dedicated
investigation team assigned to them. He wondered
how effective a primarily white force would be at
infiltrating foreign gangs that had made London
their home. The law enforcers did not come from
the people charged to protect and like any other
commuter lived in the suburbs or further beyond,
journeying home to their cocoons, forgetting their
work problems and rekindling family bonds
through the joys of home drinking and watching
box sets together. Therefore, unless Special
Operations had sufficient manpower, it posed the
question of whether commuting white officers were
capable of finding out if an ethnic city gang were
the masterminds behind it all.

Gabriel still interested him. He had arrived at
Scotland Yard without any identification, wearing
recently bought clothes and with only loose change
in his pockets. His assistant had pulled together
CCTV footage of him on the day he offered
assitance. Nothing of significance came from it.

Working backwards it showed him entering the tube at *Baker Street* and apart from a couple of glimpses on shop security cameras, nothing else. He must have walked to this tube station from the centre of town. While watching the screen, it was noticeable that kitchen workers, cleaners, street beggars, door attendants, and security guards had the anonymity of everyday commonness that both wrong doers and undercover law enforcers could use to their advantage.

On schedule, Du Gui announced that it was time for lunch. Jumping on the tube, he headed out to north London. The diverse range of ethnicities that inhabited the capital occupied his mind again.

"By political machinations, the reasons for the winning leave result of the UK EU referendum vote are effectively ignored. The current publicity-seeking mayor held traditional strong elitist views when you took time to understand what he said. World history was chockfull of supposedly men of the people gaining power, which they wheeled with incredible cold-bloodedness. Amin, Hitler and Pol-Pot came to mind. The African was allegedly a cannibal who ate the hearts of his enemies. Since they never had a voice to influence real change is it important what constituted the composition of the disenfranchised serving class. Did it matter. So long as there is a supply of personnel for low paid work to draw upon. Their use of grammar, colour, nationality or looks are immaterial. No matter the epochal socio-economic name given for it, the well-off demanded servants. It went without saying, that these new plebs did not see themselves as downtrodden, for wellbeing sake, they saw themselves as newly

arrived capitalists on the first rung of success. The real question was for how much longer the established hegemony could survive in the face of the foreign plutocrats that had made London home. It was all about show in this Versailles of the materialist world. Why not. Should not the victors have the power and enjoy wielding it. When did an enlightened oligarchy or in other words a benign dictator ever exist. Maybe a diarchy will be acceptable to both camps. The meat of it was a liberal democracy had to make an arrangement with the uber rich. After all, the purpose of an established bureaucracy with a long reach was to safeguard privilege. No matter its form, master mortality dominates human society with today's emphasis on freedom of labour used to rob the lower orders. For the sake of pretence, the plutocrats might agree that real power should remain hidden with the pomp and ceremony left to the old order; while prosperous neoliberals, on which the global economy depended, continued to freely pontificate verbal exhibitionism about intellectual values and importance of world standing, which they fussed about to the abnegation of the lives of less off subjects.

As far as mass influx was concerned, any prohibitive immigration policy is doomed to fail, as it would be akin to shutting the stable door after the horse had bolted. With ten million non-UK born residents, London is an irreversibly entangled city cohabited by the rest of the world; a city that moved money around; a year round crop not dependent on the weather but on maintaining good relations with the rich, irrespective of how their money is obtained. From being a country with the worse lingual skills, the UK is now the best and in a good position to open new trade routes with emerging commercial markets. In the eyes of the money makers, it is a modern Rome with global reach and for many of the older indigenous generations, who knew of simpler times, a chaotic Babylon. The former allowed its slaves to go free once debts had been paid and the latter ensured that that glorious day would never arrive."

Leaving the tube, Du Gui found a grill bar off *Holloway Road*. He had decided to talk to a fallen from grace chef to obtain background information, ascertain this man's feelings about the vanishings and the effect it would have on other chefs. From old recordings, it was apparent that he would encounter someone with a high opinion of himself, so gorgeous that he could eat himself. Life for him was then a piece of cake and he spent money as if it flowed freely from a tap only to lose everything on get rich schemes. Greedily ignoring that if it was too good to be true, then it was. His demise had been spectacular and left him serving a menu of bitters, bile and poison. With this in mind it was anticipated this chef was disgruntled enough to whistle blow on behind the scenes antics.

Up to now, the testimonials from friends and colleagues did not illuminate anything of value. They contained guarded narratives about the lifestyle of their friends. Some may have lied because they were frightened. Lies and evasions were necessary for maintaining self-esteem. It was becoming harder to read the character and gather unsaid information from someone's face. Everyone had become media savvy and accustomed to changing their persona, hiding real thoughts. Some may even be saying half-truths while cognisant of darker activities. Due to the popularity of TV crime dramas and crime fiction, everyone believed to know the rudiments of how the police conducted themselves and that any trace of uncertainty or suspicious responses drew attention. As a result, even if pressed the public were better placed to resist spilling the beans, letting unfavourable traits of their friends slip the mind and express amazement to why anyone would want to hurt them. Obviously, the police interrogators knew what the public perception of their methods and procedures were, and what truthful witnesses forgot and remembered with certainty. Either way, re-interviewing friends would be a waste of time.

Someone who knew trade secrets and was happy to spill the beans would be a better source for incriminating information. Anything procured would be hearsay but a new line of investigation had to start somewhere. To rule out the improbable, it was confirmed that this chef had an alibi on the fateful night, it was cast iron: a night in the cells for drunken and disorderly behaviour. The interview did not disappoint, as there was nothing equivocal in the opinion offered. Straight from the start there was a willingness to talk. He even wheedled the proposition that a demented food critic may be behind it all.

Du Gui entered a dimly lit narrow restaurant where diners were tabled in booths on one side and the kitchen and counter ran down the other side. The dethroned chef engaged with him straight away, expressing animosity, he bemoaned about being unlucky and how being good at your profession was not enough to maintain fame and fortune. The chef fried and flipped steak on a plancha as he rattled on.

"The head chef is king, a role best suited to a man. We are more than happy to adopt the role of the bully than women, who are more apt at two-face backstabbing machinations. Our own meals whether it is egg and chips or the dish of the day are served by underlings to the highest of standards, higher than the best customer would ever receive. The headwaiter is the snitch, watching everything. It has to be that way. The kitchen is a low-ceiling hot inferno of dripping sweat, clattering noise and shouting of orders, so everyone must know their place. This requires a lord of the manor to merciless work the subjects. A realm where waiters and dishwashers are the serfs. Each had their designated counter to staff; ready to go dishes on one counter and returned dishes on another. These workers are two a penny and easy to dismiss. Who has ever heard of a restaurant strike? Troublemakers go on a blacklist so who is going to complain.

We have the power to decide who makes it. Promising trainees are thrust forward, given spots on TV while established chefs are never given an opportunity to shine. No free publicity that could propel their careers. This fast track opportunity allows the best of trainees to be poached from rivals. We are the crème de la crème in a cutthroat multimillion-pound business where keeping your face known is imperative. Seeking publicity is not just about staying on top, having access to it creates a craving for more, a thirst that cannot be satisfied.

Head chefs have some things in common. We cannot afford to be humble and enjoy searching for the next big thing. Food porn is a huge industry in this country and to get on the gravy train you must create a persona that sells. The cockney rascal, the sexy cook and the organic chef have all been done. The nature of the business means if someone fails then a new opportunity opens up. The show must go on and up-and-coming chefs will relish the chance to excel. The search has begun to find replacements to fill the airtime and as far as other chefs are concerned the race is on to cultivate an image that appeals to the TV producers. To gain high audience figures, the viewer had to be given encouragement to either love you or hate you, watching your show with the prospect you marvel at or cock it up. Once you make it offers fall on your lap and invites to dine or cook arrive every day in sack fills."

"Who do you think will gain most out of it all?"

"I would guess the pretentiousness incarnate Preacher is out in front. Here is a man who never forgives any criticism and going on experience knows how to nobble the chasing pact. He is not the *Iago* of cook shows for nothing. Rumours have it he encouraged his maestro's drinking habit that led to an early demise, dethroning him as the undisputed daytime TV king. Would not be surprised to hear that he helped the tabloids to suss out my indiscretions."

"*Iago?*"

"Oh, *Othello* old man. You know the Bard, Shakespeare. You must have heard of him?"

"Yes, of course. Where I come from Molière is taught in schools. So, what about the missing chefs, did they have any shared interests?"

"They are or were members of various food clubs including the exotic eating club, an exclusive group of people that met about every six months."

"When did it last meet?"

"I do not know. I ceased being a member. The menu at *Voisins* during the Siege of Paris in 1870 inspired it. Anyway, it was losing its fascination as we were running out of new rare species to eat. On the last occasion I attended someone managed to get their hands on a pair of male Great Bustards."

"Yes, I read about the troubled start conservationists had in reintroducing the birds in Salisbury Plains with several of them lost. Renowned excellent eating and hunted out of existence in Britain in the nineteenth century."

"Chiffonade! Chiffonade!"

With the conversation interrupted, all eyes turned towards an unshaven uncouth minute kitchen helper ruthlessly slashing salad vegetables in a dark corner. The exposed hairy arms and hands did not inspire confidence.

"Ya?" Replied the small brute.

"Chiffonade! My God! Slice with less force and more finesse."

Lowering his voice again the monologue
continued and ended with:

"Once I had a young Italian stallion under my
wings, now, I am cursed with an Albanian mule
that does not know his elbow from his arse. Not
that customers would notice the difference. So long
as the food is served with servility and is edible,
subtlety is wasted on them. They only want to be
seen eating in the right places and to be able
afterwards to exaggerate the experience."

Having decided that no more useful information
would be forthcoming, the forgotten loathsome chef
was thanked for his candour. The offer to have
lunch was declined and the last words heard in this
man's private hell was a sharp comment making it
clear to a demanding customer that cheese on top of
fried steak was not on the menu and it was either,
side salad, chips or mash.

Because his hunger pains required attention,
another eatery was soon found, a tearoom.
Lingering outside it quizzing at the list of options,
he decided pastries would hit the right spot in his
complaining stomach. He settled for a delectable
high tea of triangular sandwiches, *petit fours* and
something called crumpets. Just baked comforting
sweet treats served on a tiered stand by lace capped
hair in a bun waitresses dressed in black pinafores
over white collared tops. The ordered coffee turned
out good as well, Italian coffee going by the taste of
it. The light sweet favour accompanied the
delicaties on the dainty plates.

To help obtain some solitude in the busy room and
because people watching would be superfluous in

this establishment as hardened criminals or interesting people only ventured in such establishments in novels, a bought tabloid paper occupied his eyes as he set about the treats with relish. The leading article was an undisguised attack lampooning the impotency of the authorities and the accumulating costs in the hunt for the missing chefs. Apparently, an inside source at the Met accused colleagues of taking the biscuit highlighting the amount of air miles spent by high ranking officers and other costly expenses on a lacklustre operation at a loss on what to do next. It roguishly printed that at the cost of a cuppa a soothsayer examining tealeaves would have got better results. This stinging attack would upset the digestive juices of the diners at the Met Police Officers Club. The article finished by quoting the concerns of the celebrity nominated to express the views of his peers, who used the interview as an opportunity to announce a crowdfunding to raise money to provide security for the nation's favourite stars. An enterprising personal security company had placed an advertisement on the same page offering a novel solution for those hundreds of thousands of celebs that could not afford fulltime bodyguard protection. Starting from eight hundred pounds a month, they could wear a solar powered attractive looking unisex neck bracelet or headband that streamed live 360-degree video as they went about their daily activities. A free added bonus was a secret word emergency voice activated a panic alarm to alert operators of a security breach.

A ridiculing account of a university student union leader complaining about the white bias in higher education made him think that maybe he was getting right wing in old age. Apparently she said the course material put ethnic students at a disadvantage. He wondered what white meant.

"Blatantly there is bias in education as the establishment tries to mould the next generation of adults into their desired image but labelling it as white is simplistic. This country's heritage and high culture are a mix of national and international with Western history at the heart of it. So did white mean Anglo-Saxon or did it include Gallic. Latin, Greek and other European influences. For sure, it is not as insular as many other European countries. Did it just imply that white students had an advantage when it came to dissertations? Furthermore, are not the sciences a universal subject. The common-sense solution to any dilemma would be to study abroad or by correspondence at a Black American, Middle East or Asian university. There are great ones to choose from."

Turning towards the middle section the 'Beer is Good for You' headline drew his attention. Apparently, not only do moderate drinkers live longer than teetotallers do, new research suggested the IQ of drinkers was higher. The unquestionability of the latter was just common sense in Du Gui's book but he was dubious about the first claim. A long talk with his physician had made him aware of how growing ethnic demographics in the West were skewing medical statistics. Asian men were prone to dying young due to congenital heart disease problems and their tendency to overwork. Nevertheless, it was heartening to see that the fight against a health lobby that had its roots in the Temperance Movement was continuing.

Flicking the pages back to the front of the paper to avoid adverts and an obsession with football, an article on page three sporting his name grabbed his attention. The accompanying photo was that of a middle-aged woman who according to the story was an ex-lover of his. She purportedly met him in his younger days, thrilled by his touch, spent a hot erotic month in his company after surrendering unconditionally to his suave Gallic charms. The embroidered spread described him as a man of independent means with adequate loose cash to give a girl a good time. Dinners at the Ritz, the Café Royal and the Savoy then nights at her perfumed garden scented basement flat. For the life of him, he did not recognise this woman but would not stand up in court to swear never meeting her. If he had picked her up in a bar or she was a colleague, he could only imagine that something in her personality or young looks appealed to him. His defence to being uncertain was she probably would not have recognised him on the streets if his name were not now identifiable with his well-publicised image. Looking back through the mists of time, he was full of vitality and she a good-looking lay, and that was where it should have been left.

Prior to leaving the comfort of the table and the happy clatter of returned empty plates, a check of the mobile for messages told him nothing of significance required his attention, only a brief text stating no breakthroughs or leads to report. With a contented stomach and a bounce in his step aided by a heart invigorated from a knowing smirk on the face of the waitress that sorted out the bill and being referred to in the titillating article as a prince of love in every way, he made his way to find Radu.

The meeting with Radu was brisk. Nothing to report. Where the chefs were last seen were not places frequented by beggars and lowlife but affluent districts with residents not known to stop, bend down and donate spare change. Like the monarchy, they never had cash in their pockets. Regarding kitchen staff, the opinion offered was that they were a bunch of thickies and it was extremely unlikely they could be involved in a successful abduction. A long serving dishwasher did say a mysterious stranger concealed in a long hooded cloak came sometimes late at night. He could not give any further description because these visits were occasionally observed and only lasted long enough to pass over a note to the chef.

That evening after a quick shower, picking up the novel and putting it in his jacket pocket, he ate out, opting for a shrimp curry after declining a starter in a Thai restaurant. His appetite wetted by watching the curry sizzle in the pan. Sitting silently, eating slowly, he watched the staff in quiet efficiency come and go. Only now and then did their whispers reach him. It was the perfect place to unwind and take up the book again.

The brown eyed investigative reporter dressed sharply in a dark business suit and cream blouse was an arts graduate in her first paid employment in several years: training as a horticulturist and given the responsibility of looking after the children's section and the herb and vegetable plots in a botanic garden. This work built up a strong pair of legs and hips with the scent of nature irrevocably infused in her. Due to the amount of bending involved, her straight shoulder length hair now had the tendency to flop forward to cover her cheeks exaggerating a nose, which she perceived as too long and pointy. She was very enthusiastic in her tributes to the novelist.

"Being nice all day is dull so it is good to snuggle up in bed and read about villains who leave devastation in their wake. I adore your hero for his non-violent old fashion chivalric manner, his sense of duty to find the truth. An unimpeachable character that did not trust his eyes and doubted everything. You cannot read one of your novels without learning something. A comforting feast for the mind, especially on long winter nights. Who cares if popular authors like to lead the readers through the story with all seeing narration.

I prefer crime thrillers written by men and in particular those with settings in culturally rich Europe. Tart noir on mean urban streets or hardboiled crime stories from America does not appeal to me. For literary reading, I tend to play it safe by sticking to applauded female writers such Margaret Lockwood, Muriel Spark and Angela Carter. Consistent with their style and choice of subject matter, all write in a flowing style while still telling a great story. Spark with her non-explicit criticisms of society's undermining of women and revealing men as great frauds, Carter using allusive language to conjure up a picture of the brutality of life in a seedy world and Lockwood exploring the challenges facing relationships in the modern era."

The novelist took to her kind and intelligent face and replied:

"We all have favourites among the serious writers. I cannot put down a Julian Barnes' novel. Spark is a fine example of having her cake and eating it. Lauded with honours and able to quickly write up bestselling *novelettes any time a large expenditure stretched her finances. She definitely had one eye on the money side of the business," enlightened the novelist.*

"Did you ever meet her?"

"Not directly. In the early days, I did attend a ticketed event where she gave a lecture of her work to see if any good advice would be obtained. She was a precursor of how authors would from then on conduct themselves. By all accounts although welcomed by the literati, she lived in fear of being cast out, caught out for being provincial."

"A story of yours set in Tuscany seems to have resembled a period in her life. Was that deliberate?"

"Yes, I was having some fun playing around with her plot blueprint. Except everything was reversed with all those around her character the victims and she the villain. What did you think about my latest adventure?"

"Good but sad that it has come to an end. Your man kept the spring in his step longer than most. Only thing I would query is the preponderance of negative references about life today. Could be more jolly."

During the starter, the reporter gripped the soupspoon to hide her broken nails in the palm of her hand and asked the novelist his opinion about literary critics. This allowed him to get on his hobbyhorse.

"The desire to be appreciated is the prime driving force behind all creative work. To be compared with the likes of Martin Amis or Evelyn Waugh would be the highest accolade. The need to say something and a craving of a favourable interpretation imply the existence of an audience. To maximise the size of that audience, a writer

has to be brave to brace the storm and borborygmic ramblings of paid critics, recruited from the ranks of spectators, not doers.

Anyone who is the friend of a newspaper editor, sibling of a media executive or a lover of a multimillionaire can end up destroying or illuminating a year of hard work. These self-appointed literary guardians always purport to be looking for deep learning and bold symbolism, works that have transcendent synthesis between the written word and the subject matter. However, they do not like to agree or believe in a democracy of opinion or tastes. Referring to the same piece of work some will claim that repetition of habits in a portrayed culture equates to its ethical stance and others claim it to show a lack of depth and absence of local colour.

Language conveys different meaning for the critic and the popular reading public. These frustrated wordsmiths review a novel in isolation from the reader; divorced from the emotional impact a character or plot may have on an individual as they concentrate their concern on structure, symbolism and universal morals. Romanticism to them alludes to a follower of a nineteenth century movement whereas the public think of love stories for the lovelorn bunny boiler. At heart, they are misanthropes, untouched by the need to share experiences and deniers of the fact that language in most walks of daily life is a misused tool.

The perpetual task of thinking up new witty and original phrases to applause or dismiss an earnestly created piece of work has unhinged many of them, springing fully grown Napoleon complexes about their worth. Others ply their trade by just browsing the sack of new books unloaded onto their desks then phoning publishers for their spiel and cherry picking from fellow critics the best parts of already written synopses. They resort to lazy trade tricks like referring to a well-known incident in an author's life or blowing up the importance of an extract from the work to explain a psychological meaning that reveals the personality of the writer or the importance of the work. A throwaway line is taken completely out of context or misused under the guise of de-constructivism, unconscious to the originator, to expose unique brilliance and understanding by the critic. Liberalness versus symbolism, open expression contrasted to close, transparency of thought against opacity of motive, all used against you. If none of these fall backs is deemed usable then they make tendentious comparisons with past masters to strangulate the author. They are like street vendors, earning a living by yelling at the top of their voices for attention. Parasites living off the flesh of creativity would best describe such rascals.

A common objection critics aerate about popular fiction is the overuse of lazy colloquiums, ignoring the fact that people understand and speak these offending phrases every day of their lives and their use bind people together. Instead, there is the exaltation of works that contain expressions and words only ever found in such literature; aesthetic camp sounding language confined in print for perpetuity. Any attempt to use such language in the real world would quickly condemn the perpetrator as a pompous arse. Essentially these bringers of displeasure refuse to acknowledge that the great public read for fun and relaxation. They believe in Horace's doctrine that literature should instruct its readers as well as delight them. In other words, the basis of acceptable literature is moral teaching. In complete contrast, popular fiction is a roller coaster ride intended to shock, thrill or satisfy the voyeur that exists within everyone. No matter the epoch, culture or subject Man's depravities will be *present and believed by the reader.*

Escapism drives book sales, not the search for truth. Happiness only lives in the imagined world. Sitting in a safe place with a cup of tea and a biscuit for ducking, lounging in bed or during the commute, it is mind candy to allow world woes to be forgotten. It can provide some respite from problems. It can help the reader to place him or herself in this crazy society when characters leap out of the page sharing identical dilemmas and character weaknesses as themselves. It is a comfort and consolation to find similar experiences that others find difficult to handle. Fantasy reading has an important role as well, offering the reader the chance to wrap themselves in a figurative comfort blanket and transport themselves back to an unreal time when they felt warm and protected, to a place where good and evil are clearly demarcated, people are not abandoned, can dance and be happy. Stories give people hope and re-assurance, not truth."

The blackmailer gave his endorsement.

"At the crutch of it, books that critics read and fiction enjoyed by a reading public, made up by mostly women, are oftentimes mutually exclusive. Critics dismiss popular novels and the public pay little heed to their recommendations. On the unwonted occasion when an acclaimed work becomes a best seller, it is soon revaluated, faults found and consequently dismissed as trite disguised as art."

Taking the hint to open up, the archaeologist appreciating the wine joined in.

"Winners in life plough their own field regardless what

others say. Be that as it may, success through toil alone is not possible and getting your name known is a priority. The best of both worlds you might say. Above all, to succeed you have to know your audience and manage them. Your hero is perfectly pitched for the middle-aged market. He is a typical loner that can only exist in literature. Every person he meets wants to either confess a misdemeanour or tell his or her life story as if he was a priest. In real life, the loner is viewed with suspicion and people do not like opening up to strangers. Your books are always about the joy of detection and the discovery of truth. Once a problem is solved the consequences are left, unwritten, to the justice departments, not deemed relevant. Grappling with strange cases, meeting available women and compulsive infidelity sell books."

The brown soup went down a treat and although not to everyone's taste the black pudding was tried and, except for the reporter and blackmailer, completely consumed. When the red light came on, the novelist encouraged the holding back blackmailer to drink the wine and told the manservant not to top up the water carafe. All the while the host drank from a thick bottom cheater glass...

*****

The next day, feeling the flat atmosphere pervading the operations room and thinking openable windows were needed to let the air on, Du Gui asked his assistant for her views on the morale of the officers working on the congealing Met investigation.

"It has hit rock bottom. The place is getting quieter by the day. All avenues have been explored and many officers were in autopilot mode now, looking busy when superiors did the rounds and twiddling their thumbs in between times, hoping and waiting for someone else to make the breakthrough."

What she did not say that some were spent and would not contribute anything meaningful for the next couple of weeks after popping *Modafinil* and *Viagra* to help them get through the late night shifts and extended socialising.

Moving on, her enquiries into what the paparazzi were up to on the night of the disappearances drew a blank. A notorious face within this posse had dropped off the radar. This was not considered unusual and occurred often after making a killing or an assignment out of town demanded secrecy to steal a march on a rival in the hope of getting the scoop of a lifetime. It was a competitive business with rich rewards.

That afternoon's adventure took him to Camden Town.

Several hours earlier Gabriel happily accepted an invite for an informal interview with the proviso that it took place in public. A reluctance to sit in the confines of a police station led to a proposal to have an informal word at a little café near Mornington Crescent tube station.

After an extended journey by getting on the wrong branch of the northern line, he arrived at the renovated art décor red brick station where necessity forced him to cross the busy junction and head up to Camden. The well-disguised café was initially walked past, as from the outside it looked

if it had long ago been abandoned and boarded
up. A peeling dark brown paint covered the front
brickwork, the rotting window frames and the rust-
infested sheet of metal that guarded the bottom
half of a filthy windowpane. The narrow wooden
door had a matching sheet of metal tacked on to it.

"Did they serve humans in this place?"

The door swung outwards to reveal two exiting
mawkishly cuddling and sniggering lovers in the
fashionable gear of the young middle class protester
that made this area its home. Baggy clothes
effortlessly ruffled and appropriately dirtied,
reflecting the correct mix of hippie and revival Brit
pop clothing from the market up the road. Both had
long sandy dreadlock weaved hair with brightly
coloured extensions and expensive laced boots on
their feet. To finish the effect, both wore shemaghs
tied round the neck, providing the means to hide
their faces when required. The perfect attire for
anarchists with the time and resources to spend the
week making love and the weekend travelling
around the country to support the cause of the day.
Enjoying their days of dissidence prior to settling
down to a secure future. Behind the pair, the acrid
vapours from fried food, boiling tea and the overuse
of bleach hit the nostrils.

The café was a snug with a small galley kitchen
and a poky windowless unisex toilet that shouted
out 'use at your own peril'. Five tables with chairs
were crammed into the available space at the front
next to the walls and window. Each table had a wax
cover in a black and white chessboard pattern with
a small tray holding condiments still in their
original branded bottles. Behind the counter, an old

Cypriot man with hurried hands multiplexed between the fryer, grills, hot plates and pots. From the age of the décor, the man probably had been wedged there since evicted from his paradise island by the Turks.

Two ancient long parallel strips of dirt covered florescent lights barely illuminated the scene while the thickness of the grime on the surface of the window prevented natural light from penetrating in. The dark cerise painted walls and ceiling only enhanced the claustrophobia. Other indications of the time the place last saw a lick of paint was the yellowing poster on the wall and stains from decades of grease and cigarette smoke in the corners of the ceiling. The former was a hung print of Escher's *Ascending and Descending* depicting the perpetual eternal nature of conformity within human society with a pair of rebelling outsiders looking on, watching the procession march up and down steps. A geometrical 3D *tromp l'oeil* to suck the eye into the nightmare. Even when the realisation of the impossibility of the object was accepted, the eye continued to contradict the evidence in front of it. Subliminally it cried out abstaining was futile, it achieved nothing and no matter your stance in life you must inevitably march to the drumbeat of your generation, regardless whether that be willingly or with dragging feet and slouched shoulders. A popular print of its period that the proprietor of this café refused to replace as its removal would force him to redecorate.

"Cup of cha, gov?"

This enquiry drew his attention to the fact that something had to be bought. A quick scan of the offerings indicated nothing tempting. The haphazardly displayed menu on a top shelf advertised the type of meal a hassled working class mother would give to her ravenous kids: unhealthy fun bites of mechanically recovered protein, all frozen. Tea boiling away in a large electric urn made him decide on a cup of coffee. Even then, hesitation on his face was palpably apparent when an arm reached up for a large unbranded tin of instant. Seeing this expression, the proprietor took pity on him and whispered:

"Here have some of my own, commissioner."

A hot pungent liquid was poured from a flask kept under the counter into a just washed cup and handed to him. At that moment, Gabriel materialised behind him and gladly accepted a cup of tea and a fried egg roll. When they turned round luck was on their side as the table along the half boarded up window became available.

To allow his guest to enjoy the snack, Du Gui kept quiet using the time to narrow down the age of the man in front of him. The bald bony head and open mouth while eating shouted out strong clues. Gaps between his teeth and the presence of amalgam fillings along with signs of a shrinking skull convinced him Gabriel was of similar age if not slightly older than him. Forever the detective, he could not help glancing at the other customers to see if how they ate betrayed time behind bars.

The conversation got off to a slow start.

"You know your way about?" Quizzed Du Gui.

"You have to when cash strapped, either sink or swim," came the friendly riposte.

The coffee, with its warm sweet smell wafting over his nose, tasted excellent, espresso done the Greek way, considering its strength far too much in the cup for him. His brain would be bouncing off its cranium walls in thirty minutes. To his surprise, while he watched his guest add several teaspoonfuls of sugar to his tea, he had become comfortable. The place was clean where it mattered and since everything was overcooked food poisoning was unlikely. The cheap tables and the hard unforgiving chairs along with the heat from the galley took him back in time sitting in his grandmother's kitchen doing his homework before the table was cleared away to serve dinner. The stove always had her favourite pot simmering away and ladles of its contents would constitute the main meal of the day. With fresh ingredients adeptly bought that day, she topped up the pot. That pot was a true perpetually impossible object.

After the preliminaries, Gabriel bared some scars that cut deep into his soul.

"The police are nothing but thugs in uniform. Do not get me wrong you do not want nice types in charge of guarding the wealth of the successful in society, but they could never appreciate my history. Their sociologists and psychiatrists only want to earn their living by pigeonholing me. You on the other hand, enjoy the uncommon and I promise a singular story. Allow me to indulge myself in the telling of it. It has been a lifetime in the making with many hazards encountered."

"We are made of the dreadful things that cannot be forgotten," Du Gui sympathised.

Gabriel claimed to be an orphan that grew up in a state run orphanage before being shipped out to Australia when old enough to travel, there to become slave labour under the guise of achieving a better life.

Early life was dictated by the three B's: the dormitory bell, the belt and bullies. The bell signalled the time to rise, work and eat. The belt used to install discipline and forbearance. Bigger kids relieved their suffering by tormenting the younger and smaller orphans.

Rising in shuttered dormitories, huddled together, itchy from the coarse woollen blankets and goose pimples from the chilled air, ragged, snottily nosed and perpetually hungry they marched slow and sombre across a dark yard to the cookhouse, cold always cold, as a wind cut into them like a blade. At each meal, thanks were given for the slops in front of them, whether that be a bowl of tasteless porridge, soup or some sort of hash. Tea was served in a tin cup with sympathy and compassion in short supply.

One of his early recognitions was being in a surgery where a doctor prognosed his reluctance to speak.

"Nothing physiologically wrong, throat and vocal cords intact, maybe, he does not speak because he has nothing to say?"

He had been knocked down by a car, an unlucky feat in the days when private transport was less frequent on the road. Back then, vehicles were unforgiven as a tank and he was lucky to survive. Although not remembering any details, he apparently suffered fainting fits and slowness to develop like others his age. This did not stop the belting in class when he stuttered in reading lessons. Ignorance of this and more hideous crimes against children went unpunished, as the perpetrators worked under state licence, their actions done in its name.

Du Gui found himself delving into his past around the same age. It was a Christmas day and his mother known for being a poor cook had outdone herself and laid a good table. They lived in a shabby tenement in a cobbled street that had a bakery on the ground floor and above them in the attic was a seamstress workshop. It was the family's first home and had to take what they could get. On a daily basis, the young Du Gui ran the gauntlet of women caked in flour or with threading needles pinned to sleeves as they teased him during their breaks. Suddenly above the table, there was a loud thud and the ceiling vibrated with plaster collapsing onto the table. A burglar taking advantage of the holiday had broken in, and it was said afterwards, failing to find cash decided to rip out lead shielding. Disaster for his mother but a memorable Christmas day for him. The culprit was prevented from escaping by tenants while someone ran to inform the police who duly arrived bringing Alsatian dogs with them. The whole street came out to watch the proceedings. The dogs were sent in first and when cries of pain reached the whole neighbourhood, the officers

unhurriedly searched out the dogs. Dragged and
truncheoned from the workshop, the bloodied
burglar was immediately recognised as a man that
lived at the far end of the street. All the way down
the landings and while being hauled over cobbles
name calling, spitting and punching emanating
from his neighbours rained down. The police were
cheered when this man was bundled into a van
with the dogs. There was no sign of love your
neighbour that day. Imagine that happening today.
Would the police be cheered and what financial
compensation would this destroyer of a Christmas
day lawyers demand for his human rights
violations? Aware that his eyes were probably
lacking attention, Du Gui pertinently re-joined the
conversation by commiserating with Gabriel.

"Yes, teaching methods in those days were more
robust than now with the right to be different
forbidden. In my infant class, a smack behind the
legs was received for writing with your left hand."

Nodding in agreement, Gabriel resumed his tale.

"Anyway, on leaving for the colonies, no good-byes
were said to me when the passenger ship steamed
away. With a name tag of my new owners round the
neck, belongings wrapped in brown paper tied with
string, I was put in third class steerage with
around two hundred other deported young souls. A
pitiful cargo, flooding tears, faces startled with fear,
kept below decks to emerge later into a living hell.
Is it surprising that I changed my loyalties to the
first people that offered a helping hand?"

Du Gui sympathised.

"It is a disgrace that victims are rarely fully recompensed but tragedies happened every day in this world and are soon forgotten. Best to pick yourself up, get on with life, and not let the suffering that has been inflicted spoil what is left of your time. Anywhere can become the friendliest place on earth for a man who knows how to forget misfortunes.

Why not search your genealogy to discover your birth mother? Perhaps, she tried to find you after her circumstances improved."

Gabriel was ambivalent about this suggestion, had long ago stopped wanting to punish her and accepted his fate which was not to expect happiness. After a noticeable pause, he stated he had to go. Du Gui thanked him for making the time to see him.

Gabriel left first.

Fifty metres behind Radu followed him.

In the café, Du Gui pondered.

"So his appearance is an act of mischief against a society that turned its back on him and many thousand others?"

A COLD FARE

The following day, after another morning scanning through reports, his brain told Du Gui it needed fresh air. Outside, the sensing of the presence of an observer taking a keen interest in his movements, probably a reporter looking for an exclusive, spoilt his anticipated stretching of the legs. Although accustomed to being recognised and inspected, the attention and unsolicited approaches for his happy urban stroller were starting to wear him down.

The decision was made to go to Kew Gardens to get into the open. Entering the tube station, a shadowy figure followed behind him.

All the way down the district line, his senses persisted in alerting him to the presence of watching eyes. These belonged to a passenger choosing to stand next to the doors despite the abundance of seats. Because it occurred to him that his unease was probably a manifestation of paranoia brought by being recognised, a plausible reason made more so by the restrictive width of the seats for this standing passenger's girth, he fought the irrational feelings. Meanwhile, the eyes that had looked away when observed looked again in his direction a few moments later.

In Richmond, under a hot early summer blue sky, the cherry trees planted down the avenues stood undisturbed by any mischievous juvenile behaviour. It was still blossom time and the pinks complimented the pastel browns and yellows in the bricks of the detached houses and luxury flats. The no ball game signs obeyed when in his day kids would have used a prohibition sign as a goal post with the other end marked out by a pile of jumpers. Apart from tourists and office workers taking their lunch, the green places were the realms of the raptor and seagull to torment the feral pigeons.

In the gardens, after paying what was thought a high price for a walk in a park, he took a straight tree lined path towards the Pagoda, removing his jacket and folding it over his arm, annoyed that he had not left it back at the Yard. Behind him, his shadow unsubtly tried to keep out sight. This encouraged Du Gui to have some fun by advancing slowly, repeatedly stopping to listen to the birds or to examine a woodland lily, always looking back to see if the fellow was still behind him. Although dark shadows lay across the path diminishing his field of vision someone seemed to fret; impatient twitching from someone who was clearly not a lover of horticulture.

The large frame of the greenhouse on the right reminded him of a classic comedy film starring a 1960s British comedy duo. In the film, God lived in such a glass house, and the Devil had an arrangement with him regarding capturing souls. In a sketch, the devious one enlightened his current prey the reason for his fall and banishment.

"Imagine you are in heaven and I am God, parade round me praising my beneficence."

After a few minutes of play-acting, the tiring human expressed his feelings of getting fed up with this.

"That is what I said!" Exclaimed the Devil.

The sight of summer orchids and wild mint starting to flower in late April was a sure sign that it had been a long mild spring. It was a time of year when the bellies of the peregrines and sparrow hawks were full, and magpies flash mobbed trees one at a time wiping out the chicks in the passerines' nests. The striking impression or lack of one was the want of strong fragrances. The only hint obtained when bending down to cup a bluebell or ramson in his hands. This, after all, was a working campus and not intended to be merely ornate. The Kew Garden curators of the day aided Darwin in classifying his plant samples by genus and species, a task they still did today.

At another spur-of-the-moment stop in his ambulation, Du Gui's eyes dwelled on a silent wood pigeon resting on an exposed branch of a black popular, and then another was spotted on the neighbouring branch, and then another one, the tree was riddled with them.

At the clearing around the 300-year-old structure, he pulled breakfast rolls from his jacket pocket and enticed the pigeons towards him. He could not help thinking that the loud frequent drone of the flight path above his head merited a good discount on the ticket price.

Should he return the way he came and confront this inquisitive fellow or continue to give him more exercise? Not ready to eat, he swung right to follow the signposts to the pond. The decision was to get his money's worth and go on strolling with his thoughts. A high walled perimeter, security guards at entrances and keeping to well-trodden paths reassured him that nothing underhand would happen, unless, of course, it could be made to look like an accident. Halfway to the pond, shoelaces were re-tied again to allow him to raise his eyes back to see if the stalker was enjoying the pleasant idling walk under a warm sun in the air of a meadow located in the middle of the most congested city in Europe.

Stopping to observe the water lilies with frogs relaxing on their broad waxy leaves floating on water masked black by this foliage cutting out the light, the impulsive laughter from a pair of love birds holding hands on the other side reached him. It occurred to him the charge to enter this oasis did have a major benefit. The pedestrian was allowed to appreciate the ambience and zig-zag or loiter along the paths without the nuisance or interruption of thoughts from cyclists and runners racing past.

Looking at his watch the decision was made to return towards the tube station and have something to eat at a restaurant seen near there. In

the chosen café-bar, Du Gui was impressed with
the choice. Beer hand pumps had accompanying
notes that described to the discerning drinker what
to expect when the nectar hit the lips. Another
remarkable change from the old days when only
mild, bitter and lager were on offer, two of which
served warm and the other tasteless and heavily
carbonated. He ordered a small roast served crispy
at the edges and pink in the middle along with
boiled baby potatoes, a melee of greens, mushroom
gravy, and a large glass of porter from a brewery
that claimed superior quality by using water drawn
from an underground source lying deep beneath
mineral and pebble beds. The order was taken by a
two-toned dyed red haired, tattooed roses covered
barperson sporting a large nose ring and dressed in
a pair of light cotton floral cropped trousers and a
sleeveless khaki top. The recommended beer from
this person, described if created by her generation,
was a beverage that she probably drank regularly.
All said from an immaculate red lipstick mouth and
powdered face, straight out of the 1940s.

The beer turned out a surprisingly good match for
the red meat dish. For afters, there was a sticky
toffee pudding served with *crème anglaise*. At the
next table, a female customer voiced the opinion
that this must be a gay bar because none of the
men had glanced at her. That thought did occur to
him when observing a ceiling populated with
cherubs looking down on him and fresh cut flowers
adorning every nook and cranny, but his main
query was where did the non-chic hang out.

Dabbing his lips with the provided paper napkin
and sipping his coffee after eating the last morsel of
an excellent pudding, the tail who had been

scrutinising him from the bar took this as his signal to finally approach him. Above the bar noise, a haunted looking stranger spoke with the recognisable intonation of an African, a Nigerian.

"Commissionaire Du Gui?"

He nodded.

In front of him was a middle-aged man dressed in a charcoal wool blend casual jacket, blue trousers and a white shirt opened at the neck. The latter exposed an even tanned skin. His receding forehead was not detrimental to him as it enhanced his strong facial features. The remaining cut short hair was thick and black. On his wrist was a *Hilfiger* with a wide face dial. A big watch for a big man with a soft drink in his hand. A broad upper body and a height of nearly two metres gave him a natural powerful strength. When the stranger spoke a baritone voice sounded diffident with a hint of desperation, it also came across as Christian.

"What can I do for you?" Enquired Du Gui.

"My daughter is missing. Her name is Cerena. She left for school and never came back. Our lives have been torn apart. My wife is on the verge of a nervous breakdown. We are frantic for news and any help would aid us. If it were an accident, then there would have been news by now. You can appreciate the stress we have been under. My wife lies awake recounting anything that may have had troubled or unsettled our daughter."

"Please sit down."

The man put his mineral water on the table, placed a panama on his bending knees, and immediately continued his story.

"I know you are a sagacious man and will do your best. She has led a sheltered life, still young in many ways, and not the young adult that the police claim her to be. They have her details on their database and a DNA sample, and now she is just another missing person going down the list of priorities until completely ignored."

The distraught father passed over a photograph of his daughter and in a voice that had difficulty in enunciating words mumbled she liked to paint then recovering his voice he went on to say:

"I have been told to be patient and that she will turn up on their own accord. The whole family is hysterical with worry. We just want her back home, we all do. Why does she not contact us? Not knowing makes each passing day harder to bear. Her room is still the way it was, her hopes and dreams left to gather dust."

There the man ceased his entreaties.

"I will look into it, but cannot promise anything," said Du Gui gently.

After giving his personal details, a recent photograph and a note of the case number, the Nigerian parted. Alone again, Du Gui sipped his coffee and found it cold. He put the cup down, put his jacket on, left the table and went to the bar to pay the bill. He hated saying platitudes, more so when it concerned a missing child compounded by the hallowing fact that the time allocated by the police to investigate had expired. The truth was unless his sudden celebrity could be put to good use, he was only in a position to offer a sympathetic ear. Mind, considering that children were now normally bigger and stronger than their parents, the girl would be by this presumption hard to miss. Simply by sitting, the dining area had been rendered cramp by the Nigerian making it difficult for the waiter to go about his business.

Outside, walking back to the tube station, the need to act dawned on him as his feet felt the pavement beneath his feet. Of course, he ought to help, no question about that. Besides, it would not waylay him from the task that he was headhunted to aid. He also wondered what it was like to be a man of faith in a city where material corruption was omnipresent, the jewel in the crown for the rich and liberal minded. Every type of biblical sin and new ones openly enjoyed and celebrated in front of their eyes. Sybaritic princes and the nouveau rich enjoying any pleasure so desired. If they came voluntarily perhaps they accepted the state of play or if they came from the fringes to bring back the Faith they were up for the challenge. Prudish evangelists with a strong belief in traditional gender roles presumably faced a greater up road struggle; and what about the monarch, as the defender of the Faith with an upright rigid upbringing and champion of the older generations, did the mores of the young urbane cause concern.

*****

More to relieve his conscience than with hope of

success he gave the case number to his assistant
and asked her to review the missing person dossier.

Nothing suspicious found. At fifteen, she was too
young to have acquired a detailed database profile.
Social services never had reason to be suspicious of
untoward behaviour. Her social media accounts had
the usual young girl nonsense. On her homepage,
there was a nice picture of her with a pet rabbit
against her cheek. School records showed good
attendance, a top student and a medical history
had the normal list of growing up ailments. Her
parents said there had been no quarrels or fall-outs
of any kind. They have made a comfortable life for
themselves in London and adopted an acceptable
blend of *Naija* pride and English conformity. She is
their only child. Both parents highly educated
professionals, *Redeemed Church of God*
practitioners and owned a nice property in
Southwark. One worked in the health service and
the other, the wife, an IT consultant. She left for
school, spent the whole day there, teachers noted
nothing out of the ordinary, left friends at the gates
and that was the last sighting. May have cut
through a park, but that is a presumption based on
her normal routine. The school uniform is quite a
common sight at that time of day. Not been in touch
since or active on social media. The *London
Standard* printed the customary missing person
story about the police asking for help and her
parents being worried sick. Intelligence reports on
the family background came back clean with no
known ties to the criminal world, corrupt tribal
leaders or political families in Nigeria. Now that
the first seventy-two hours had passed since she
disappeared, the inquiry was effectively on hold,
not due to negligence or lack of respect but costs.

Du Gui asked if there was a family photo on the system. When pulled up onto the screen it confirmed that the man in the café was the father and that the girl took after her mother. They were on paper an idyllic family. This on face value should mean outside familial influences had come into play but in these sceptical times apparent goodness could be treated with suspicion.

"I got the impression from speaking to him that the father was a disciplinarian without any intended malice."

"Perhaps the pressure to succeed got too hard for her."

"Mind, even if what she wanted went against the wishes of the parents, it does not necessarily mean anything. Behind closed doors, families quarrel with no holds barred and it is only to be expected that the teenager would be irritated by the foibles possessed by her parents. They have the intimate knowledge to hurt, be savagely direct. Even outdoors, overheard family conversations to a neutral observer can sound rude and lacking respect. Of course, this did not normally lead to harm and in many ways allowed a healthy release of tensions. Anyway, motive and opportunity does always lead to an offense. Otherwise, society would have collapsed centuries ago."

The assistant did not reply to these remarks and aired her latest findings.

"FGM is not prevalent in their social group, worse offenders associated with rural communities and poorer northern African and Arab states. CID and Special Branch indicated no gang activity near the school attended or her home. Just the usual gang warfare activities of Nigerian gangs with their East European associates contesting against the *Yardies* for control of the narcotics trade and money laundering.

Kidnap of children for ransom, although common in Nigeria, not yet known here. If this were the start of such a caper, the absence of a demand from the abductors suggests something went wrong. Black magic abuses do occur but these tended to be within superstitious families, which does not seem likely with this family. It is used to control the weak minded by installing irrational fear into them. Nothing stored about her school friends. Would have to get permission from the chief investigator to get resources assigned to obtain information about them and to get access to their mobile phone recordings."

She also provided him with an up to date assessment of organised crime activity in London from the National Crime Agency, primarily to indicate the many nefarious groups out there and secondary to say finding the girl was equivalent to the needle in the haystack problem. Each community had youth gangs that protected their turf. Organised ethnic crime lords' tentacles reached into these gangs to recruit soldiers. The *Yardies* dominated the hard drug and prostitution scene with Asian and Turkish crews rising fast behind them because of their contacts in Afghanistan. East European and African mafias are increasingly using London as their base. The Albanians, although smaller in numbers, were ruthlessly violent in chasing their goal for an increased share in the criminal trades, conservatively estimated to be worth a tax-free sum of 30 billion a year or double that if illicit money brought into the country is included. Trading in illicit advanced anti-ageing drugs, steroids and cognitive enhancers should reach the same proportions as hard drugs once costs and availability made them affordable to the masses. The gangs' strength maintained by a strong bond of kinship and the fact that crime lords could swiftly retaliate against family members back home if any disloyalty occurred. These 'businessmen' illegally specialised in theft, counterfeiting, fraud, sexual exploitation, drugs, firearms trade, money laundering, people smuggling, kidnapping and extortion and that unspoken word in the UK, corruption. Traditional Chinese and Irish gangsters continued to prosper. It went without saying many gangs had strong links with rightwing and foreign nationalist politics. Extra policing to monitor and depreciate the impact of the actions of these criminals on mainstream society cost the taxpayer around 500 million pounds a year. This figure excluded the cost of housing captured foreign felons in this country or through international agreement to pay for their confinement back in their homeland.

"The girl could be this very moment working the streets in any city in the world," said the spot-on assistant.

"It is interesting that she spent the day at school," concluded Du Gui.

"Her parents appear not to be big cash spenders with no suspicious items purchased," chipped in Williams after browsing printed off bank and credit card statements.

Before leaving the office, Du Gui got the photograph given to him uploaded then along with the one already stored on the computer downloaded both onto his phone and had several hard copies printed off.

*****

Not fancying a heavy dinner, he popped into a deli-restaurant near the South Kensington tube station and had a selection from the cold tray with a Portuguese dry white to go with it.

Afterwards knowing it would be fine to do so, he called Radu to find out where Gabriel went after his meeting with him and to ask him to use his street contacts to see if anyone knew anything about the Nigerian girl. The Romanian gave news about the former and raised doubts concerning the latter.

"*Mon ami*, I will be of limited use to you in finding this girl. I rarely venture into her community and my contacts tend to not have any dealings with them. But I will keep my eyes and hears open."

"It cannot hurt to look," he hoped.

In the hotel, he chatted with a young female managing the hotel's reception for a few minutes which gladdened the spirits then headed up to his room to pour a large cognac and take up the novel.

The blackmailer sheepishly ate the tartare, thought it had a unique taste and wished for an unaccustomed boldness to leave the dish unfinished. His discomfort compounded by a wine glass that seemed to him overly refilled by the archaeologist who was making a night of it.

"I like your detective because of his single mindedness, honesty of expression and flawless courage. Your sleuth has a well-grounded personality and takes on everyday villains. A man not afraid of making his face known to draw the criminal out into the open. There is also an authentic premise to the crimes in your books. If the number of murders recorded in the towns of novels written by some writers occurred in real life, a special Home Office task force would have commandeered the running of the place. In saying that, I liked the futuristic story about the group of geneticists who thought it their prerogative to mix together human DNA with organic life surviving in the most punishing conditions on Earth to produce yeti-like creatures capable of surviving in extreme environments, hot, cold or dark, with the future aim of using them to colonise and work on other worlds. Potentially intelligent and capable of exercising free will creatures condemned to a life of slavery by having neural paths blocked. A modern day Dr Moreau tale where the brutal deaths of mauled mountain wolves by an escaped creature put your man on the trail of mad scientists."

An interpolation came from the aristocrat.

"It is too late to stop it. Enhancement technology through drugs, implants, biological twerking of cell structures and DNA splicing is understood and available. Metamorphosis will be driven by the rich demanding greater life spans with good health."

"A theme behind Frankenstein is Man's hubris. No matter how clever he thinks he is, he cannot grapple with the enormity of what he is playing with. The impact of sentient rivalries and perversions will result in an outcome beyond his feeble imagination," the novelist replied.

The reporter referred to examples raised by H. G. Wells.

"Through his predictions of things to come and time travel, you can take your pick between a world run by an elite of super-intelligent scientists or a world inhabited by the Eloi and the Morlocks."

"The future beckons woe for us. It is a form of mass suicide. Science is hell bent on transforming the human species into an artificial super-alternative and we will be become pygmies, unwanted decrepitudes forced out of existence. Irreverent in the future as aboriginals are today. May as well trash the place before the new rulers of the planet are created," mockingly joked the archaeologist.

"No more need for babies or experiencing second-hand the joys of childhood fun I cannot see that. Missing out on a family life would be too much to bear for a lot of women. We are mammals after all."

Moving on, the blackmailer gave an abstruse compliment to the novelist.

"You are one of the few modern writers I read. Because your plots are intriguing I tolerate the grammatical errors and the tendency to overuse the same prepositions and adverbs. I have read all my life but tend to stick to sci-fi, detective stories and classics by Victorian writers. Tried to read the likes of Martin Amis but the subject matter

had no attraction for me. Well-written and great insight, I suppose, but the manners of the promiscuous middle classes just do not interest me. A subject dominated with the angst of public school raised writers."

"You cannot criticise Amis, he is an icon," protested the now preoccupied novelist. His eyes were caressing the changing contours of the bulging breasts of the black-eyed femme fatale, which she noticed. They had always been her first line of attack. She knew that men knew that there was nothing accidental in the way a woman presented herself.

Unexpected support for the dull guest came from the aristocrat:

"Just because he is on the college reading list for literature students, does not make it necessary for the reading public to like him."

"Your books sell faster than his classics!" Confirmed the reporter.

"Cannot argue with that. Suppose we cannot help reflect our own generation and post-war writers excelled at rebelling against the mores of the establishment," admitted the novelist.

"Has anyone got to the end of his novels without skipping a few pages," voiced the femme fatale feeling left out of this conversation.

The one thing agreed upon was the heyday of reading for pleasure was truly over. The effortless distraction of continuous access to work, throw away information, friends, music, videos and on-demand TV had resulted in the creation of a more is less culture.

The blackmailer, desperately wanting to make himself appear insightful, rested his glass of wine and with ebullition veered the conversation on to a well-rehearsed topic.

"Believe Arthur Conan Doyle deliberately or more probably unconsciously inculpated himself in a sort of belated confession when 'The Problem of Thor Bridge' was published in the Strand. The lovers in this story were none other than a veiled Doyle and his young mistress. Simply put Doyle wanted to free himself from a loveless marriage with an ill and aging wife and openly be with his new younger love interest who by all accounts was pretty devious. The same trait as the beloved mother of the famous creator of Sherlock Holmes who aided and abetted the extramarital relationship of her son, done in front of the oblivious wife..."

You could hear a pin drop. The force of delivery raised eyebrows.

"...considering the fact that Doyle was a doctor and as such must have had the opportunity to prescribe hard to detect poisonous vials, at the very least, his wife's death may not have been completely due to a natural cause. The slowness of the poor woman's death backs up the premise of small potions frequently given to aid her passage to the next world. I quote these words from that story published in the Strand in 1922, sixteen years after the death of his first wife:

'I guess most men have a little private reserve of their own in some corner of their souls where they don't welcome intruders.'

Is it not strange that a man who believed in spiritualism only sought out correspondence with a dead son and none with a dead wife that bore him two children?

All this compounded with the well-documented fact that Doyle was a man of action and would naturally hate being chained to a sickbed.

In later life, Doyle became estranged from the daughter of his deceased wife.

I will not bore you with the other clues in his writing."

"Too late for that," whispered the reporter.

"Maybe others before you reached these conclusions but kept their silence," suggested the baffled female fatale, well on her way to merriness.

"Would you be the one that betrays Doyle? You had better watch out, the legions of Holmes fans would not take kindly to the maligning of the creator of such revered stories. In fact, you are speaking to one just now," said the novelist.

The surprised and incredulous blackmailer involuntarily released an exclamation.

"There has been no mention of this in any of your biographies?"

The novelist's face gave a hint of hesitation before discussing this oversight.

"I will make sure my publicist addresses this detail in the next update of my official biography."

The tact of the conversation changed with a robust intrusion from a bemused archaeologist.

"What has become of any brains that God has given you? If this is not edited out, then you can expect hate mail and twitter abuse. You will be hunted down. Get out more and enjoy life. Reading is not doing and does not necessarily lead to comprehension. Travel and experience life. Books cannot express the heat, the colours, the sounds and smells of different parts of the world. A culture is not its heroes and historic monuments, it is expressed in daily life by its distinctiveness, little things like its post boxes and advertising boards tell you so much more."

"Live a little. Take a long holiday. Push yourself. That will sort you out," concurred the aristocrat.

In jest the archaeologist demanded to know if they were addressing a librarian.

"No! I am an information research officer at a university bibliotheca."

The blackmailer wanted to go on to say that participating in life stopped you thinking clearly, it affected judgement by either enjoying it or stirring emotions. But aided by consuming above her normal quota of wine, the reporter got in first with an attempt to lighten the mood with an impromptu rendition of climb every mountain with the femme fatale joining in with the chorus.

*"Climb every mountain
Ford every stream
Follow every rainbow
Till you find your dream..."*

A grand finish accomplished by standing and pirouetting round their seats, leading to applauds. The soiree had lifted off just as the main course was served. Braised meat easily pulled apart with a fork negated the need for steak knives which given the explosion of pent-up fervour released by the blackmailer was fortuitous.

Turning over to sleep, the book fell on the floor, a critic's glowing endorsement on an inner page facing upwards. An entertaining tour de force it was not. Maybe the best was yet to come. If not, it would end up on the regretted bought pile then given to an unsuspecting friend as an interesting read or taken to a charity shop during the annual tidy up.

"Was it not Molière who said writing is like prostitution. First you do it for love, and then for a few close friends, and then for money."

*****

Another day, the same story. Nothing concrete came out of the new initiative to focus resources on ethnic criminal gangs. A wall of silence was met, not even a denial obtained.

Bang on one p.m., he strode out of the building, rode the tube and got off at Leicester Square to look round the second hand and antiquarian bookshops. The reason for hiding in a bookshop for an hour had nothing to do with an infatuation with the written word. He did not intend to buy anything just wanted to enjoy the aroma of old hardbacks and to pick up a rare copy of a then popular author whose archaic style of writing now dissuaded anyone but a scholar to read it. In a future where the written word has regressed back to a standardised hieroglyphic text, how will this century's prose be judged, will it be classified then also dismissed as outdated and longwinded.

For lunch, a takeaway was fancied to munch while walking the streets to people watch, amuse himself with a game deducing the background of milling passers-by from their appearance and attempt to remember as many small details as possible. This idea led him towards Soho to a fish and chips shop called the 'Best English Chip Shop' served by a pair of happy smiling young Algerians. Once there, an abrupt change of mind resulted in the purchase of steamed bao buns from a next-door restaurant.

Next, his afternoon appointment with Radu took him to Aldgate, a place historically known as a roughhouse area, a haunt for recent arrivals to London. Gabriel had been followed to a flat in this district. An interpreter was brought on board for this expedition. A cheerful, slightly porcine round faced man with matching round spectacles, called Neerja Chopra, who looked as if in his thirties and was of Indian extraction. The prolongation of puppy fat around his cheeks suggested a spoilt domestic life.

Meeting at a tube station, they walked east for five minutes then went up a side street where all the flats were rented out by established ethnics to recently arrived ones, mostly northern Africans, Arabs and Asians; these tenants had something in common: they were here to find menial work. Many boastfully professed to speak at least six languages but knew not to understand English when it suited them. In their native home, they were accountants, cooks, butchers, stonemasons and the like. A few of these new residents lived on the wages of women but most were dishwashers, cleaners, fast food servers and waiters. Richer ones drove unlicensed taxis or were petty crooks. Few had come to benefit from or appreciate a rich culture that centuries of freedom and free speech had bequeathed to a nation.

Deprivation was not forced on them but accepted because they wanted to be with their own kind in a new country and to allow most of their earnings to go to their families back home. It reconciled them that they might bring them to this country or return rich to their homeland. For the present, working all the hours possible and reading the Quran sustained the devoted while smoking, card games and standing at street corners watching perceived loose western girls amused the less religious. In return, any passing woman only saw the bad side of the watchers with their disdainful mocking behaviour and periodic displays of loud guttural clearing of the throat, retching of mucus through blocked noses and spitting; habits deplored by western sensibilities. For some of these bored men jesting in raucous ethnic slang led to name-calling, groping and full *Taharrush Gamea* molestation.

"On arrival, they gravitate to the east end and usually only know holiday words and phrases learnt from Hollywood movies and porn sites. Most cannot read or write in English. They delude themselves into believing their own lies. When not working the lack of leisure opportunities and habit of clinging together make them look lazy and dangerous. Boredom drives them to the same street corners as it costs nothing to use your eyes. Trapped within a few blocks and cut off from a rural setting from which they came," conjectured Neerja.

The more cynical Radu expressed a commonly held view that it cost money to get to London and many here would have been sponsored with later repayment in kind or had hide what was left of their wealth in foreign banks to use after state benefits helped to establish them.

"These youths are ambitious but do not possess empathy and only see an emaciated society. Trafficked to London and herded together for cheap casual work, they feel no gratitude to the host nation. They are modern day workhouse paupers, living in poverty, forced celibacy with hours full of idleness. Free women do not condescend to such men. Their only comforts will come from drug addicted prostitutes or young sex slaves marshalled into their abodes under the cover of darkness by unscrupulous masters."

"Disillusion makes them easy prey for rogue muftis," added Neerja.

Ignoring Radu, Du Gui tended to agree with Neerja.

"Yes, rather than accept not being cut out for it the ones that uprooted themselves and spent all their savings only to fail to find riches may vigorously blame others and go down the radicalisation path. When life gives no pleasure, men become eager to give themselves to a cause to release their frustrations, but remember, just as many as the haters of the West eke out a living and go on to make a success of it. Their first major step on the ladder to success is gaining a bank account. With hopes raised, they move on to greater things. They open barber shops, convenient shops and takeaways which are not only their place of business but where family and friends can congregate away from the street corners; establishing their place not with the gun but with the captivation of a nation's taste buds."

"Yes, best to bear gifts than the bomb. For the enlightened, migration is a natural phenomenon and is a key way of refreshing society. Even so, many traditionalists see the arrival of so many young men from different cultures as the first stage of an invasion force. These latest migrants have no association with this country and do not see how it has evolved. It is just all foreign to them. It is not the fault of religion. All religions have duplicitous relationships with empire building and we have to be wary of those who throw the first stone. Muslim history came out of migration when their prophet took flight from Mecca to Median. The subsequent years in Medina building up an army and the victorious return are what puts fear in the minds of the West as radical muftis use ancient struggles to achieve God's Will as the reason to justify the rejection of modern life with its advancements and promotion of the rights of all sexes," sighed Neerja.

The flat was in a block that the postman rarely entered and populated by new arrivals with no relatives to come and pick them up. The entrance,

stairs and landings had the unmistakable smell
of body odour, urine and tobacco. The latter made
life tolerable for the poor with its power of addiction
to take the mind off earthly woes. Few of the
tenants knew the landlord was one of the biggest
slum landlords in London. According to Neerja, this
property entrepreneur ran a trust to house young
immigrants and asylum seekers. A life in the
charity sector had brought great wealth to this
man. Money and influence can quench unwanted
publicity as well as satisfy a thirst for it. Here, it
hid duplicity concerning the misuse of public funds
by skimming cream off the top and leaving low-fat
for those in need.

The flat was situated at the rear of a landing at the
top of several flights of stairs. A push button to
light the stairs was vandalised. On the way up, it
was evident that the whole building was in a state
of dangerous disrepair, crumbling in decay with
cracked tiles and steps, smeared walls and ceilings
obliterated by cobwebs. The landlord blatantly felt
impervious to repercussions from building
inspectors or social security inspections to see if the
tenants got value for the rents paid out for them.
There were squats in run-down streets waiting for
demolition in better condition than this place.

Quiet whispering emanated from many of the
closed doors, as if praying dominated the passing of
the day. Then suddenly, the loud cries and shouts
in an African tongue flooded the air.

"A married couple arguing on the phone about the
wife's behaviour back home," whispered Neerja.

It was unimaginable how anyone could rest with

such tenants living next door. In fact, nobody probably managed a good sleep in a building overflowing with young men coming and going day and night.

Once they had clambered up the dim stairway to the top floor, they halted outside the rear landing door. Du Gui put on gloves and knocked his fist against it, nothing. After waiting several seconds, he decided to force entry which turned out not to be necessary, as the lock had been already circumvented with the door free to open.

Doing this a fetid stench hit his nostrils.

Du Gui insisted on entering the flat alone to gain a first impression without anyone's influence. With a sharp intake of breath, he looked inside the dark room, the air was sickly. Flicking the light switch made no difference. Nothing happened. The meter must have run out. The only window was caked in filth and old newspapers probably going back twenty years. Stepping through the cramp abode with a pocket spotlight scanning the space straight in front of him, he treaded carefully, remaining vigilant with probing eyes for the smallest sign that might be useful. A grubby mattress placed on wooden pallets and badly cut carpet remnants that had the grounded in dirt of many different footprints nearly tripped him up. Every step taken was accompanied by a loud creak from a rickety floorboard. In a corner, a jumble of dirty clothing consisting of tee shirts, cheap jeans and the obligatory baseball cap lay festering away, nothing that would keep a person warm in winter. Fully within the bedsit, the full force of the reek from scores of unwashed socks that littered and hid in every inconceivable corner almost made him throw up. Grime covered every fixture and ornament. Starving lice, multitudes in their death throes, jumped into the air for one last time, hopping from a chair and the old mattress to reach Du Gui in the hope of a last supper. It was hard to believe a man of Gabriel's age lived this way. The man may have had an understandable resentment against the British establishment but did not come across disenchanted about life and being an ex-sailor would have the discipline to keep his belongings clean and well ordered. Scanning the spotlight upwards, the extent of the filth in what was no better than a pigsty struck him. Thick festering mould covered the cracked ceiling and invaded downwards to meet advancing damp. Donated furniture for charity commandeered and used to furnish the flat, a blend of uncomfortable *Formica* and fabricated woods manufactured in the sixties seemed dumped rather than placed. The stand-alone toilet was indescribable with excrement in places where it was difficult to image how it spread there accidentally. The small kitchen sink was completely inadequate for the demands placed upon it. A toothbrush and comb lying on a ledge above the sink were put into an evidence bag pulled out of his jacket pocket.

Radu entered next, saying the obvious.

"It's a shit hole."

His attempt to open the window failed due to it being nailed shut. He then took it upon himself to rip away the discoloured newspaper sheets off the windowpanes, tap the walls for secret hollows, turn out drawers and examine bare floorboards for hidey-holes. During this robust search, a pensive Du Gui removed his gloves and stared at the well-thumbed Quran that fell onto the floor from a pulled out drawer, someone's solemn and sober possession. Neerja remained at the entrance, the unoccupied flat was a sign for him to relax and catch up on text messages.

It was left to Radu to state the obvious again.

"A waste of time."

"Pourquoi faire cette allusion?" Rhetorically slipped out of Du Gui.

"A false lead, *mon ami*," as Radu read the face in front of him as being miffed at making a mistake.

"Maybe it is shamefully irrational to go on a hunch, a mere gesture of a wish to do the right thing other than just do nothing. Nevertheless, why go to this trouble to lead us up the garden path. Trails that go nowhere also tell a story," came the reply, adding:

"Surely, a Muslim would not voluntarily leave his holy book behind."

They withdrew and rapped on the neighbouring door on the left to ask some questions. Nobody answered so they moved on to the next one. An occupant with truculence showing on a suspicious bilious face responded after a persistent knock on his door by opening it a few centimetres.

"Hello, can we have a few minutes of your time?"

"No inglesh," as the door started to close.

Neerja swung into action and asked something in what turned out to be a shared language. A few moments later as they made their way down the stairs, talking in a low voice the translator explained the conversation with the evasive Eritrean resident.

"From what I gathered he believed the person who rented that room was from somewhere in North Africa, a young boy escaping persecution, probably homosexual and earning money as a rent boy. Not seen or heard him for weeks. Not sure how much of this is true. Got the distinct impression the fellow did not like this neighbour and lying is obsessive for many people."

*****

The next day, Du Gui passed the evidence bag to his assistant asking to get it processed for DNA to see if it tallies to a name. Using ingenuity, she walked across the floor and stealthily came back with another evidence bag with a label stamped Floyd on it, filled in the request for forensics to examine it and attributed the request coming from the liaison officer.

"Suspect very much it would get any priority if we sent it, best to infer it is an approved request," she explained.

In the late afternoon, a phone call came through instructing Du Gui to go immediately to a deputy commissioner's office, which he did. Whereupon, the deputy continued with more important business, forcing him to wait in front of a large oak desk. It was mentally noted that the Met chief and this man both had uncluttered desks. The deputy was effectively in charge as the top man, not animus against advice from his American colleagues, had crossed the pond to learn how they dealt with civil unrest there so would miss out on the dishing out of a severe cold rebuke.

The deputy looked up as if just aware of someone else in the room.

"Oh, it is you Du Gui."

The tone of voice signalled a rough ride ahead. In the soup again, time to eat humble pie and let the anger directed at him be vented; best not rile a bear in its den.

The displeased deputy with flaring nostrils went on to inform him in short outbursts that did not leave any doubt of what was on his mind that Du Gui's unconcealed presence in a sensitive area displayed a foolish reckless attitude. The complete lack of tact of the overt act of forcing his way into a dwelling in broad daylight compromised the effort of others. Long running operations were put at risk due to him, making it difficult for agents and informants painstakingly embedded in Aldgate to flush out malcontents and provocateurs.

The errant consulting advisor immediately apologised. He was smart enough to know when to knuckle down.

"Look! We have to bear the consequences of your

blundering informal snooping. The amount of possible blowback due to your escapade is inestimable. Any hint of ethnic involvement or cries of persecution will inflame the situation to the detriment of everyone. You had your chance to aid us and have blown it, had to tinker. You are no more than a meddler masquerading as a detective. In fact, a fire raiser who reports his own arson."

Pausing for the moment to study the expression on Du Gui's face, the deputy recommenced his put down, exaggeratedly emphasised by waving his right hand about his chest in the copycat manner of a PR taught politician.

"Understand this, threats are everywhere so stop meddling, your task is to appease the press. You are on thin ice. Now go. By the way, did you learn anything?"

Without waiting for a reply the deputy shrugged his head and with a final wave of a right hand towards the door signalled Du Gui's dismissal.

With a show of circumspection, Du Gui trudged out, rubbing a small chunk of resinite in the palm in his hand. The mineral, a passed down heirloom that his father found when working the coalface kept in his pocket to remind him that whatever circumstances threw at him life was harder for his ancestors. The supposed long walk of shame took him down a lush carpeted corridor with portraits of distinguished knighted gentlemen looking down at him with fixed disapproving stares. It may have been worse the reprimand could have come from the xenophobic commissioner.

Back at his desk happier news was waiting for
him: a call taken by his assistant from Neerja
invited him to dinner that evening. The offer was
accepted, a Frenchman was always more upbeat
after a good meal and a few glasses of wine.

*****

Nodding to the hotel receptionist, he went straight
to the lift, this briefest of recognition normally
enough to allow a guest into the upper levels. On
this instance, the receptionist called him back. An
ordered basket of exotic fresh fruit was waiting for
him, a neutral gift to take with him to the dinner
date.

An hour later while dressing after showering, the
phone rang. The receptionist informed him that the
booked private cab was waiting. A few minutes
later, just as it began to drizzle, he jumped into the
waiting cab. The Basque driver punched the name
of the Walthamstow address into the route finder.
After tutting and in broken English saying the
address was outside the city centre so was going to
cost a bomb, the driver set off in a happy mood: the
clock would run for at least an hour with a
surcharge to bout. Du Gui watched the streets,
buildings and passing traffic as the car drove out of
central London. Cosmopolitanism, Portland stone
and yellow brick, Lamborghinis and Aston Martins
gradually replaced by segregation, ubiquitous red
brick, *BMWs* and Nissans. The further out the car
travelled the more often long avenues of similar
sized houses and front gardens came into view
down side roads until the driver turned into one
and parked outside a well-maintained semi-

detached house. The front cut off from the pavement by a low pebble dashed wall fringed with rose bushes. Between gaps in the closed curtains, patches of light escaped from the living room bay window; a frontage once seen as a mark of success by the petty bourgeoisie. A time when a rotund waist signified wealth and good health, when generals and admirals through exploits printed in the front pages of newspapers were known to the general public, and when rows of such houses were built to house school headmasters, branch bank managers and doctors.

The front door was a solid hardwood construction with a small circular central glass panel in the top third and a brass letter flap with the family name of Chopra engraved on it. The decoration of the panel looked like Sanskrit. He did not have to wait long. The door swung open almost immediately and a warm welcome from his hosts and the central heating greeted him. Entering he engaged in small talk by asking if the panel inserted into the front door signified everything.

Neerja, out of his formal work clothes wearing a ruby kurta shirt, white cotton flannels, and sockless in his scandals replied:

"It is a mantra to bring good luck and keep away evil. Now, may I introduce you to my wife, Riya."

She too wore a fine mix of European and Asian clothing with the addition of gold jewellery that enhanced the colouring of her skin. They shook hands. Riya betrayed being accustomed to meeting strangers by ensuring eye contact was maintained when their hands gripped with her thumb squeezing the back of his hand. The gift of fruit was taken from him with thanks.

His immediate impression was that of a charming nicely proportioned woman with a light Indian complexion face radiating large brown eyes. Not what you would call classically striking nonetheless there was strength about her, a glowing confidence, creating the impression of a beautiful woman inside and out.

After his jacket and hat were disposed on a coat stand, the couple directed him to a door on the left, straight on the aromatic smells indicated that the kitchen lay beyond and on the right where stairs. They entered the front room, which had the trappings of a couple well on the way to gaining respectability within their community. The back wall bordering the kitchen had a hatchway. The table near this part of the large lounge was superbly set while in front of the bay window a fine example of a Jade plant in a grand ceramic pot graced the space. In between, the furniture and settees were of a modern style that reflected their age group, with artefacts, pictures and throws exhibiting their heritage. A spotlessly clean setting, lit with colourful table and wall lamps reflected off furniture polished to a bright sheen, unless at boarding school, a sure sign of a childless household.

Riya broke the urban myth that a woman preferred a strong male to the company of a man fond of her. Enlightened parents, acknowledging a stubborn independence of character decided to allow their daughter to use her own volition in picking a future husband from a list of acceptable candidates. She interviewed them via social media and video chat lines until satisfied. Neerja was by far not the best looking or dynamic. His strongest points from her point of view were trustworthiness, same London location and social opinions. A risk adverse reliable man for a woman intent on giving working life the highest priority. Children would have to wait until a high enough position was secured to negate the risk of the impact of pregnancy on her career. Meanwhile uncomplicated snuggling with the cat would calm any brooding spawned by the internal clock.

A vase of freshly cut flowers was the centrepiece of the dining table laid out with sparkling glass, cutlery and white porcelain plates and dishes. Pickles, chutneys and chopped cucumber ready and waiting for the arrival of warm poppadoms. The heady aroma emanating from the latch indicated that dinner was ready to be served. Fragrance seeped into the fabric of the house and the occupants.

"That smells good."

Seeing the anticipation on his face, Riya's words further pleased the guest.

"Home cooked is the best way to sample Indian cuisine. The chefs in restaurants over spice everything with the intention to get customers to drink more. Besides, a restaurant does not guarantee that Indians run it. Authenticity and quality are important. We also use hahal meat as it is untreated."

"Did it take long to prepare the meal?"

"Working all hours, my wife only normally has time
to reheat frozen or ready meals during the week.
But everything is pukka. Tonight, my mother
prepared the dishes. She is the queen of the kitchen
and my wife an alchemist in high finance,"
answered a proud Neerja.

"I am looking forward to it. Your house is spotlessly
clean for a couple that have busy working lives."

"Again, you can thank my mother, she is a wonder."

"Would you like a drink? We have French wine and
Indian beer?" Asked Riya.

"A beer please and maybe a wine later," said the
diplomatic guest.

"Let's sit down at the table, on my right
commissionaire."

The guest was about to be presented with the best
Indian meal of his life, a meal enhanced by cooking
it in a wood fire masonry oven set up under a
sheltered backyard patio. A gentle happy evening
in a comfortable household setting was just what he
needed.

A somewhat solicitous old looking woman served it
in traditional Indian costume. Du Gui took this to
be the aged mother of Neerja and contrary to her
deportment was only slightly older than him. She
lived an independent life in an annex at the back of
the house.

As promised, unlike restaurant dining, the food was not overly spiced or immediately tricked the stomach into believing that it was full. Large dishes placed in the centre of the table allowed him to have as big a portion as his heart desired; a meal so good that while eating, he barely engaged in conversation with his hosts, nodding to everything said as Neerja described the Punjabi heritage of their families, the basket bread and dairy centre of India.

The pleasure of watching the man enjoy their offerings completely outweighed any umbrage taken by the hosts from his silence. The starter was a chicken kebab coated in yogurt batter with crisp coriander naan bread and a creamy dal side dish for him to try. Riya preferred a tomato salad. The second dish to savour was a lamb biryani. Dessert was a cardamom-favoured pistachio halva served with French roast coffee.

The conversation restarted after the demolition of the food.

"Must be a good time to be a translator?" Expressed Du Gui.

"Yes, never been out of work since quitting my college lecturing job and going freelance. Diversity to aid economic fecundity has been good for me. Bit nervy at first but been with the Met fulltime for several years so feel secure. We had decided that I would work in the public sector and my wife would advance in the financial sector, balance the risks during boom and bust cycles, but as it turned out the public sector not safe. Fortunately, the demand for translators is booming, so we decided just to go for it. Riya is doing well at an investment trust company in the City, she is a senior consultant."

"Let's return to the sofa and enjoy that wine now," butted in the praised woman.

After Neerja's mother cleared away the dinner dishes, she brought in a tray of snacks to go with the poured wine. It was a good wine and the titbits of delight sated the tongue. Du Gui thanked the woman for the delightful meal and received a genuflect acknowledgement in return.

Riya explained that leaving the EU made life at work harder but not impossible as trade and protecting London still remained the main concern of Parliament. Furthermore, she admitted to being a Francophile with the married couple spending many a vacation in his wonderful country. They were surprised to hear that due to the nature of his work, Du Gui did not possess romantic notions about his homeland. He politely did not mention the hard upbringing in a coal mining region of France, his natural sympathies for the lower orders and that a good life and opportunities were not open to everyone when he was growing up.

The talk then commenced being about how London had changed over the decades with it being an attraction for so many different reasons with Du Gui asking an open question to gain insight.

"Does pluralism not continue to blur national identity and only works if every citizen adopts it?"

Riya voiced the usual concerns.

"Yes, the attraction of London despite leaving the EU continues. Individual and collective unease has not gone away. The only shared gossip between the different communities as always is about house prices. We feel we are losing our voice. The trouble is that in many ways our distinctiveness is becoming harder to protect. Although my community would not like to admit it, we have done well. The old British Empire made us indispensable and multiculturalism protects our gains. Yes, we moan a lot but if you do not do so this can lead to the weakening of your privileges. In many ways, we cope better with modern living as well. We are multilingual and accept that equality in human society is impossible. The caste system in India is repulsive to western eyes but it reflects the truth that some humans are valued less.

We are also well acquainted with the polemics that erupt within the Muslim world. As far as we are concerned, it is not a problem rooted in eastern culture. Islam with its one god justification for attacks against other faiths and offering redemption to the impious for acts of martyrdom came to India from the West. You see it all depends on your perspective. The Christian variation has had centuries to accept its role confined to providing spiritual bliss but imagine what the early popes would have done to England if they had the atomic bomb. One thing is for sure, there is no anodyne for life."

"The thought of coming back as a dung beetle is a mighty good deterrent for stopping evil being done, and yes, it is a dreadful thought to imagine the *Borgias* having access to weapons of mass destruction," concurred Du Gui.

Riya reiterated her feelings.

"Immigration is still a thorny issue. The promised new policy was supposed to favour highly educated professionals rather than the low paid unskilled from Eastern Europe and beyond. Restrict access to those that bring greater value to institutions like the health service, science and education. Unfortunately, cheap labour by hook or by crook finds its way here, causing concern and negating the good work done by migrating professional Asians."

Although never been invited into the inner sanctums of the EU where alliances were made and deals struck, Du Gui knew this news gladdened many in Brussels. Changing the subject to something lighter, he asked Neerja:

"Do you visit the other nations in the UK that often?"

"No, all we need is in London, all our families and friends are within easy reach. A rich life is interwoven with them and in our case they are the one and the same. We have brought rented out properties up north through the *Asian News* but an agent manages them."

"You should be able to retire and move to India to live like a maharajah?"

"My father went back when he retired but to be honest it will be too foreign for us, full of superstitions."

The chitchat flowed with the wine and ended around midnight.

"Thank you for a good meal. It was marvellous."

"I am glad you enjoyed it. It was a pleasure and my wife wanted to meet the great detective."

They were a happy couple.

When Du Gui re-emerged into the night, the rear lights of the waiting cab directed him to his transport back, moving off at a gentle pace, the driver recognised him.

"Ain't you that Frenchman, mate?"

No verbal reply, just a polite smile.

"It is innit. Who is your favourite TV detective?"

"No one."

"Surely you have one."

The driver went on to recount some of his own adventures. The circulation of hot air imbued with human sweat and the smell of stale beer from previous customers promised an uncomfortable trip. After noticing that this was a family car that doubled up as a private hire, the sleepy passenger sat back, let the driver settle down to his ramblings and gazed out of the side window at the passing night-time scene. The rhythmic clinking of the windscreen wipers and the low volume beat of *folkpop* coming out of side speakers eventually lulled him. Exterior life continued regardless as reflected streetlights on wet pavements created the illusion of gold, fool's gold. Red double decker buses and black hackney cabs ferried the populace. Smooth changing of gears at traffic lights and calm reactions to the build-up of traffic testified to the experienced gained driving in this congested city.

He was going to ask if the cab had CCTV, as unlike the outward bound one no warning of its use to prosecute unruly customers was perceptible. However, the possibility of a prolonged conversation deterred him so he opted to continue looking into shut shop doorways and dark recesses, trying not to think but finding himself searching for a dark face that could belong to the Nigerian girl. A needle in the haystack but he could not help himself. The lights of passing cars and the fleeting stares of ghostly passengers in other cars broke up his thoughts and reminded him of where he was.

"The city can be lonelier than any deserted island. Violence infuses the intimate and domestic settings, causing many to bolt, moving around, drifting, forced to take shelter wherever it can be found. Spotting pulled back corrugated iron sheeting intended to block an outside door, they grope through dark corridors, pushing open smashed doors, to sleep in a dank cold empty room littered with the discarded rubbish of previous sleepers. Cold and dirty, never knowing whom to trust and what was wanted in return. It is inevitable that people on the edge have extreme outlooks and take greater risks, any poor decision leading to fatal consequences.

The city does not hate, discriminate or exclude. It

existed and would continue to exist until the age of Man ended. On that day, the need for the law becomes defunct, along with the death of envy, greed and viciousness. Until then, each of us kept a finger in the dyke to maintain our personalised illusion of civilised life."

The driver had chosen a different route back. The earlier cab went east along the Embankment; this time the journey was north of inner London along the *Euston Road*. The cab joined a slow queue when traffic navigated past King's Cross railway station; a notorious red light district dispersed when impressively modernised. Not going the expected way reawakened the passenger's interest in the outside world. Life being life, after dark, sex trade workers had returned. It reminded him of being mobbed by the unwanted attention of African prostitutes outside Oslo railway station, all of them speaking good English. Unless the cause had titillation value, no interest would be generated when any of these marginalised street workers went missing.

The driver pulled him completely out of his reveries by asking if there was any desire to go down *Baker Street*.

"No thanks, unless it is the quickest route."

The exchange jumped to a different topic entirely when the driver exclaimed a disbelief at the behaviour of a jaywalker stupidly not looking when stepping on to a one-way lane designated for hospital bound traffic. Obscured by being completely dressed in black and obviously drunk he just missed being struck by a speeding Mercedes thanks to a friend having the wits to pull him back in time.

"Madness, why waste your money getting drunk like that," tutted the driver.

The last notable events of the journey back were the flashing of a bare bosom from a well-out-of-it young white female at a pedestrian crossing and having to pull over to the side when siren blasting emergency service vehicles ploughed a path through the centre of town.

In the hotel hallway, the lights were dimmed down. The sound of a string instrument, being learnt by the sound of it, came from the room marked staff only behind the reception desk.

Lying in bed, the wonderfully capable and astute Riya came to mind.

*****

Waking up early the next day, he picked up the novel.

"I am a fan of the matter of fact approach taken by the hero in your books. The milieus he finds himself in, his tenacity and single mindedness, almost autistic in his stubbornness to find the truth. Emotional trauma and grief are only felt by the victim, for everyone else there is the correct mix of reactions. For the professional it is immaterial how grisly the scene of a crime, there is a job to be done. People whether naturally cynical or empathetic protect themselves. If they did not, they would suffer themselves. Yes, you hit a rich lode with this

series. Any possibility of a movie deal?"

Putting down his knife and fork, the novelist thanked the aristocrat for the praise and to the delight of the guests told them a TV studio had bought the rights to the detective series but as yet only scripts had been produced, nothing so far in the can.

Beaming at the novelist, the tipsy reporter expressed her thoughts about how life had its ups and downs and how her work has given a fresh perspective on everything.

"Purpose for organic life seems only to be the need for nature to have mobile seed spreaders, carry other organisms and be fertilisers. To cope on an individual level, we grasp things to believe or love to make life bearable. Your books are a prime example."

The aristocrat expanded this new thread in the conversation to his way of thinking.

"If by chance life gets better after years of struggle the chosen sacred thing gets the credit for rewarding the endurance shown. An unwavering faith credited for allowing a straight path to be ploughed. For all practical purposes, this sacred thing can be anything. Myths are consolatory nonsense but just as valid as anything else."

"Van Gogh was ignorant of the answer but the night sky conjured up a numinous experience as he wandered along the shoreline in a cloudless Mediterranean with the different hues of blue reflected from an ultramarine sea, Prussian blue land and cobalt sky as stars sparkled like emeralds, lapis stones, rubies and sapphires. He thought these shining distant dots might be where the dead went as it was obvious Man could never reach them while alive. To him, dying quietly in old age meant a slow

peaceful leisurely journey to the beyond whereas a violent or sudden death due to conflict or a nasty illness propelled the soul at great speed to the afterlife."

"Well said," applauded the femme fatale to the novelist's defence of spirit over the material body, adding:

"Perhaps heaven is where you remember achievements and happy moments and hell is an eternity going over regrets and cringing moments."

"Thank you, I do like to make a point now and again that my detective and I are two different people, one analytical and the other artistic. Is the whole of life visible to us I am not sure, or isn't it rather that on this side of death we see one hemisphere only?"

"It looks like we will not have long to wait to find out. The final conflict between men of progress against faith believers may be happening soon," retorted the aristocrat.

"The end is nigh," announced the trying to be funny blackmailer.

The aristocrat explored this probable likelihood.

"This truth has been proved, let me explain. Back in the middle of the last century, astrophysicists started searching the Milky Way for radio signals from extra-terrestrial life on other planets. To date, nothing has been found. Without bogging you down with the mathematics, the chances of detecting life were based on the multiplication of seven parameters, one being the length of time an alien civilisation is technically capable of producing radio signals. It was assumed that this

195

period would be at least in the thousands of years. Going by the values of the other parameters which recent research have shown to be remarkably accurate then other intelligent life forms should have been detected by now. Therefore, the absence of signals strongly implies that civilisations do not remain in an advanced technological state for long, a relatively short period it seems. Something disastrous happens. A singularity occurs, a conflict that stops scientific progress in its tracks. My opinion, the adoption of rationality as the driving paradigm for any organic life in the need of afterlife reassurances is doomed to self-destruction. Playing god has far reaching consequences. The integration of synthetic and genetic bio-enhancements with nanotechnology whether that be in somatic or reproductive cells is an unintentional disaster waiting to happen. Do not be too sceptical. This apotheosis has been an aspiration from the day Man became self-aware. Eugenics is part of evolution. The survival of the fitness and all that. State led eugenics to create super beings may be out of vogue but the liberal free market allows the individual to pursue it and the rich have the money to pay for the resources. Even philosophy can be used to support its use. The Enlightenment view to life was to use it to develop into someone worthy and post-modernism adheres to the principle of the right of individuals to choose what they want to be. So both permit human engineering, the former to produce good citizens and the latter to enhance desired traits. The emergence of a new superior is inevitable and let's be honest the less fortunate have always been regarded as an inferior subspecies."

This raised a reaction among the other dinner guests.

"We transmute animals so why not humans."

"How will natural Man respond to his position at the summit of the animal kingdom being threatened by those who are by science superior to him and will they see us as a different species with no compunction to our vanquishment. If history has taught us everything then our greater numbers will be immaterial. Although few in numbers, pioneering ancestors used their advanced technology to overwhelm and wipe out the natives of the Americas and Africa. Why would they want to preserve a race that has copiously shown itself not susceptible to reasoned argument?"

"Perhaps they will not be totally ruthless, say, culling or castrating the males leaving the pretty as pleasure pets. I am sure that happened in the past as well."

"The new being will have its dilemmas to suffer. Its society may not be as collective as you imagine. At a personal level having a brain able to instantly recall everything, good and bad, will bring its own set of problems. Imagine being born in a test tube with no family or shared history to fall back on. The real truth we will never know how it will turn out."

"Malfunctions, mutations or deliberate misuse of invented amoeba or nano-machines could rapidly eat the host then spread to all life forms turning everything into goo."

"If civilisations on other planets became so clever their great thinkers should have invented time travel and gone back in time to stop the spread of disease or alter their philosophical and religious texts to explicitly state that murder in any circumstances should never be committed."

"Maybe they did but screwed it up or like Frankenstein's

monster came back to destroy its creators for making them suffer from even greater ennui that we have to endure."

The aristocrat offered a solution to the cognition corundum that showed his age and bamboozled the reporter.

"Cognitive control will allow upgrade of memories by adding and deleting events as seen fit. Virtual learning will replace the need for arduous time-consuming study or to physically partake in leisure activities. Joe 90 stuff. Of course, mass control of society will be a drawback if not used responsibly."

"What are you on about and who or what is Joe 90?" Frowned a perplexed reporter.

"H'm. Look it up on YouTube."

"Mumbo jumbo brain implant words which boil down to the controlling of mental prowess or mood with stimuli which is the same as drug taking. No better than the happy pills consumed like candy in 'Brave New World'. The problem with visionaries is they only picture super versions of themselves and not the opposite and depraved part of humanity."

The aristocrat went on the re-offensive.

"No different from reading for pleasure which is a slowed down virtual reality to escape into whereas the future will offer 3D real time visions without the need of consoles and screens. Future possibilities are hidden from you by a fettered imagination."

The other guests came down on the side of the reporter.

"I can see a problem with this. It is called multiple personality disorder. After each change in mindset, some residue will be left behind in the subconscious which will lead to mind sharing issues or even schizophrenia."

"I for one am happy to admit that my subconscious dictates me and it does not like to be messed about with."

"You know what I believe, it will not be our problem. Why worry about things that will happen beyond our lifespans? As I said earlier, why not just enjoy ourselves. Memento mori and all that. Anyway, why create super beings so that they can work longer, seems silly. Let's have another drink," as the archaeologist topped up the glasses.

Feeling out of it and alone with his thoughts the novelist murmured under his breath.

"Strange but I would like to see the end of the world."

*****

When it came to the turn of Du Gui to stand at the rostrum and speak at the news conference some reporters had already made their way out of the room. New faces had appeared in the shrinking gathering as top reporters left this task to junior colleagues or to *Reuters*, opting for better pickings elsewhere for their papers' front page. A sure sign that support for the official investigation was waning.

He had given his word not to divulge information relating to the chefs, but the disappearance of the girl was a different matter, so illuminating the screen behind him with a photo of her he implored the public for help by contacting the police if they had seen this person. When questioned why she was of interest, the reply that at this time it was not possible to say anything more but information concerning her whereabouts would be very useful to his enquiries raised expectations and achieved the desired coverage.

In the afternoon, another word with Gabriel in the Cypriot's café occupied his time. This time he arrived a few minutes earlier due to awareness of the correct route and spent the time to take in the surrounding area. The bland exteriors of the brick built tenements marked them out as British built. Ornate finishing considered too vulgar for the prudes of Europe, or, could it be they believed in a form of beauty beyond the elaborate, a functionalism that would go on to dominate the modern world.

The ground floors of the tenements were dominated by small businesses. Mainly, hairdressers and convenient shops catering for the owners' ethnic group interspersed with tattooists and second hand clothes shops rebranded as retro chic. There was even a rival Turkish coffee shop nearby, a narghile café offering various flavours of sweetened tobacco to try. This proprietor expanded his serving area by placing decorative small round tables and chairs on the pavement. The front window displayed smoking accoutrements for water pipe smoking and making roll ups. Painted tobacco tins, pipes, paper rolling machines and legal highs were scattered around the glorious looking water pipes. Above, the rows of identical dark lifeless windows void of any indication of a house owner's pride clearly cried out privately rented flats where neighbourly acknowledgement was rare due to the preoccupation of young tenants to be only interested in themselves.

On entering the café, he could not but notice a framed newspaper cutting placed proudly on the wall opposite from the Escher. It showed an image of him with the caption 'notable customer of the café' below it. Everything else was identical to the last time: same good coffee from the flask, table and feeling of comfort; and the air heavy and warm from the heat of the fryers and human bodies. The faces of the others customers differed from last time, but the mix of the customers remained the same: the pretentious young, pensioners and street traders. For different reasons, nobody rushed to drink up nor did the proprietor ask them to. The body language coming from the table seating a young couple bode ill as a subdued, slightly trembling and cowed girl sat submissively sipping a mug of tea with both hands round the rim while the boy with quiet aggression spoke down to her. She answered his questions in the affirmative with a quivering little voice. At another table, from the overheard conversation a jobbing actor was complaining about waiting for a phone call.

This time, being hungry, a soup and crusty roll was ordered with the coffee. Du Gui made it two soups when Gabriel appeared and indicated a liking for the same. The smell, taste and thickness of the broth set off more childhood memories for both of them, the past again. He in his grandmother's kitchen again and the orphan back to a cold

winter's day in an unheated sparse dining hall.
After finishing the soup, Gabriel took up his life
story by talking about his jack-of-all-trades work
experience which involved never saying no to the
opportunity to earn a living.

"On the boats, I witnessed a seaman being thrown
overboard. *Ta'aroa* received another soul that day.
Without knowing why I thought the man was
considered a Jonah and blamed for the poor fishing
that time out and not the fact that the winds were
not in our favour. In the South Seas, natives
dispensed their own justice and believed the great
spirits decided one's fate.

On land, scullion work was exhausting. Only a
double door separated the *stalag* of the kitchen
from the splendour of a spotless dining area.
Pandemonium during peak serving hours with
peeling vegetables, washing, polishing, scrubbing
and re-stocking cupboards in between times.
Ordered to run errands or sweeping up trampled
food if nothing else could be found for me to do.
Petty spite to get the maximum out of you for the
few francs earned. Drenched in sweat it was a
wonder that we did not taint the flavour of the
served food. At peak serving times, everyone raged
to let off steam as we rushed to get orders
completed, anger always directed downwards
bypassing the cockroaches to reach me."

"You left the boats for kitchen work?" Queried Du
Gui.

"Oh yes. I was always available for bread and
butter work and the chance to work in a hotel with
lodgings was too good to turn down. It left little

time for anything else. The effect of long hours of toil made you lazy, lethargic, and oblivious to the outside world. When my head hit the pillow, sleep came immediately..."

Parting, Gabriel was asked to look out for the Nigerian girl and was given a photograph; likewise, the café owner was given a missing person flyer to hang on a wall.

TOO MANY COOKS SPOILT THE BROTH

As part of the charm offensive Du Gui accepted an invite to guest on *My Life Story,* a BBC radio programme. Prior to the recording, a young able researcher came round to his hotel and they sat in the lounge going through the ropes: a set of questions accompanied by pieces of music to reflect his personality. The problem was he only possessed a single recording, an original LP of *Kind of Blue* by Miles Davis purchased over forty years ago. When in a nostalgic mood, the nocturnal sounds of the trumpet and bass reminded him of being an overworked *jeune flic* cruising along unsavoury Lille streets as headlight irradiated rain pounded off the windscreen.

"We cannot play music from one recording. Anyway, according to the track list it only has five tracks. What other music do you like? You have to remember our listeners are mostly *OAPs* so you cannot be too experimental or say anything that will upset them."

"Hard to tell, comic and rustic operetta but mainly

just this *LP*."

"You can only have one Miles Davis track. OK, if you go order another drink, mine is a large white, I will have a list ready for you when you come back. As a suggestion, why not choose a track from his *A Day in Paris* album. It will give the transmission the continental flair the producer will be after?"

Standing up to go to the bar, Du Gui insisted it had to be from *Kind of Blue*.

True to her word, with the aid of a laptop, the list of musical pieces to play and crib notes on what feelings each provoked was ready.

"Right, here are your choices and the questions you will be asked."

The list contained a bit of jazz, a Flanders folk song, a French songster, comic and rustic operetta overtures from Offenbach and Mascagni, and works from Ravel and Strauss. She even included a favourite Vaughan Williams piece to win over the English audience.

"Thanks, you have been very helpful. Have you been doing this for long?"

"Couple of years now. After Art College, I did my internship up in Manchester when my folks contacted some of their friends. Essentially, it was inevitable as I have the right pedigree to work for the BBC.

You know I meet one of the missing male chefs.

Was on the show about a year ago."

"Oh. What was he like?"

"Rude bugger. Pinched my backside."

Du Gui turned down the kind offer of a chauffeur driven car to come round and pick him up to take him straight into *Broadcasting House,* explaining that it would be easy enough to get there as according to his map it was a manageable walk up *Regent Street* from Oxford Street tube station. It would also give him the opportunity to wander into the next-door regency church he had spotted on his previous visit to her employers. The unexpected sight of a stone circular columned vestibule holding up a prominent spire intrigued him.

After, another drink, the researcher said good-bye and told him the show would be an enjoyable experience, a charming hour fronted by a darling of a woman with a sooth lullaby voice.

Several days later, he found himself sat at a table in a studio wearing an earpiece, with a cup of lukewarm tea and chocolate biscuits in front of him. The biscuits shared with the iridescent host when the selected music aired. The young researcher was right about the host's voice.

"Today's guest is the redoubtable inspector Du Gui who is synonymous with explaining baffling incidents. Hello inspector, do you have a first name?"

"Alfred, thank you for asking. It is the same first name as my father," after politely ignoring her mistake.

The presenter in front of him was beautiful, not in a young way but with that refined middle-aged air that came from having a comfortable existence. In a low husky voice cultivated by smoking twenty cigarettes a day while attending a fee paying all girls high school, she asked the next question on the crib sheet in front of her.

"You are a self-made man that has dedicated his life to the protection of society?"

"I would love to say yes but I am a product of my upbringing and education. When young, becoming an artisan baker was my only real ambition and I drifted into crime investigation."

"Yes, the French system is much admired, unlike our system which has many critics."

"I would say your system is highly regarded. It gives the young a broad education before specialising. You are Scottish after all?"

"Oh, you have done your homework, inspector. May I remind you that I ask the questions. Now, what are you listening to at the moment?"

"That is easy. My constant companion is Miles Davis's *Kind of Blue,* which I bought over forty years ago. Such purity only exists in music. The sound remains immutable as I go through the swings and roundabouts of life."

"What are your personal mottos?"

"No mottos just common sense. Use your eyes
and ears and have humility. There are none so
blind as those who will not see. You must listen
well to understand people better and do not believe
it is true because you said it. And remember if it is
possible, it will happen."

"Do you like sport? You have the build of a scum-
half."

"Rugby, no! If you watch children play, you come to
realise how primitive it is. A toddler when rolled a
ball picks it up, attempts to run but falls over; an
infant will kick it and a youngster tries to do
something skilful with it. So, on the scale of human
development, it is at the lowest rung."

"Biggest fear?"

"Going soft in the head or becoming a miserable old
bugger. I find the older I get, the more neuroses I
pick up. Every day someone tells you what is wrong
with your lifestyle. I drink to relieve stress but
alcohol is bad for my liver. The list goes on and on.
You have to be strong minded to enjoy pleasure
nowadays. On a more serious note, the deliberate
release of a rapidly spreading pandemic or a
warped zealous faction getting their hands on a
WMD and justifying its use to harm innocent
bystanders because their leader had a dream
supposedly from God to reap revenge. Maniacs
believing in destiny and forever trying to outdo the
previous worse atrocity. In short, end of humanity
acts perpetrated by disturbed individuals seeking
their own macabre form of celebrity without
understanding the irony that there will be nobody
left to remember their evil deeds. Like most

malcontents if you could search deep into their psyche what you find is not a monster but a disturbed child unable to accept the world as it is."

"We all agree to that. Let's hope the process to gentrify man in all societies gathers pace. Now, do you think about your dead parents?"

"*Bien sûr!* Nevertheless, less often now. Due to their generation dying out and the change in clothing style and fabrics used, I no longer mistakenly think I have glimpsed one of them out of the corner of my eye when on the streets, which used to bring them back to life for a few minutes. Although dulled and untrustworthy by age, I have stronger early souvenirs of my grandmother, a woman with busy hands, lively eyes and a strong backbone. This is because I was left with her while both parents worked. I never knew grandfather. She lost her husband early when as a young man he joyfully marched off to war, ironically glad to get away from the misery of the pits to die several kilometres away as a sapper digging tunnels to plant explosives under German trenches.

I can never forget *'il faut avoir les dents longues'* coming from behind me as she did her housework and I my homework."

"Have big teeth?"

"No. Be ambitious. I digress. When I go back to my youth, I do not see poverty as everyone was in the same boat. I see the old lady in her kitchen. She lived and died there. A person who installed a strong sense of right and wrong, and stopped me brooding about teenage angst and listening to the existential talk that was dominant then. One moment she was busy and the next sitting in an armchair placed in the sunniest spot, smoking a cigarette; that chair stank of tobacco. Always ready to give her opinion. She had a unique way of folding socks, which I have never seen again. The early death of her husband saved her from the misery of being a baby factory rearing seven to nine kids, but it forced her to be the breadwinner until my father started earning. She seemed ageless to me, short pitch-black hair cut around the neck, strong body draped in her accustomed housedress, a faded green cloth with a pattern dissolved after years of many washes. Old fashion and insisted on being called Madam. She never understood that study required peace and quiet."

"How did she die?"

"Of a new cooker. For years, she was pestered to get a gas cooker and then she finally relented. She must have turned the gas on without lighting it then later lit it."

"Oh!"

"Do not be too concerned, she would have seen the irony of it."

"Being French, you will be passionate about your food?"

"Not really but compared to many, yes. My favourite meal is fish soup with fresh bread. Like most great gastronomic dishes, it started off as peasant food made from leftovers, good old fashioned comfort food. I could eat it every day."

"And who is your favourite novelist?"

"Do not possess a passion for anything. I have what I call a healthy general interest in everything. I find people that take a passionate interest in something tend to restrict their time to one or two subjects. Getting back to your question it must be Guy de Maupassant. For two reasons, I like stories about everyday people and believe novel writing peaked at the end of the nineteenth century. Undeniably, there was Zola but his preoccupation with expounding *Darwinian theory* in human behaviour overshadowed everything, whereas, Guy de Maupassant touched upon the souls of people."

"Souls. Then you have Faith?"

"No, I find it impossible to believe that there is any divine purpose to life or that heaven guards the righteous."

"But, you of all people have been given the gift of being a guardian angel?"

"I cannot prevent crime, no one can. It does not occur but recurs. I only reveal the cause by finding facts after the event."

"Any ambitions left?"

"No, childhood dreams should remain locked away. I am content with the life I have."

"No regrets?"

"Well, the trouble with me is I know nothing about music and would love to be a natural at dancing, singing and playing the blues. But I suppose you cannot fight what you are."

"It has been a pleasure to talking to you. Your last answer leads on to your final music choice. Would you like to explain it before we play it?"

"The music of Miles Davis so cool that the man could have been French."

"Wonderful, quite wonderful."

Afterwards, he mused that instead of him Gabriel should have appeared on this show, immediately on all fronts, dismissing the idea of a person surviving on a day-to-day existence having any appeal to the producers of this show.

In the green room, there was a questionnaire to complete. Only four questions related directly to the show, the others concerned his beliefs, gender, sexual orientation, religion and colour. To help them out he ticked an assortment of boxes. The slanted sunlight falling into Broadcasting House through electronically controlled blinds and the abundance of empty news gatherer chairs signalled it was long past mid-afternoon and time for something to eat and meet up again with Radu.

*****

At Convent Garden the warm spring air augured a good evening, which would make up for the hustle and bustle experienced on the tube ride. Standing silently as pedestrians crowded the plaza, the unique atmosphere was absorbed. From the pleasure on the faces of outdoor diners, the pinnacle of luxurious living remained a long lazy late afternoon spent sitting in a *chic* café-bar.

The young were embracing life as stall vendors, many selling tack made in China or Bangladesh, tried to earn a living. Seeing the manifestation of the old Norman *'les trois chats'* emblem blazed across tee-shirts and mugs made him smile. There were also bespoke traders selling cheeses, honey and retro mementos but these were not the sort of stalls bargain hunters would find much joy.

The open space attracted all genres of sellers including those that sold their talents: street entertainers consisting of lone musicians, choral singers, jugglers, human statues and magicians competed for the attention of the passers-by. Not much money came their way. A conjurer got his retaliation in first by mentioning during his performance that in a theatre this would cost them over forty pounds to see and as a professional his efforts deserved remuneration. A toothless last of his kind grotesque senile looking octogenarian cockney playing the spoons fared even worse.

Rickshaw pullers seemed to collect here. Many a tourist shunning their offer of a ride, being warned beforehand in their guidebooks that this unmonitored trade was a rip off.

Pickpockets applied their trade, playing catch and mouse with undercover law enforcers. The rapidity of sleight of hand and being an unknown face made the difference between easy pickings and a night in the cells. A risk worth taking especially if the quarry was a Middle East or Chinese tourist carrying a wad of banknotes.

He saw Radu mingling amongst the crowds. Taking an envelope out of his coat pocket, he approached him to give him his pay packet and pass the time of day.

"*Mon ami*, London is always a good place for the rich to live and now also a mecca for the world's poor seeking handouts and work without any hard questions asked. The downside is increased competition and a lowering of the standard of begging. Many know nothing of tradition and how begging should be done. They beg without putting effort into it. The days of tramping to avoid punishment under the Beggars Act may be long gone with tramps replaced by rough sleepers, but some traits continue, like the genuine English beggar still has a self-pitying living by hand to mouth deportment while the migrant, mainly the younger males, expect the rich westerner to gladly empty his pockets of any annoying coinage. Maybe, eventually, they will lower their expectations to become lifeless bundles of blankets that are rough sleepers snuggled in doorways, sheltering under railway viaducts and sleeping along the Embankment. For them, it must feel like death by a thousand cuts. They only have the right to walk with little expectation of a welcome at the end of it. Anyhow, increased dislike for the foreign beggar means the time has come for me like you to retire or at the very least move my operation to Frankfurt. Such as life, if you do not make decisions, circumstances do it for you."

As Radu melted back into the crowd, Du Gui
shrugged his shoulders. It was amazing how
getting to know someone fortified the impression
that in each unique way everyone at heart was
essentially verging on insanity; a widespread
affliction as a reaction against reality.

*****

Lying in bed that evening, the sluggish progress in
his chosen approach to bring light to the so far
unfathomable conundrum did worry him, and
although reluctant to admit it, the myriad of minor
medical complaints associated with getting old were
also playing on his mind. His acknowledged
strength was as an observer of human life, an
unaffected outsider examining interactions in a
closed system. Now with weakening mental
strength emotional contagion had seeped through
once impenetrable defences. Conferring with
witnesses and suspects took more of his time, a
good ploy to allow people to divulge details that
could be important but now more and more these
dialogues brought comfort to him as well. It even
made his day coming across people that still
possessed a sense of goodwill to others after years
of struggling themselves. The truth be known, he
had not been on fire for several years, relying on
hunches, based on well-earned experience, but
guesswork when said and done to resolve
mysteries. Thoughts of his retirement and
inevitable mortality disturbed his nights. One thing
for sure, dealing with death on a daily basis had not
diminished the discomfort of his approaching
demise.

He grabbed the novel, found his page and read.

"Good how a drink makes you ravenous," she said tucking into the succulent meat and crunchy vegetables. The femme fatale was enjoying the freedom away from the family home. It had not felt like a home since the children went off to college, more like a prison, a solitary confinement. Her husband arriving punctually each evening from work at the same time seldom had anything interesting to say. She was bored and if approached in the right manner would not say no to a fling. Life could have been different if the right breaks happened when she was modelling. Being attractive and black was in demand back then and her upbringing as a tomboy that played Sunday league cricket in her father's team made good copy. Although not a natural, her presence on the field distracted many a batsman, a stunner she definitely was and from an early age was gloated on by boys and men. It was a good training ground to learn how to be seductive in her dealings with the opposite sex. An unambiguous short curly haired beauty, internally grinning with pride as her presence caught the eye, teeth shining brilliantly in sharp contrast to her dark Caribbean inherited skin; a perfect fit for European high street chain catwalk events with electronica music blasting as she made her youthful struts and turns. Shortlisted as a candidate to become the face of a national advertising campaign for a new premium perfume she just missed out when a well-known alternative was chosen: it was decided at the last minute not to risk going with a fresh face. Even today, she had strong facial features and exceptionally round held high breasts with firm nibbles that poked through her tight floral cotton dress. She was fully aware of intimidating the reporter who was in need of advice on how to best present what nature had given her.

Seizing the moment, she offered her contribution to the novelist's desire for good feedback.

"A quote from you about your novels has stuck in my mind. Two hundred and fifty odd pages are about the right length, otherwise it would be like a dinner guest who has overstayed the welcome."

"Yes, I hold by that. Experience has taught me that this length is sufficient. A good publisher should insist his editors cut a novel to a readable length."

An easy throwaway comment for him as it was the publisher's decision on what the layout and font type of the book would be and the editing required to keep the target audience interested; as a general rule the smaller the font the more serious the subject matter.

"What would you advise a new writer to do to make it?"

"One thing you should never do if you are a budding novelist is to tell an established writer your plot. Writers are magpies ever so ready to steal or use anything freely told to them. I remember at a book fair a depressing looking chap lamented that his idea for a children story of transporting animals to different continents to see how they would react was used by a writer friend without acknowledgment or financial compensation: polar bears in a rainforest, elephants in the Arctic and so on. I just wrapped my arm round his neck, squeezed his shoulder and gently said what did he expect. Then I would say choose wisely where you write. Take northern crime writers, pasty looking fellows who sit in a dark room in grim city apartments with incessant rain hitting off the windows, earnestly typing down plots that reflect the sinister side of life. I, on the other hand, prefer to write in *a comfortable setting with a warm sun brightening an airy room. Finally, if you want to make money from your writing it is imperative to attract the female reader. To this end it helps to have a suave available male investigator or better still a strong female lead embroiled in relationship issues. I have created the former because for authenticity the latter is best written by the opposite sex. Accordingly, my protagonist enjoys food, the company of women and travel, no draft-ridden bars sitting alone while downing a mass-produced mood modifier for my man. Of course, my protagonist has something in common with all detectives loved by the public: besides experiencing at least one serendipitous moment per novel, he is a stubborn addictive searcher of the truth, overcoming many obstacles to find the perpetrator of a crime."*

"So are you saying most detectives created by men are loners because it removes the need to write about what they perceive as mundane family and domestic issues?"

"Yes, I believe you are right."

Meantime, the other guests were merrily keeping themselves amused by gibbering about this and that.

"If I had a time machine then it would be used to go back a few decades, buy confectionery, bring it back and compare it with what we get today, then let see them deny that their products are not smaller."

"I don't like the way they force feed animals to infuse flavour and colour in their meat. I am sure a food critic would enthuse about it but I could not tell the difference. If there is, it was too subtle for my palate. Anyway, you do not eat meat on its own so the taste is affected by what else is on the plate."

"Rat east rat, chimp eats chimp and man eats man,"
chipped in the aristocrat as he nibbled meat from a bone.

Rolling her eyes," how disgusting!" Winced the femme
fatale drawn into the free for all discussion by
participants unaware of the break in recording and the
seamless efficiency of the manservant in clearing away
the empty plates of the main course and bringing to the
table ample portions of suet pudding oozing the juices of
wild berries with a dollop of honey ice cream on the side.

Between mouthfuls of dessert, the aristocrat explained
himself.

"Why waste protein? Only religious opprobrium denies a
common sense use of a food source in harsh times.
Dead bodies should be used as butcher meat. If not for
human consumption, then given to our pets."

"A chillingly fascinating subject," remarked the now
engrossed novelist.

"Cannibalism has been a feature of human life
throughout history. It was widespread in the Iron Age and
today it is associated with sadistic psychopaths," chipped
in the blackmailer.

"Not just psychopaths. Placentas are sold to
pharmaceutical companies to make prescription drugs,
organ transplants are a form of cannibalism and there
are also people who go to the extreme to try something
different to preserve their looks," concurred the
aristocrat, happy to find an ally.

"Apparently the discovery of preserved mummies in
Egypt encouraged Victorians to believe that these

artefacts would bring extended life benefits when ground and used as a tonic," voiced the novelist.

"Once inhibitory mechanisms are broken a human is capable of anything. Depersonalisation and treating others as objects is seen throughout life. It allows decisions that are unethical to become justifiable."

"Taboo-breakers get a high out of it."

"I read somewhere that the young make better eating!"

"Cooked trussed with an orange in the mouth."

"Stop it!" Cried the reporter.

"Why be surprised. The animals we eat rarely get beyond infancy."

"If you ate the brain of a bishop would you become holy?"

"No, it will have nothing to do with a person's profession. More likely, it is a chemical thing. So, if you ate the brain of a manic depressive than you will become one."

"To stop men from being such pricks, maybe, they should feed the brains of deceased women to them!" Whispered the femme fatale to the reporter.

"Double portions would help," retorted her confederate.

"There are stories in the tabloids about the rich having regular transfusions of blood from the young to keep their brains active. Does that not remind you of something?"

"Vampires!"

"Would any of you young women like another full-bodied red wine?"

Du Gui's eyes, which had been half-shut with drowsiness, sprung open. They were bright with delight. He christened the author of the novel *'mon ami'* and cried aloud:

"Mon Dieu! Je parle comme Radu."

*****

Next day started and ended slowly. The only good news from that day's press conference was the absence of bad news about the fate of the chefs. The chief investigator later told Du Gui he was happy with his performance at the previous press conference. Getting the press to take an interest in the girl got the newspapers off their backs for a few days at least.

At one p.m. precisely, punctual to the minute, he put that day's report down, leaned back in his chair, stretched his arms, and looked to see if the minder was occupied, smiled, put on his jacket and went out. His assistant looked up and also smiled: it was good to have a hands off boss that only worked half a day and took long weekends. It was also a signal for them to stop work. Lunch for the couple had become an hour in the gym and a refusal to eat the stodge options served in the staff canteen, preferring a fruit smoothie instead. Bread and butter pudding was not for them.

A brisk stride quickly got him out on to the streets. Most of the afternoon was spent looking at the Iron Age artefacts in the British Museum and meeting the departing Romanian in Russell Square to say their farewells, next stop was Paris.

Drawing in cigarette smoke sharply, Radu aired his final views.

"*Mon ami*, nothing to report. Can I tell you something? I have a bad feeling about this girl. She probably held somewhere within her own community. There are many reasons why she may have been taken. Within the African communities there are many types and tomfooleries. Witchcraft, Islamic barbarities and slavery are known to happen. We Romanians believe in premonitions, evil and that some people are destined for bad luck. She is pretty so could now be hooked on drugs by gangsters and forced to apply sexual services on the streets and brothels. These men make girl dirty, turn her into whore, and now has lots of uncles to please. Death will be her friend."

Du Gui articulated his dark thoughts about the human organ trade.

"*Mon ami,* in the meat trade the offal of the animal is considered worthless compared to the prime cuts, but, in the organ trade they are the money end and the meat is just an unwanted by-product. The bush meat trade could be the ultimate destination for this by-product. Yes, I am sure cannibalism exists in London."

With that and a roguish wink, Radu bade farewell.

An hour after Radu left to catch his train at St Pancras, Gabriel sat down, happy to recommence his adventures.

"At one restaurant, working long hours in the kitchen got my face known to an up-and-coming chef. Eventually a rapport developed when he cottoned on that I could improve his English. From there the kindness and respect shown to me from this man did me the world of good. Taking under his wing he trusted me to go each morning to the market to buy the best and freshest vegetables, meats and fish available."

Du Gui interposed and asked if he heard anything about cash for organs within the transient work community.

"Not personally but it goes on. A couple of thousand pounds is nothing to some but a fortune to others. You have discovered something?"

"No, something I read."

The conversation lulled giving Du Gui the opportunity to check his text messages. Nothing was waiting for him.

"Do you fancy a bite to eat, Gabriel?"

"If you are paying, I could eat a horse."

"Let's find a bar that has a good wine list and an impressive selection of hors d'oeuvres."

Forever the considerate egalitarian, the pair had a

culinary experience more comfortable to Gabriel:
jellied eels and pie and mash followed by finding a
bar serving a good navy rum. After a few libations
to assist digestion, a mutual love for fishing and
other things kept the chat flowing in a manner that
only the same generation could have without
causing offence, being misunderstood or labelled.
Gossiping about a time when everything was
simpler and, of course, grumbling that it was
harder. Back to an age when discipline not
wellbeing was society's cry word and a teaching
profession occupied by sex starved spinsters due to
the shortage of men. An age when young unmarried
mothers had their babies taken away from them if
no one within the family offered to bring the child
up as their own, nothing like the mollycoddling that
went on now.

"Spinsters and thugs masquerading as teachers
bashing the spirit out of you," recounted both of
them.

*****

In bed, the mattress refused to be a friend to the
tipsy boarder so the radio was switched on and
accidentally tuned to a music request show instead
of the intended news station. He left it on when
listeners announced to the bubbly DJ what they
were having for an evening meal along with their
choice of song for that night's theme. Hearing that
people still ate late when the latest health
guidelines insisted on a light snack was reassuring
to hear. Mind this might just reflect the fact that
the audience for this station were generally young
and easily capable of sleeping through the night
without waking up in the pitch dark with a lucid

alertness unmatched in the daytime. There was a loose correlation between the genre of music chosen and the type of meal prepared. Eating leftovers and ready meals dominated the Americana following, freshly prepared food the old songwriter musicians, steak and curries the rock fans, while soul aficionados preferred Italian dishes.

Still not relaxed enough to sleep, he switched the bedside lamp on, sat up, rubbed his eyes, put on his reading glasses, picked up his book and opened it.

Near midnight, as the blackmailer slumped against the armrest of the chair, sputtering incoherent nonsense, coffee and an assortment of cheese were served along with brandy to toast the passing of a friend.

In his short interview, the archaeologist had spoken about the novelist's modulus operandi: specialising in crime, avoiding the psychological and the overuse of metaphors, the copying of the Shakespearean trick of adding comedic skits to his stories and in later novels expressing angst about where society had ended up, which he stated was fair enough as life was perplexing with elements of farce.

The man preferred a good plot to rich language and read on his commute back and forth to work with a book pressed against his face.

"As far as the latest novel is concerned the ending needs more punch, more shock factor and less of the explicit preaching which is unlike you. Usually you leave it to us to make a final judgement."

The party was noisier and happy to freely express

opinions. Even the blackmailer and reporter had become less self-conscious and had started to look the others directly in the eye. During a toilet break, the amorous femme fatale had moved seats to be closer to the novelist.

"The magazines say you are a Don Juan and your tropical home is a love palace."

"You must not believe everything you read."

"The pictures show you on the beach with women half your age."

His early career saw him working in Fleet Street but when literary success arrived, he moved to France on to North Africa, Thailand then the South Seas.

"Mere publicity shots to get my name in the media. Anyway, these women are around your age group."

The gossip columns attacks called him a silver-headed operator with a tongue to match the colour of his hair. Some accused him of being a pompous egoist that happily used people. A libertarian that immersed himself in primitive cultures, like others before him in search of an exotically unconstrained existence in the islands he now called home, rolling back the clock to a time before Captain Cook arrived. Each morning after breakfast, he would feed the Rottweilers, turn off the electrified perimeter fencing and order the outer gates opened to allow the waiting gardeners to enter. In the afternoons, bimbos from beach bars were picked up and given a good time on his lavish yacht, never in his house, which was out of bounds even to his friends.

"Who loses sleep over the poor?"

The latest interruption came from the archaeologist and the topic capturing the interest of the others was a discussion about a theme of the novel.

"You just lack sympathy. Your soul is at the bottom of your feet compress by the weight of indifference," retaliated the aristocrat.

"Gravity brings everything down," came the snappy riposte.

"More yin and less yang please," from the reporter.

Someone played footsie with the femme fatale; she hoped it was who she hoped it would be and not the pretending to be asleep blackmailer.

"Nowadays, it is difficult to remember anything for long. Mind games to improve memory do not help either but definitely think the series had become dull. The last few novels have been off the boil, mere pension pot fillers." contested the archaeologist.

"Hero has lost his mojo," asserted the reporter, adding: "first couple of novels were the best. He was an aging playboy when the series started and it was the discovery of a son that rejuvenated him."

"Rehashing of previous plots as well," joined in the awoke blackmailer, and "it is not a good practice to let your detective develop a social conscience that attacks the people who buy books."

"What you should have done is refresh the series with cases involving him when he was a rookie, a pre-sequel," proclaimed the archaeologist.

"Spin it out..."

Switching on the smart TV, he searched for information on Captain Cook.

"Ah, English explorer, first name James..."

THE MEAT OF THE MATTER

Du Gui was looking forward to this next jaunt away from the capital and had happily taken jibe when it became known to the liaison officer.

"Summer creeps in slowly up there. Better pack your long johns."

He had replied:

"The best way to renew oneself is to head out of town, re-energise, start afresh and redirect thoughts to good use."

The short flight above the neglected heart of England abundantly illustrated the effect of the varying climate in this north-stretching island with blue skies and broad streets replaced by the monochromes of a grey alleyway infested city once populated by troglodytes and named after an Anglo-Saxon settler. The dearth of colour and light explained the popularity of Calvinism and the dour character of its older residents and parliamentarians.

On his arrival, he found that the mystery of the missing chefs had a political slant. The Scottish nationalists were using the situation as the basis for that week's call for another referendum. The papers were replete with this demand. Words over substance perpetually bounded about a regional parliament set up to provide local accountability but instead spent its time stirring up divisions and blame. Many made a good living out of it with the expectations of greater rewards to come in the adamant belief that Europe was fixated on the desire to send its riches north without anything in return, ignoring the adage that there was no such thing as a free lunch.

He mitigated the chill in the air by keeping to the sunny side of the gaunt streets when possible. On the promise from them to leave him alone thereafter, the local press congregated to meet him for a photo shoot at Edinburgh's most famous tourist spot. The clicking cameras played a tattoo as he stood next to the upper parapets. He was treated like loyalty, loved every minute of it and pictures of him on the ramparts of the castle next to *Mons* Meg appeared in all the Scottish papers. The impressive cannon, the most famous of its day, so powerful that it shot over the heads of the English in Northumberland and hit some unlucky cattle grazing in a Scottish field. Although the man of the moment stated not having any intention of debunking the legend of the Loch Ness Monster, this story was too good not to print.

The realisation of a dream had likewise influenced him to come to Scotland next. Therefore, the first

thing done after meeting the press was to head
straight to one of the many kilt outfitters that
thronged the city centre. Having no ties to Scotland
proved no handicap with the outfitter deciding that
this Frenchman was entitled to wear the tartan of
the ancient society of Jacobites exiled in Paris.

"You've got a fine pair of legs for wearing the kilt."

"You will be soon roaming in the gloaming," teased
the other and older of the sales attendants.

"If you're on shank's pony you will be needing
boots?"

"And a Harris Tweed jacket," added his colleague.

The last pieces of business were a request for the
immediate alteration to the off the peg items to
improve the fit and the paying of the final bill
which was kindly not itemised and charged under
the nondescript heading of all-weather gear.
Several hours later, a man in the full regalia of a
Highland gentleman, as found in old Hollywood
movies, hit the streets. Walking in the late
afternoon round Gothic streets on the mound of an
extinct volcano reassured him as no queer looks
came his way and he even took pleasure in having
pictures taken with friendly tourists.

Getting confused about where he had ended up a
passing taxi was flagged down. It found every
traffic light back towards his hotel. They even
managed to pass the parliament building which
according to his tourist guide was in the opposite
direction.

"Are you from this area?" Asked Du Gui.

"Nae from Glasgow. The traffic is so bad here it is worthwhile coming across for the fares."

"If we are doing the tour then you may as well drop me off at Carlton Hill cemetery."

"Daenae get yerself inta a fankle, sit back and enjoy the view. The difference between the Scottish lasses and the Europeans is their bums. Our lasses' bums hang down and your lot sit up."

At one set of particularly slow changing traffic lights, the driver gave his opinion about the missing Scottish chef.

"A gobshit that nae heard o' plain English."

At the requested stop, the fare was paid.

"Ta bud, by the way, you know David Hume is buried in there?"

"Yes, I know. He was a friend of Voltaire."

That evening's meal was enjoyed at a bistro off the Royal Mile, near St Giles. The desire to taste Scotland inspired him to choose a starter of ox cheek braised in an ox and horseradish jus served with a neep and tattie hash. This was followed by pan-fried sea bream with smoked haddock kedgeree and curried sauce. Vegetables were Chantenay carrots and crispy onions. To finish, he requested the cheese board and ordered a glass of dessert wine to go with it. The Scottish produced blue cheese and Australian wine turned out a perfect

match, causing him to mull over the fact that the
rest of the world with its well-placed new
generations of entrepreneurial artisans could
compete with the best that France offered.

In the morning, rising from a bed in a hotel along
Princess Street, he was surprised to see exercising
Japanese tourists from a bedroom window that
looked down to an uncovered roof patio. A moment
of guilt about being comparatively idle flashed
through his mind as the group gracefully performed
in synchronism their *Tai Chi* movements. A routine
probably done like clockwork every morning.

The undisclosed part of the journey was to take him
beyond the Great Glen on a double carriage diesel
train that slowly inch by inch steadily zigzagged
round the base of heather-covered hills, across a
rugged landscape with steep ravines, riddled with
mystic standing stones, crisscrossed by streams and
rivers that had forced the inhabitants to become
renowned engineers by building bridges that could
endure the elements. A journey that passed the
Black Isle rumoured to be a place where the
unwary met their doom, desolated by collective
migration seen at the time by salon elites in
Edinburgh as the necessary removal of a diseased
and damaged part of the Scottish population. The
trip made longer by stopping at every remote empty
small halt at outlying hamlets, exaggeratedly called
villages. The driver took his duty of care to his
passengers very seriously indeed, probably knew all
their names to boot. Including himself, the number
of passengers in this final lap was less than ten
souls. No conductor came to check tickets.
Uninhibited audible conversations allowed

everyone on the train to learn the life stories of
the others. Needless to say, the locals had an
unrushed countenance, taking life as it came,
enjoying a mode of transport that saved days of
trekking on foot or a tiring car journey. One, a
teenage mother with child on toll was off to hospital
in Thurso for her twelve-week pregnancy scan.

He got off the train at the stop for the east coast
township of Lyndale, hidden from the halt as it lay
below the cliff edge. The panorama from the
platform of the featureless station offered a
magnificent view of a sea surface twinkling in the
evening light. Reaching the internet booked hotel,
the weary traveller numbed by hours spent staring
out of a moving carriage had a warming whisky in
its bar dubbed the *Silver Darlings* then went
straight up to the room.

The next morning, the smell of toast and cooked
bacon pervaded the bar, which doubled as a dining
room for guests. The splendid full Scottish stuck to
his ribs for the rest of the day providing the
necessary nourishment for the planned exertions,
not his normal way of breaking the fast but a
necessary one for rural dwellers. Thanking the
sleepy-looking toast munching black haired
waitress when she came to take away the plates, he
perceived a very young woman with the perfect
combination of imperfections that made her
attractive whatever she may have felt about
herself. Small talk between them related to how
quiet it must be to live in this coastal village, and
with a Polish accent, she replied that the only
noticeable disturbance was the helicopter that flew
out to sea during the night or when there was a
haar.

"Haar?"

"A sea mist," proudly replied the Pole.

The omnipresent young Poles were everywhere. East to West, North to South, they went where rent was cheap or came with the job.

A friendly chat with the English hotel owner informed him that this man had brought his family north in the search for a better life.

"How do you find life here?"

"Life is like the rest of Britain with the bonus of beautiful countryside, real wild lands, untameable due to its unique geology."

Later using directions pointed out on the map by the hotel owner and taking the man's white terrier for company, he headed out to realise a childhood dream. The departing pair immediately chummed up.

Passing a front door, a friendly voice called out from a small white-haired stout woman wearing house slippers in the cartooned shape of pandas.

"Off to see how the day goes? If you fancy trying to catch old Stottie, then best to work your way several miles upriver until you come to the falls of sorrows. The creature should be lying deep somewhere in the pool below. Mind you keep to the path on the north side of the glen, as the Russian estate owner is robust with unlicensed anglers on his side."

Old Stottie was reportedly a six-foot-long pike that ate the fish that an angler returning home empty handed would have otherwise have caught. The legend did not interest him as fishing was not on his mind. A brisk walk in the fresh air was what the doctor ordered and off he went as the woman maintained her position to watch the sway of the kilt until it was beyond her sight.

As expected, the hardest part of the hike was the start. Without acclimatisation and warning to his muscles, a steep incline laid ahead to the top of the cliffs. Coming down from the railway station the night before with the full weight of a rucksack on his back increasing the pull of gravity should have reminded him what to expect this morning.

After some considerable effort, the out of breath sexagenarian rested at the cliff edge, inhaled deeply the fresh air and appreciated the mild weather as such a labouring climb would have killed him if attempted in the sweltering heat of a continental summer's day. Once his breathing and heartbeat settled, the intensity of the silence hit him. Eastwards, a bituminous North Sea seemed still like time itself. The dog came back from its forward advance position, smelt the ground and pointed its nose upwards to sample the air, forensically determining what the holdup was.

"Marchons! Marchons! Time to forge on," roared Du Gui.

He hummed the French national anthem as they travelled westward. With a map and compass, the destination on a paved surface was about ninety minutes away but hillwalking changed that with periods when it seemed like no progress was made on the energy sapping peaty turf. Out of town and away from the protection of coastal cliffs, the force of a rising westerly wind caused the temperature to drop, sending a chill all the way up his exposed groin. The anorak pulled out of his rucksack provided a crumb of comfort but what was more on his mind was the realisation that the thick pair of tweeds that he had turned down at the outfitters would not have gone amiss.

They initially searched for and walked beside the meandering river where an occasional fish leaped out of it. A short while later the river was left to follow its own path as their route took them upwards. There, in front of him, was a great expanse of a tree bare moor, a wide upland of heather and coarse grass, deliberately lacking of predators, unlawfully exterminated to keep the habitat ideal for game birds. As if to make a point, a hitherto unseen ground nesting bird flew up in the air when the dog came too close to it for comfort. Admiring the bleakness of this atmospheric landscape, he addressed his new friend.

"*Petit Milou*, life is full of boundaries. Geographical, regional, cultural right down to personal preferences and beliefs that make a prisoner of you. One thing is for sure, facts are found in nature, while held truths only live in human society."

Looking down at the disinterested dog, he shook himself out of an encroaching melancholy and announced that they were here to walk. The spry companion led the way, as he trailed through the

boggy ground by attempting to find a secure
foothold on raised tufts of heather, but on occasions
his forward foot plunged deep into sludge, leaving
his full-length thick coarse woollen sock soaked.

The combined effects of the bracing wind and
energy-sapping terrain exhausted both the walker
and dog. His legs and back severely tested, as the
stop-starts in a busy city had not provided
sufficient stamina for life on the hills; it only gave
him a false indication of his strength. Now hip and
back pain informed him of the true state of his
health. Gritting his teeth, he reminded *Milou* that
he was the master by leading it up the remainder of
the slow rising summit. Squalls of rain had left
exposed rock wet and slippery. There, they hide
from the worse of the wind by taking cover under a
lee of a protruding granite boulder invaded by
green patches of moss and lichen.

This high vantage point put everything into
perspective and plugged him into the glorious
creation of nature, spontaneously awesome and
humbling. The sublime created by dramatic
geological cycles, and another reminder that Eden
did not exist in the City of Man; and that all epochs
have a start and end point, even the Anthropocene
era.

It was an opportune setting to enjoy the provided
pack lunch. It consisted of half a roast chicken,
presumably to be shared, an apple and something
called a *Tunnock Caramel Log*. Just a bite of the
latter told him it was too sweet for him, and it was
dropped down to *Milou*, who gratefully recognised
the treat.

The whole glen opened up in front of them with the ever changing vista altered by brighter skies with iridescent lenticular clouds in the troposphere replacing rain clouds. The previously closed off by mist hills revealed festive colours of blazing patches of green, golden brown, reds and purples. Burns swept down into the river, which in winter must be in continuous spate. The landscape dissected by these arteries and by narrow leading upwards trodden footpaths. A sheltered lonely birch or was it a larch and crags of metamorphic and igneous rocks broke up the barrenness. Getting out his trusty binoculars, he observed across the glen on a hilltop, a doe and a buck scrutinising each other while fifty odd metres below them, the carcass of a bloated and stinking stag attracted the attention of a mountain fox, like them enjoying *al fresco* dining with a grand view.

Below, just off a bend in the famous salmon river lay the buildings of a hunting estate that amply told the history of the district. The majestic hunting lodge possessed many of the original fortifications of a Scottish Baronial castle, a tall forbidding windowless edifice impregnable until the arrival of cannon. Later occupants had enlarged the entranceway, grafted on a Georgian Palladian facade and laid out manicured lawns around it. A Victorian built stone road provided access to the lodge and the many newer outbuildings that housed sporting paraphernalia and kennels required for a well-run estate.

The noise of a helicopter passing overhead attracted their attention. It was a *Bristow*. It passed straight on and lowered itself onto a pad. In

this part of the world, a helicopter was the best
way to traverse across it and to see its grandeur.
One moment flying low across the bleak tundra, the
next a dramatic drop of several hundred metres
revealed glens carved out by retreating ice with
silvery light glimmering off lochs and distant seas.

A group of passengers digressed from the opened
hatch to be received by waiting porters with trolleys
for baggage and wheel chairs for two of the arrivals.
With London only four hours away at cruising
speed, seclusion was found in a secure hideaway
that would take a unit of special forces to
successfully lay siege. Seeing covered up persons
helped towards the castle, implied two things to the
detective, they had something to hide or were not in
the peak of health.

Further up the glen, a white-tailed eagle came out
of the sun, ringed the flowing river then like a bolt
of lightning fell, returning upwards clasping a
squirming fish in its stretched out talons, taken it
to its own crag to enjoy.

With the hands of his watch pointing to three
o'clock, it was time to get back. Prior to standing
up, the rested hill walker rubbed his legs to get the
circulation going again. The dog took its cue from
these actions and stretched its limbs. This response
encouraged the man to take a last long avid inhale
of a cigarette, stand up and stretch in unison. The
swarm of midges that had followed the pair needed
no invite or encouragement to follow them back
homewards. It was going to be a bumpy return.
Clambering across wet granite to regain the
summit, a slip and loss of balance brought home
how unforgiven the rock beneath the feet was when

a wrist jarred and palm scraped against it as he tried to break a slide by stretching out a protective arm. In the same movement, a back foot dislodged loose gravel and send a flurry clattering down the side. On the rim of the hill with the light shining directly on them, they were as visible as the stags had been. They stood there for a few minutes with him swivelling his hurt hand and rubbing the palm to tease the pain away.

Retracing the route back, spirits rose on the knowledge of knowing where he was going, and with the improved weather. His mind freed itself from worries, went blank then dwelled on abstract thoughts. Before the romance of the setting swept completely over him, he brought to mind that foreign lands looked sublime to the tourist, that the wilds of Jura and the Sierra Nevada were just as outstanding. An overheard conversation between a tour guide and a young Arab in a northern museum then flashed back to him. The guide asked everyone in the party where they came from and on hearing the origins of this young man and that he was going to be studying at the local university she apologised for the persistent rain. In response, the young man announced that he enjoyed her country's climate and walking in the rain was a great pleasure. The relaxed Commissionaire then soliloquised Schopenhauer's thirty-eight stratagems, compulsory reading for spin doctors, politicians, bureaucrats and other paid deceivers. He was not sure why as he had never considered them for a very long time. The idea to do so just popped into his head, a sure sign of blissful peace of mind; past knowledge rediscovered in a tranquil moment. Seldom over the last few weeks had he been in such good spirits.

Following the river downstream, fatigue and hunger made themselves known again. Up ahead a human figure was distinguished by its movement against a dulling sky. The blast from a gun and the rush of a frightened terrier to hide behind his legs signalled an inimical intrusion.

"Keep him on a leash as it will not be so lucky next time," came the coarse shout from what was assumed a gamekeeper in the shape of a gorilla on the other side of the river.

Bending a knee and like a father to a distressed child he smiled and gently said "a narrow escape for you, *petit.*" While rubbing the back of a quivering *Milou*, he shot 'I will remember your face' look across at a man who should never have had been given a firearm certificate.

Clenching his fists and mindful that he should bite his tongue, he did not, instead his left hand tucked into the tweed jacket side pocket as he walked to the edge of his side of the riverbank to engage with the armed man on the other bank. Back in a locked drawer in Brussels, his unloaded *Glock* handgun lay undisturbed.

"There was no need to fire your gun, the dog was doing no harm."

"It was frightening the birds and it is my job to protect them," from an Asiatic looking brute.

"Humm...a bit overzealous I would say and we do have the right to be out here."

"This is private land."

In a lonely lifeless setting two outsiders had an exchange about the right of way until the gamekeeper slowly treaded backwards before turning round to go up river back towards the estate.

Stroking the calmed head of the dog with his empty left hand, it occurred to him that he was not the only one that was having a bad week. At least during the remonstrations, he found it interesting to note that there was a protective vest underneath the jacket of the great ape. It also occurred to him how it was odd that a gamekeeper with a sporting rifle could miss from close range. Was it just a routine warning shot to deter nosey parkers and did the outward bound helicopter drop the man off ahead of them?

A warming plate of soup and a dram of *Old Pulteney* waited for him back at the hotel. For a small hamlet at the ends of the world, the bar was busy. The burning log fire was scorching for those sitting nearest to it. With their legs open it reminded him of roasting chestnuts. Happily, his drinking arm was unaffected by the earlier mishap and the planned drink turned into a third of a bottle as he spent several hours listening to yarns about a seafaring past when the fishing fleet returned to the harbour with hulls brimming with herring, familiar tales of catches and of great storms. Music provided by kinsmen playing a hand pipe, a mandolin and a fiddle accompanied the loud gossiping chatter. Folklore through airs and jigs retold tragedies, romances and infidelities. Glasses

of amber nectar passed to them as a reward.
They played with the emotions of the crowd like
experts.

With a serious face and fiddle wedged under a chin,
a lament for the lost and gone sobered the drinkers.
The moment was broken when the barman sent an
old drinker packing back to his table after a failed
attempt to short change the bar.

"You ken well that you're not sufferin' from
dementia, you're just an auld git trying to get cheap
drink."

The bar greeted this wisecrack with rising
crescendos of laughter and cheers.

In spite of the amount of drink and the lateness of
the hour when heading upstairs, he woke early
after falling into a drunken, heavy, dreamless
slumber. Because there was plenty of time before
breakfast and his departure back to Edinburgh via
Inverness, it was decided to stretch his stiff calves
and hams by taking a slow stroll down to the small
stone harbour.

With high waves ramming against the walls,
anorak wrapped tight round the collar, he reflected
how unsettling it was in the bar last night to see
the exact double of a past friend. It was as if he had
been transported back in time to another country.
It was one of the musicians, the youngest by many
years and those forte was the pibroch. This
instrumentalist had near identical stature, skin
and hair colouring, head shape and facial
expressions. Understandably, that person would be
a lot older by now and could not play the hand

pipes. Was this proof of the Celtic gene?

The sound of footsteps drew his attention. Turning round, the low rising sun shone straight into his eyes causing him not to immediately distinguish a pensioner that spoke with him in the bar the night before. A fellow perhaps in his eighties with skin moulded and dried by sea air, nature's preservative. Dressed in clothes which once may have had fitted him perfectly and which now hung loosely on a body shrunken by wizened ligaments. The outer layer consisted of a donkey jacket and leather cap that kept his thick fisherman's jersey dry while a dark thick pair of tweed trousers and sturdy boots provided protection from the elements for his lower half. In a relaxed quiet matter of fact manner, this man spoke.

"By Jove, it is blowing a hoolie. The spirit of the sea is in a bad mood today and will not be pacified until it has received a sacrifice. It may just be the Norse blood in us but in the old days we believed that the sight of a clergyman on the way to the boat foretold that sacrifice would be you."

Touching the Commissionaire's arm, the old timer laughed.

"You have picked the wrong time of year to visit us. Too late for the lights and too early for the long days."

"The place gets busier?"

"Not really. The truth be told not much happens nowadays. The laird's salmon is not for the likes of us. The herring and the need to go out to catch them are long gone. We finally got what is left of the fishing back and Holyrood immediately want to return it to the Spanish to appease the EU. All for nothing did older generations worked hard and died to create a thriving community. It is a poor country that cannot fed itself. Even the gulls have given up on us. Better pickings for them at land fill sites where they can spend all the seasons gorging on free food. Did you know it is said that the same species of seagulls never bred with their urban counterparts?"

"Natural segregation probably due to smelling differently," suggested the Frenchman.

Rain started to pour down and the pair went their separate ways. The Commissionaire always took great pleasure in casual conversations with men who had carved out a living.

"No sane person revered a bureaucrat but a person that made something with their hands was envied."

Heading back, he realised that all the houses were alike and built with the surrounding grey stone. On an overcast day, the village in its unending Sunday morning peace dissolved into the background.

At breakfast, the offer of a full Scottish cooked breakfast was turned down and he settled for toast and scones. He asked for coffee but to appreciate fully the local blackberry jam accepted the recommendation of Scottish blend tea. In this part of the world, they ridiculed the notion of putting cream on your scone. He appreciated the gesture of boiling bottled mineral water for the tea. The local tap water with its brownish colouring and smell of peat would not have done his hangover any good.

On the way back on the train, he was hoping the gossip might be about the outcome of young Morag's medical consultation.

*****

With renewed vigour, he strutted into Scotland Yard where the lovers were still eye smiling at each other.

"Did you enjoy your break?" Enquired Williams.

To deflect the conversation away from his activities, he humoured the liaison officer's prejudices.

"When it was not raining, the weather was bearable to fine, but it was unfortunate that when caught for ten minutes in pelting ice cold horizontal rain the pleasure in getting about was spoilt by drenched clothing."

"I did warn you. It is why northerners stoop and have a chip on their shoulders about the South, not because it is richer but because it is warmer."

After the pleasantries, the Commissionaire asked for a land registry search for the largest rural landowners in Scotland and to check aviation traffic around Lyndale. The liaison officer stood behind his assistant as she fired off the requests. Although suspicious of her loyalties, he had to acquire this information and when all things were said and done she was a productive worker, willing to search through records and only report information of importance.

Her latest endeavours filtered out land owned by the Church, Ministry of Defence and National Trusts. Her fingers were slender and nimble ideal for a computer keyboard. Data sorting and that dreadful misuse of the word 'mining' was her forte. Maybe, when her days of vanity and lust were over she would make a good bureaucrat after all. Meanwhile, she played with the chain of her necklace by folding it in her fingers and biting it with her front teeth.

On seeing the small list of names, he reflected that for a country seeking its independence within the governance of the EU, it seemed strange that there was a reticence to complain about why a few foreign tycoons owned the vast majority of the land. Effectively, these few individuals had created their own kingdoms, patrolled by their own armies of game wardens. The landowner most curious about turned out to be *East Highland Hunting Estate* owned by a venture capital company registered in the Bahamas. Digging deep she found out that the parent company only had a single shareholder, a Chechen, not Russian. A query for information on intelligence databases about this individual returned an access denied message.

"This fish has found a large rock to hide under," mooted his assistant.

"See what property is owned in London by this company and if any extensions have been done to them, look for work in the cellars, big enough for a large oubliette," the Commissionaire replied.

The trip north informed him that this missing chef, known for putting on airs and carrying on as if an earl was the son of a gamekeeper and had spent most of his youth up at the estate, and as one old timer had put it:

"He wass nae born with a silver spoon in the mouth but rammed wan up his ain arse."

*****

A communication on an information board in the Yard had drawn his attention to the workings of the Thames River Police. He accordingly arranged to go down to the Pool of London to see them in action the next time a dredging occurred, which was the coming Friday. This facilitated, from Tower Hill tube station, a saunter round the White Tower, his planned exercise for the day pass a symbol of power built with imported Caen stone to solidify the establishment of a new capital away from the defeated Saxon stronghold of Winchester. The location of the most glaring *cui bono* murder of young royals that Tudor misinformation pinned on its defeated rival.

Predictable tides and currents allowed the Marine Policing Unit to know which spots to regularly dredge for drowned bodies. It was a patient affair waiting for the river to eventually give up its dead. At this location, an underwater metal grille trapped debris in front of a renovated wharf supported on concrete pillars drilled into the riverbed. For the involved personnel, it was a routine operation as punctually conducted like the passing of the keys by the beefeaters in the bastion above them; every

movement done in slow motion to give decorum
to the grim task and for health and safety reasons
too.

Wearing polarised sunglasses to cut out glare, he
observed the men at work, done without
exchanging a word. Without fuss or drawing
attention to their work, all knew what to do, it was
just another day in the office. An outboard
motorboat positioned itself fifty metres downstream
before two divers entered the water. As expected, a
body was found. It was pulled clear from the grille
and towed towards the quay. At the water edge,
colleagues used gaff hooks to drag it towards them
onto the quayside pontoon. A preliminary
examination showed no visible pathological
evidence for the cause of death or signs of parasites
attacking the flesh. The absence of damage done by
collisions with water traffic pointed to a short
distance travelled to this debris trap. The corpse
was that of a young man and the onset of rigor
mortis once out of the water along with other
indicators suggested that death occurred around a
few days prior, long enough to obliterate the
serenity which it can bring to a sufferer's face.
Personal effects consisted of soaked banknotes,
coins and a credit card.

After the paperwork was completed, the body was
bagged and put on a trolley by attending mortuary
staff, rolled up the gangway and lifted into the back
of a dark blue van. The van shot off. Once the air
tanks were safely stacked into the back of the
diving unit van, some of the men had a smoke.

"Another rent boy slung over the side of the House
of Westminster terrace bar. Mind you a lot less of

them since the Liberals were routed."

Black humour to relieve the sombreness of a job
well done. The truth of the matter was it was a
common occurrence for intolerable emotional stress
to lead to the most devastating self-harming action
to finally end the pain.

He thanked the departing crew and lingered
westward along the quay, letting his mind drift
with the lapping waters, allowing it to travel miles
away as several men, unobtrusively approached
him, surrounded him, nudged him, knocked him
sideways with one jumping him from behind,
strangling his throat and forcing him to the ground.
Winded and sore, his wallet and wristwatch were
snatched from him. Fortunately, a posse of young
tourists hastened to the scene. Their commotion
and maybe the possibility of capturing the incident
on smartphones and cameras encouraged a retreat
by the assailants, a withdrawal done in an orderly
defiant fashion, slowly pulling away, not running.
Why these rescuers were off the usual tourist track
remained a mystery but it went without saying that
he gratefully received the assistance.

Left lying on the pavement with a gash on the
forehead and a nose dripping blood, giddy, he
politely refused an arm to lean on, and with
determination got to his feet, straightened up but
only managed to stand shakily. He did have the
forethought to ask if any of them were filming at
the time. The affirmative pleased him and they
watched a replay of the captured scene from a
camera's high-resolution LCD screen. It missed the
beginning of the assault but did have a good image

of one of the attackers.

With a final thank you to his rescuers, he made his way back to Kensington, given the circumstances a difficult task. Keep moving, he told himself, and slowly but surely with the Thames on his left side progress was made walking beside a busy road. His attempt to flag down a taxi made awkward by a closed right eye. At every fifty yards or so, he stopped and physically turned to look at the oncoming traffic.

"Never can get a taxi when desperate for one."

It dawned on him that this was a dual carriageway with no stopping lanes and so the decision was made to try and get across it to be closer to the city centre. Thus at the first pedestrian crossing encountered, he got himself on to the north side of *Lower Thames Street*. To get away from this busy fast moving artery north by northwest he went, up *Monument Street* which took him into *Pudding Lane*. Not before a car horn blared at him for walking across the adjoining road without looking. Accidentally finding the spot where the Great Fire had started did not go unnoticed but the sixties built concrete office blocks nullified any pleasure. The next turning was more fruitful. A busy pedestrian thoroughfare with its safety in numbers was a reassuring sight. Finally, a tube sign caught his good eye. The compactness and anonymity of rush hour traffic aided the concealment of the dishevelled Frenchman who pulled a cap out of his jacket pocket and lowered his chin to his chest to further reduce the chance of recognition.

*****

At the reception of the hotel, slurred speech initially taken for the customary drunkenness of a returning guest hampered the attempt to get some first aid with medical attention only forthcoming by removing his cap to reveal the wound above the eye. This act made him notice his hand, still shaking from the events that happened well over an hour ago.

A Congolese hotel porter turned out to be a good night nurse by checking up on him and supplying ice and sedatives, a contented man who liked his job, the hours and the solitude in the middle of the night allowed him to quietly contemplate the next life and freely play his violin without interruption.

Sore, exhausted and drained, it took several minutes to peel off his clothes and step into bath water. His damaged sunglasses placed inside his jacket pocket fell onto the floor. They probably protected his eyes from being squashed. This thought caused him to shudder. He loathed violence, notably when conducted on him and reproached himself for again neglecting his safety. It was the first time in months since he bathed, normally it was a quick shower. Shutting his eyes, by turns he submerged his head under the hot water to bathe his wounds before coming up to breathe and reapply the ice pack. The constant supply of hot water was much appreciated. After several hours of this restorative cure, anger soon subsidised as his natural countenance took over.

Drying his hands, he lit a cigarette, the gamble taken that the steam would disarm the smoke detector. Soaking in the hot water, topped up every few minutes, the incident was mulled over. The wise decision to deny himself a large glass of cognac and spend a couple of hours bathing to reduce the swelling on his face and leg helped him to get on the mend and to reflect. The assailants did not smell like muggers but if the assault were reported, it would go down as an attempted mugging. Knowing differently, he knew his activities must have touched a nerve. He had brought himself into the orbit of those sought, which in the final analysis was his intention when he had decided to use himself as a lightning rod to attract invisible forces. The question was what happened to earn this warning, and from whom. Firstly, as the possibilities were imponderable, he vouchsafed no encouragement to take logical analysis to its limits by considering a reprisal resulting from previous cases. This aside, four potential reasons crossed his mind: people smugglers alarmed by his request to find the girl; abductors belatedly reacting to his presence; a hit ordered by the Chechen and a security services response after being alerted by a trigger raised on one of his assistant's database searches.

On the actual assault, it had told him the perpetrators went unruffled about their business, smelt British and had the training and strength to dispatch him if that were the aim. They set upon him in a controlled planned manner. Firstly, nudging him as one of them pushed past him to draw his attention while another pulled his arm up his back and snatched his head back with a hand over his eyes. Men under orders just doing their job, delivering a firm message with the understanding that a stronger one awaited if his current enquires continued. Collusion between the security service men and the Chechen seemed the best bet. Security service involvement would explain the lack of recovered digital footprints for the crucial hours after the last confirmed sightings of the chefs. Whether this was the work of approved spooks, special protection services or clandestine ghosts in the machine working for renegade units within intelligence departments, he probably will never know. This supposition relegated people smugglers and abductors down the pecking order. Mulling helped him to focus, regain defiance and remain implacable in continuing his investigation.

He spent the rest of the night trying to find a comfortable position in bed that did not irritate his sore body. With aches and adrenalin flowing through him, a deep sleep only struck just before dawn. In the morning, he took a hot shower to get the blood circulating again and ease the stiffness in his body, noticing black and blue sores on his right arm and side which developed overnight. For the remainder of the weekend, as the rain poured down outside the window, convalescence and watching the red swelling over his right eye turn dark purple absorbed him. The promised email from one of the tourists with an *mp4* attachment arrived on his mobile phone. Unfortunately, an error message informed him that the file was corrupted.

Waking early on Monday, the irritation around the eye had abated, the headache gone and a rub of his cheek informed him a shave was definitely in order after two days of lounging about living off room service. The blood shot in the eye and the swelling around it had started to clear. Although, the last person to judge, no after effects caused by concussion were felt and it was time to face the world again.

He had hoped the broken leg of his sunglasses stuck back onto the frame with strong tape and a slight limp due to a bruised leg would be the only noticeable impairment. However, these were all secondary signs compared to the black eye, which he tried to convince himself would be obscured by the dark lenses. Second thoughts forced him to replace the damaged glasses with a pair of reading glasses. This intact pair was a poor substitute as the prescription strength made them no use for general activities; not that he would be taking interest in other lines of enquiry.

Downstairs, a kind receptionist applied some man makeup to further disguise blemishes. A hand mirror pulled out from under the counter to show him the finished result.

"Parfait, vous êtes beau."

A final touch-up softened the applied mascara; prohibited by regulations for male officers and, in his case, by old-fashioned male pride.

He left the hotel to find that blue skies had returned for the start of the working week and made his way to the tube station.

In the Yard, his assistant and liaison officer exchanged a quick surprised look then tried to make light relief out of it.

"Some shiner. On the sauce? Lucky nobody raised a complaint," chuckled the liaison officer.

"Quel dommage," from the assistant.

"Nothing self-inflicted. Caught up in a brawl," clarified Du Gui.

To commiserate Williams added:

"A sign of the times."

He reassured them.

"No real harm done and I never carry anything of value. Only lost some cash and a cheap wristwatch. Why spend thousands on a timepiece when one for a few euros does as well."

*****

In the afternoon, after some shopping on *Tottenham Court Road*, a prearranged meeting with Gabriel was honoured. There was now a relaxed familiarity between them.

"From the outback sheep farm, I hid in a cattle truck, got off when it reached a slaughterhouse, made my way to a port and jumped on a ship, slept for several days in the hold, woke up in sunlight that sang and danced. From there on, instead of walking the gangplank as I feared, the steward drafted me onto the crew to earn my keep. The cargo ship was bound for Chile via the islands, dropping off and picking up cargo on the way. In some places, we anchored and waited for natives to come aside. Not just goods came aboard. Girls hosed down before taken below decks to entertain crew members. A razor blade had yet to touch my

cheeks but curiosity got the best of me. Looking
through a porthole soon told me what was going on.

I spent most of the voyage in the bowels of the
vessel working as a greaser and stoker, but being
covered in muck and oil did not deter the unwanted
attentions of the chief engineer. All his spare time
seemed to involve chasing me round the engine
room or trying to ply me with drink. I soon learnt
how to run on swaying decks and punch in the right
places. All the other crew members thought it was a
good laugh.

The cargo ship puffed out across the blue from
Australia heading for New Caledonia, Fiji, Samoa,
Cook Islands until the day Tahiti came into sight. I
gasped in awe at the natural beauty of the islands
nestling in clear blue seas. The rocky shorelines
peppered with black volcanic sand strips. A land of
coral reefs, tranquil lagoons, atolls and motus with
smiling unhurried lovers disappearing into the
woods."

"Ah oui. Cook came to the islands to observe the
transit of Venus, which was appropriate as this was
the land of the fun loving native, the new *Cythera*
as the earlier French mariners described it," butted
in the Commissionaire.

"Yes, a beautiful place. As I watched the break
waves hit the beaches and reefs, the decision was
made to jump ship. My naivety got the best of me
as swimming to shore turned out a dangerous and
exhausting affair.

Thankfully, a departing native boat pulled me out
of the water, laughed at my foolishness and took me

back with them. My journey in life now truly looked brighter.

Living there it could not be forgotten that water was the key to life and it was where the old gods dwelled. The expanse of the Pacific meant something when boats were made of wood. Remote undiscovered islands only reached if currents with divine guidance led you. The ocean brought the first Europeans to our shores. War, pestilence and exploitation soon followed. From then on, we suffered the curiosity and righteous indignation to a way of life that had sustained the people for millennia.

Tahitians are marvellous seamen and ingenious in the way they keep old diesel boats going. Working the currents demands long hard hours with short breaks to grab some time to eat and catch a few hours sleep. Loading and offloading passengers and goods along shorelines navigated by experience. Death rates high for those lacking intimate knowledge of sea currents, shorelines, safe harbours and hidden dangers.

Out in all-weathers with the possibility of capsizing in a storm on a rolling overloaded boat is a terrifying prospect. Sealegs learnt quickly otherwise slipping over the side, never to be seen again. Even vessels manned by the most experienced of men went out to sea to never return."

"So you speak French?"

"Pigeon French like the natives, nothing fancy."

Later the Commissionaire's last bit of business that day was to phone his assistant to ask her to do the impossible: see if photo recognition software against custom control records could identify Gabriel entering the country. After a strongly worded protest that this could take months to do, he agreed to restrict searches to times after the start of the year and for those arriving from Europe.

That night, a hotel meal of *steak-frites* satisfied him, and keeping an eye out for the night porter he thanked him again for his attentiveness with a gift of a collapsible music sheet stand given to aid the man when playing his violin during the night.

*****

A night spent at the hotel allowed him to finish the novel, tick another one off.

Several weeks later, a ninety-minute heavily edited recording of the soiree which embarked on a soliloquy in praise of the novelist was uploaded and made available to the world on the day the final version of the concluding novel in the series was published. The recording went viral causing the headlines in the press to make fun of an artist giving his all for his public, in this case literally. Sales rocketed with books lifted off the shelves as fast as they could be put there. The outcry was correspondingly ferocious with demands made to get the recording off cyberspace. As it turned out the novelist although present was not the host, that place was taken by a similar in appearance close friend and anonymous contributor to the detective series, who was soon questioned by the police. When on the island paradise he lived on the yacht to give both writers some personal space to think.

When is cannibalism, not cannibalism? The unconscionable closing shot appended to the recording of the co-writer confessing to serving cuts, blood and suet of the deceased friend to the unaware guests may answer that question. Also, murder it was not as a signed statement from the terminally ill novelist consented to the consumption of his body while small print in the agreements signed by the guests stated the use of meat sources from any creature in the animal kingdom. Being less fatty and more tender, quality horsemeat was used in the tartare, otherwise, the novelist was served in all the other courses. The co-writer went on to surmise if this was any more immoral than the consumption of products once fertilized by human excrement and bone meal gathered from battlefields.

This last supper was a publicity stunt to maximise revenues for the final book and to increase interest in earlier works. Fearing that his opus would not be a remembered legacy the decision was made to create a more lasting fame. Furthermore, the other landowners on his beloved island were bought out with the proceeds of the book and it was renamed after him, left unoccupied to return to a natural state with rumours of what was left of him being quartered and buried at its furthermost points.

The novelist's last will and testament stated that he wanted to give his audience something special, a unique moment that would give them memories forged by experience rather than acquired through reading. It was a characteristic of him, having made his mind up, to throw himself into the task with full enthusiasm. His energy and resources used to get the desired result. To this end, his ultimate act was to satisfy the incessant greed of the public to have more of him. As a resolute atheist, he had no soul to give them so the next best thing was to share his body amongst them. It was the epitaph sought. Not being able to eat himself, the next best thing, was let his fans do it. His critics were right about something, the taste of the book buying public was not discernible.

It was not all plain sailing for the novelist's friend who was left the yacht and a healthy lump sum. A freelance journalist made it his mission in the hope of getting the biggest scoop of his life to prove that the person claiming to be the novelist at the soiree was in fact really him and that it was the friend who was consumed, allowing the recluse novelist the sought-after footnote in history as well as the remainder of his life free from the demands and the attentions of his fans and publisher.

*****

Although the opposite was true, it felt like a hot night in a stuffy room even with the window open. The unthinkable inkling that bubbled in his subconscious finally frothed to prompt him to stop dodging the unpalatable link between the suspects and his possible part in unwittingly abetting the disposal of evidence. Although not pretending to have unravelled all the ramifications, everything came together: motives, viable suspects and Gabriel's role in it. The sailor come hotel jack-of-all-trades worker told truths but truths that revealed only what was required for him to know, just a tableau to reel in his curiosity and to infer the capability of seeing what was confessed. Buying time by spinning half-truths to give his story plausibility. There was a clock ticking and the Commissionaire was aware of it. If Gabriel was involved, his accomplices had already been come across.

His drowsing in bed continued to peruse his hypothesis with vivid swirling apposite visions that shook him up to find himself in a room where everything was crimson: the walls, the carpet, the bed and quilt, all soaked in blood as it ran down the walls and trickled down from the ceiling. Another vision placed him at a banquet, seated at a table with five shapeless guests. The surroundings reminded him of the French Polynesian restaurant. One of the guests was recalling Captain Cook's death and recorded incidences of cannibalism on life rafts. After each course, the diners became more mutilated with sinews ripped and limbs cracked open.

Awoke for real, he lay silently, contemplating until the breaking dawn encouraged him to stir and turn off the forgotten lit bedside lamp. He wanted to get out and walk to clear his head by using his legs to encourage the heart into action and pump blood around his body. There was a destination in mind. The time had come for the investigator of strange cases to act, to let his solution see the light of day. He was determined to put an end to this vile incident.

Still bleary-eyed, he made himself a complimentary coffee using three sachets and all the available sugar then he sat on the edge of the bed to electric shave, while wishing his consciousness had the ingenuity of his indomitable subconscious in the way it pulled together everything that was disturbing him and not let anything remain buried.

Prior to leaving the room, he scanned his clothes and shoes looking for bugs. Outside, the accustomed route to the tube station was followed but on this occasion the walk continued on up *Brompton Road*. For the next fifty-odd minutes, he meandered in and out of shops, went along pedestrian precincts and passed art galleries, furnishings boutiques and interior design specialist dealers for the uber rich until satisfied that it was safe to enter the Knightsbridge hotel that faced him.

His loathing to disclose intentions so to avoid any unwanted deliberation or to alert adversaries had a flaw. For a lone man without firearm or means to call backup or to expect help from a wingman protecting his flanks, it was not the brightest thing to about to accuse the head chef in his own kitchen of being the linchpin to the mystery that had stunned a nation. Surrounded and outnumbered by sous chefs and kitchen lads possessing knives, carving forks, ladles and rolling pins as sparkling polished aluminium worktops, ovens and masses of stainless steel pots and other utensils reflected imminent danger, he found himself in the soup again. Not sure what was going to happen next, he drew breath and stated his suspicions along with the fact that Gabriel had similar tattoos on his arms and hands as the French Polynesian kitchen helpers.

Perplexed and angry, the head chef uttered his defence in French.

"I did not attack you or ordered it. Yes, I know the fate of the chefs but for my own safety and that of my staff, I had to keep it to myself. Knowing that you were investigating the disappearances and being recognised dining here panicked me into the decision to trick you with a false trail, delay you by planting Gabriel on you. Your well-known love for listening to an interesting life story and his joy in reciting it seemed like a perfect match. All done to quietly gain time to honour my contract at this hotel..."

Grabbing the bull by the horns, another supposition tossing in his mind had to be resolved by returning to the plague pit, which now gave the impression of a landfill site with all types of domestic and commercial waste discarded there; emphasised by the increased numbers of gulls arguing about who should get the best pickings. To reduce costs, local businessmen fly tipped in the exposed pit, usually in the middle of the night through the many gaps that existed in the surrounding fence. The poor long dead reeking once more this time from waste and putrid organic matter dumped onto them by market vendors and local fast food sellers. There was also evidence of the modern phenomenon of doggers looking for a risky spot to indulge in rough sex.

With construction workers and hordes of gawkers gathered round the fencing, a called out forensic team worked away discovering human remains: bits of fingers, toes, and crushed larger joints thrown out with the rubbish. The task engendered an eerie silence. Even the gulls went quiet or flew off. Like the archaeologists before them, they painstakingly examined partitioned areas by

working on hands and knees through the filth.
From a distance, the scientists initially looked like
maggots feeding off carcases then after just a few
minutes, the disposable white boiler suits covered
in muck camouflaged them.

Contamination due to the movements of site
workers, dumpers and the crawling around of the
scientists negated the chances of bringing criminal
charges. Made more difficult as organic evidence
dissolved faster in soils copiously mixed with lime
centuries before to purify the plague bodies. The
best to hope for was the collection of human DNA to
link samples to known missing persons.

RECIPE FOR DISASTER

The Commissionaire with a bit of arm-twisting encouraged the Tahitian to talk.

"You only have a modicum of proof that I was involved in the demise of the chefs," insisted Jordan Lemanu.

"The link to the chefs may not hold up in court but I could still easily destroy your reputation by making my opinion public. Now, if you tell me precisely what occurred and there were mitigating circumstances, I give you my word that I will not air my findings so long as you leave Europe, never to come back."

"I will be most grateful to get the events off my conscience and leave this mad continent behind."

Throughout the revelation, the Commissionaire's face remained thoughtful and neutral only betraying traces of feeling afterwards.

"I regret ever becoming enmeshed with them, should have given them a wide berth when initially approached about advice on roasting large joints of meat. This led to an invite up to Scotland to stay a few days as working guests of an Eastern European acquaintance of the Scottish chef."

"Was exotic food prepared?"

"Yes, it included a large assortment of endangered meats like caribou, sea turtles and a skinned carcass of an apparently marijuana fed panda.

The place was a fortress, something straight out of the movies. There were an armoury and the presence of black suited men stationed in a bare stone entrance hall. A glimpse into a side room revealed some of them helping themselves from a large pot simmering on a stove of what looked like meat on the bone and thick noodles. A staircase and lift took you up to the host's quarters while the dungeons housed the guards and stores.

On entering the upper apartments, everything to sustain a rich man in splendid isolation was at hand. Luxury hit out at you. It was blatantly apparent the host did not believe that the simple things brought the greatest pleasure in life. The facilities ranged from cinemas to fully equipped medical surgeries.

I spent most of my time in the kitchen preparing the banquet. When I did adventure about, I lost my bearings and ran across by chance a young pallid fevered Egyptian promised money for donating a kidney. He looked out of it and no longer aware of what was going on. Duped into multiple transplants, the boy's flesh looked drained of vitality, warmth and colour, his eyes red, light fading from his pupils and smelling of disinfectant. A muffled sound came out of his lips when he first saw me. It took all his strength to get his story told. According to him, he was once a healthy teetotaller and now suffered from the consequences of his donations to the world's rich in need of a quick medical fix. Going by my instincts, a lot of young men must have been butchered this way. It put the fear in me make no bones about it. Thankfully, none of the gathered guests or the host took much interest in me, giving the distinct impression that I was regarded as a mere ignorant helper there to aid the other chefs. This suited me fine."

"Did he tell you anything about who performed the operations and the recipients?"

"No, after our brief meeting, I never saw him alive again. His last words were a request to send his personal mementos to be found in the London flat back to his parents. I got Gabriel to lead you there hoping you would take an interest in the fate of this young man.

The following morning, a helicopter ride took us to the west coast to explore a scallop bed. Unknown to me, body parts of the young Egyptian came along with us."

He took a deep breath prior to resuming his account of events.

"We arrived at a place called Hellenabrich, the next part of the tour was a boat trip down the coast, undertaken before dawn broke. This was an isolated settlement of identical white painted cottages with black slate roofs. The setting was calm, gloomy and cold with hundreds of thousands of stars above us. The awesomeness increased by the absence of the familiar company of the Southern Cross. This clear holographic show new to my eyes was about to leave the stage after another outstanding performance.

From the outside, our boat was a battered ten-metre length ready-for-the-scrapyard fishing trawler with warping deck timbers and corroded gear. Inside, the cabin and galley had been gutted and refurbished to the highest standard. The caretaker crew who had brought the boat with full fuel and water tanks into the harbour the previous evening left us and hurried up the hill to jump into the departing helicopter.

We stove away food and drink then quickly set to sea before full light. Our movements cloaked in secrecy because the plan was to harvest a scallop bed in an area of conservation. The only witnesses to our departure were a bull harbour seal and his harem, disrupted from sleep, silently observing us while bopping up and down to keep their muzzles and whiskers above the waters; strange inquisitive creatures accustomed to the cold northern seas. The other moored vessels mainly pleasure cruisers and open boats showed no sign of life. Even, if our departure were noted, the grainy half-light would have made identification difficult. So the calm harbour was left behind and the boat headed towards choppy waters.

The early morning was spent riding the waves on a

greenish-grey sea, going through kyles and coves. When the rising sun gained strength, the early cold stillness gave way to a stiffening breeze with the light changing the character of the land as darkness was replaced by pastorals then earthy colours. Intermittent strong sunbeams blazed the land. Deserted shorelines of rock and extended deserted beaches flanked by hills with clusters of gorse in bloom adding specks of yellow to the browns, violets and greens. The only movement seen was from rollers hitting the shores. The raw beauty described to me as full of skerries, underwater reefs, and lagoons made from disused slate quarries. In the southwest, the Paps of Jura poking above a mist were pointed out. On the sea, tourist excursions and trawlers came into sight but never got close to us.

The boat seemed sluggish and deep loaded by the alterations done below deck. Our constant companion gulls hovered and laughed at every sudden jerk and high crosswind wave that struck while porpoises occasionally rode our wake. Scuba diving commenced when the boat entered the desired cove. If anyone asked, then the reason given to being out on the water was to observe basking sharks, not search the seabed for shellfish. I refrained from the waters disregarding insistences that the sea was just as warm as the air temperature. In fact, this put me off entirely. Afterwards, the Scottish chef prepared lunch using stolen bounty from the sea larder and treats from packed hampers, served with cooled bottles of white wine.

The destination in the late afternoon was a building

called a bothy near good anchorage on the western shore of Jura with the aim to dine in front of a glorious sunset shimmering on the empty expanse of the Atlantic Ocean, a purportedly wonderful treat due to an atmospheric effect that caused the evening skies to clear in this part of the world. I dare say the locals held this view more in hope than fact.

There, I was later told I was expected to roast prime cuts of the poor Egyptian soul. This revealed after a dessert of snorted cocaine stupefied them and loosened tongues. I must have stared at them in disbelief for a full minute, waiting for one of them to indicate that they were making a joke, but no, they were philistines that would have happily destroyed my revival in French Polynesian cuisine. Pagan barbarity brought on by the stupor of drug taking. They, like you, thought I was an expert on long pig culinary.

Fate took a hand that island was never reached. The weather turned for the worse with this ship of fools veering into troubled turbulent waters. I along with the women approached the helm to voice concerns. My own reservations increased when a rogue wave crashed over the deck. Although not unanimous, the belief that this weather would blow over by early evening could not be dispelled.

Knowing definitely, the gulls made for land. I later found out that the weather forecast was for west to south-west gales, tough weather for any boat."

Another brief pause ensured as he retrieved his recollections.

"The first signs were a drop in temperature, increased moisture in the air and the strait becoming even more choppy.

To our right, an enormous wall of rock rose up into thick cloud. Hidden cries from the shores conjured up the impression that this was the home of sirens. Its shelter provided some rest bite from the weather. There I noticed another vessel making anchorage to ride out the coming storm.

Indifferent to the signs of the change in weather, my hosts contrary continued to carry on regardless. Away from the protection of the rock, the force of the winds hit us. The engines seemed to have a seizure brought on by its fight against the elements. Fright started to engulf everyone. The ailing boat plunged into the troughs and laboured on the rises. Beyond us, the sea roared and seethed with menace. The winds added strength to the Atlantic swells carrying in an overwhelming amount of ocean into the narrow strait. The sea rose and closed around us. Darkness completely fell upon us when low black clouds moved in. For a few moments, a strange awesome exhilaration filled me but that soon turned to despair in the deeply unsettling atmosphere.

Bashed by waves, flooded by water, blinded by foam and rain, the wrath of the turbulent ocean reached its zenith. Stability, already compromised by alterations below deck had worsened further by taking on water. Then a massive wall of water collapsed on us. It was apparent the boat would soon flounder when the rudder jammed causing complete loss of control of the steering. I decided to

abandon ship and took a small fibreglass launch
at the stern to make an escape. I tried to pull a
terror-struck hyperventilating female drained of
body heat and front covered in vomit with me but
she refused to budge from her slumped corner
position on the deck floor against the guard railing.
The others I could not see. Some may have had
already been swept overboard or could have been
only a few metres away but my terror along with
the spray and foam that riddled the air hid them.

With a backing wind, I left the want-a-be cannibals
to the mercy of the sea and tried to find with all the
strength and endurance my body could muster that
anchored vessel. Behind me, the boat continued its
path to destruction towards the centre of a roaring
kraken to plummet as if a plughole opened below it.
The swirling boat sank from sight. In my opinion,
the incapability of keeping an even keel caused it to
capsize and if there was an automatic release
beacon, it failed to reach the surface.

I did not expect them to be such bad sailors. For an
island people, they demonstrated a complete
incomprehension of the awe-inspiring power of the
sea or gave any impression of inheriting seafaring
skills that allowed ancestors to rule the waves and
conquer lands around the world."

A final draw of breath allowed him to the recount
the final chapter of that horrendous day.

"I powered away in time and when the motor
packed in then spent several hours rowing in the
dark searching for that vessel. It was a foul night,
blowing hard and raining. At times only a tolling
bell guided me. I eventually came upon it, a moored

deep-sea trawler. I banged the side of the hull to draw attention to my presence. My exhausted face looked up at the crew when they came up on deck to see what the banging was. They were Filipinos who lived permanently on board and came to my rescue by throwing down a life preserver to pull me up.

After being surprised to see me they quickly assumed that a rogue captain had honoured a threat to throw a crew member into the sea. They pitied me, dried my clothes, fed me and in the morning got me off the vessel onto the mainland. There, the crew grouped together to give me cash to pay for a bus ticket to Glasgow. After an earlier phone call, Gabriel came up to meet me and bought my rail ticket back down to London. Since then, I maintained a low profile. Yes. I was afraid, who would not be."

After listening to this catalogue of the events, the Commissionaire was satisfied.

"Your story ties in with my own deductions. There is justification for your reluctance to come forward. When all said and done the ill-maintained craft scuppered from poor seamanship, misadventure due to not taking care on the seas. Without power and steering, the tempest controlled the boat's destiny and it probably broached, taking everything down with it. Saltwater and electric ovens do not make good bedfellows.

I did find out that the owner of the highland estate was a Chechen who had the same financial accountant as the chefs, while the DNA samples taken from the Aldgate flat indicated the tenant to

be male and from North Africa. I will presume
the bodies of the deceived transplant donors
normally ended up weighted and dumped in the
North Sea. Their organs harvested to prolong life
for rich recipients that travelled wide and far to the
estate. Yes, and more besides, reckless prohibited
rejuvenation treatments and the helicopter
probably picked up drugs and other contraband out
at sea."

Happy with the decision not to blight the life of a
man for a spur of the moment indiscretion, the
Commissionaire made his final farewells. His
parting shot was the recommendation that Gabriel
disappeared asap as the Met might link him with
emerging new information. They did not believe in
coincidences and would tally any developments
with previous statements. He received the right
reply.

"Do not worry. Gabriel has already flown the coop
and looking forward to being home. He has a
romantic image of the life that awaits him. Plans to
carve out a canoe from a wide log and go fishing
every day in the hope of catching the big one. All
his wages have been spent on buying tackle.
Animosity for the country of his birth has not
deterred acquiring its fishing tackle.

I plan to follow him soon. It is only a matter of time
before a sub machine gun blasts in my direction.
Home to me is busy Pape'ete with its five star
hotels for rich tourists and modern box houses for
the natives where the French and Chinese
entrepreneurs hog the key commercial interests.
The natives only remain foremost on non-
commercial outcrops like the English aptly named

Disappointment Islands, a marginalised people in their own country.

Yes, my ancestors were cannibals that ate Captain Cook and gave the bones back to the British in an attempt to appease them. You have to see it from their side. Cook arrived not only to observe the transit of Venus but also to claim the islands in the name of the king, his king. To discipline the natives in the way of the civilised man the order to cut off the ears of errant natives was given and for good measure huts and canoes were burnt. In a strange way, eating him was a sign of respect to gain the strength of a ruthless warrior.

Gabriel thinks you too will be calling it a day soon?"

"Maybe, maybe not, I have not made final plans yet. Is Gabriel his real name?"

"No. I chose a name with connotations to a carrier of messages. He has a Tahitian name. Do you want to know it?"

"No, best not too."

The Commissionaire could not remain untouched by the integrity of this man. Later, in an internet café, a search on the web for the location where the unseaworthy trawler sank revealed it most likely to be the Gulf of Corryvreckan, known for strong underwater currents and famed for containing a whirlpool that could become very violent. Vessels should only make passage through it in benign sea conditions. Looking at the map and starting at the named hamlet, the boat travelled south down the

west side of Luing, along the Firth of Lorne then
huddled near the inhabited island of Scarba before
being exposed to the full thrust of the weather.
Another search, this time on fishing weather
forecasts, found a warning to seek shelter on the
day of the disaster. With high spring tides and a
westerly gale, it was not an evening for small boats
to be out. Beneath the whirlpool, a 100-metre-deep
trench captured all lost souls. This piece of
information caused him to muse on the fate of the
drowned chefs.

*"In this deep darkness, never to be in heaven or hell,
time no longer existed, forever caught in cold waters,
swirling round in nature's great mixing bowl,
blanched faces froze in terror, murky chowder, their
only release from limbo is to sink down to
unexplored depths to the mustered wrecks below to
become a gourmet lunch for appreciative congers."*

He finished the internet session by getting in touch
with a reliable trustworthy contact in Europe to
pass on a plausible last sighting. The credible sent
communique to Scotland Yard stated seeing a boat
carrying the chefs going out to sea when on holiday
and that he had only now become aware of its
significance on their whereabouts. The date seen
tied in with the actual trip but the location of the
capsize remained a mystery that would become part
of folklore.

Elsewhere, the results of the DNA analysis from
the plague pit justified suspicions. The area
sampled contained human remains with genes
indicating ancestries from various continents but
only a few related to known missing persons. Any
further findings from the pit would have to wait

fifty years when it would once again see daylight.

At his last press conference, addressing deaf ears, an astringent Commissionaire for the record left his sting in the tail.

"Soyons serieux...despite CCTV cameras, neighbourhood watch schemes, GPS, DNA identification and credit card trails, a quarter of million people in England disappear each year, of them, many are asylum seekers and foreign students but nevertheless an under sixteen-year-old runs away every five minutes. Thousands upon thousands of 'totally out of character' people that once led ordinary lives for one reason or another divorce themselves from a past life and go walkabout. Many are eventually found, others remain hidden while the unidentified bodies of five thousand a year remain lying in morgue stabs, until they can be legally disposed of with the associated paperwork condemned to the dark recesses of the unsolved archives. It is quite astonishing that media obsession with *cause célèbre* disappearances has suppressed serious concern for why so many cannot cope with modern living and the artificial pressures that it creates. Is this grim reality too much to bear?"

*****

The investigator of the unusual left London and returned to Brussels ready to sign off, clear his desk and move on.

A puffed-up *Geschäftsführer* Brüning called him into his office.

"You see, Du Gui, modern scientific methods and information gathering can solve the macabre. No accolades for you this time."

"Yes, with perseverance a viable explanation was found."

As usual the collar button was the focus of his attention and the soliloquy that followed by-passed him.

"Du Gui! I said go write up your findings and tell Mademoiselle Vermeulen to come and see me."

"Merde, elle travaille encore à Londres," murmured Du Gui under his breath.

His face answered for him when asked outright where she was.

Overall, he enjoyed his last adventure, a concoction of perverse cravings and abuse of those seeking out to enjoy the fruits from the tree of forbidden knowledge and that of eternal life. A gruesome tale that would have to be abridged in his memoirs to get through legal departments. Its publication will be his graffiti scrawled with personal biases and hidden attacks on the fortress walls of bureaucratised totalitarianism, started after disappearing for a few hours to walk the neighbour's dog.

THE WASHING UP

All the chefs had been invited up north to be
handsomely rewarded for preparing a banquet for
the Chechen and his guests to celebrate the
birthday of the wife of this toppled warlord who the
intelligent services put under their protection for
services rendered. His finances initially came from
plundering funds while in Chechnya and gifts
bestowed on him from Riyadh for raising jihad
against the Russians. Thereafter, his criminal
connections, lack of morality and assumed impunity
from the host country's law allowed him to increase
his wealth.

The period Gabriel was in France before arriving in
England did coincide with those of the head chef,
and of course, there was the kitchen experience.
These facts were not picked up and his vanishing
act ended interest in him.

The lost at sea story and subsequent inquiry
confirming the disappearance of an old trawler

owned by the Scottish chef got the ball rolling to close the investigation. Although without bodies wilful murder by some person or persons' unknown could not be ruled out, the coroner at the inquest returned a verdict of misadventure; a catastrophic accident highlighting Man's ignorance of the perils that nature could throw at him with the bodies claimed by the sea. This verdict in a way satisfied most. It allowed the press to insinuate the possibility of the chefs faking death allowing them to fill their newspapers in no news days with reported sightings of them from as far afield as South America to Outer Mongolia. Conspiracy theorists could spend all night on the net postulating the worse, consensus with the tabloids occurring with the assertion of the possibility of alien abduction to provide chefs for *Elvis*.

To officially terminate the effort in finding the sunken boat, a bereft looking Prime Minister gust out a panegyric at a weekly press conference praising the contribution the chefs had made to British wellbeing, gone from our sights but always remembered for feeding our souls, adding the time had come to allow families privacy to grieve. In a public house in a Cornish coastal village, a box was placed on the bar to allow customers to donate subscriptions for the erection of a commemorative plate. The House of Parliament had a day when all the restaurants and cafés within it served only traditional British fare: mince, tripe, faggots, spotted dick and Eton mess all on the menu. Following this lead, every restaurant across the land closed their doors in a national day of mourning. Such platitudes were unnecessary as the public had already accepted the inevitable fate of the chefs. Prior to these announcements, unease about costs and deliberately leaked unfavourable details about the personal and financial affairs of the chefs had weakened public affection.

The Commissionaire did not expect punishment to be meted out but believed the vile schemes would surface. Details turning up even in a nation notorious for white washing unsavoury events. The 'my country, right or wrong brigade' willing to hide evidence in the service of the greater good were a dying breed. More often than not someone will have said something to a friend or relative and that something will be dynamite in the right hands. Even the bullheaded on their deathbeds have been known to seek absolution by telling all. Something leaks out, initially denied but persistent rumours and tickles of information force a change of stance, especially if a once protected friendly foreign ally becomes a foe.

In the meantime, avid attention to the mystery of the disappearing chefs faded leaving a small band of conspiracy theorists to keep it alive. The popularity of cooking programmes temporarily declined as disparaging sensational news stories and books about the trade secrets of restaurant kitchens, social security frauds and dodgy dealings of celebrity chefs flooded the market. Many switched off watching daytime TV and instead took to partaking in locally organised activities or swarming into the countryside. The latter caused environmentalists and farmers to unite to demand that TV executives show something that would return the populace back to the goggle box. The sure fire solution put forward by an ideas team was a daytime show where a chef made an unannounced visit to the home of a celebrity, ascertain the treats a precious pet loved to eat then prepare a dish enjoyable for both the pet and its celebrity owner.

On the streets, demonstration took on their normal hoo-ha form. Orthodox feminists campaigned against transwomen wanting recognition of the right to join their ranks, a postmodern take of the born catholic superiority over the converted to Catholicism argument. No sugar in the tea or milk of human kindness from these vanguards. In their moment of triumph over a male-dominated society, this front line of womanhood was in no mood to share the spoils. Some of the surgically reassigned males-to-women achieved martyrdom when strangulated with 'Real Women Bleed' banners on Parliament Hill during a particularly violent internecine clash.

"It was good to see that in a world where half of humanity was starving that some people got their priorities right. Always fighting for more rights instead of enjoying life, asking for too much out of life made them bitter.

As far as involuntary harvesting of organs and blood from living donors was concerned, one day medical advancement will make this trade obsolete with new laboratory created organs available, who knows, maybe organ harvesting will be classified as a crime against humanity and past culprits and benefactors prosecuted in the International Crime Courts at The Hague, then again pigs might fly."